G

**IT WAS A VOYAGE FILLED WITH TERROR ...
TO AN UNFAMILIAR DESTINATION ...
WITH A WOMAN WHO KNEW NO FEAR ...**

The first rainsqualls hit at about nine o'clock that evening. The seas were already heavy. The high winds and thunder and lightning followed. Wails of terror went up from the Creek children. Their parents huddled frightened on the deck, chanting to their gods. They knew that if the ship foundered, they and their children would drown. The men were manacled. Many of the women and children did not know how to swim.

A rush of water breached the port side and blanketed three sailors. Moultrie hugged one of the huge stays supporting the mainmast, fighting for hold against the surging water.

When the water cascaded from the deck back into the sea, the three sailors were thrashing about on the ends of their safety harness like hooked fish.

Then the force seemed to take the bow of the ship. The bow wave grew higher and spread out, lifting the ship, then dropping it like a stone. Moultrie's knuckles whitened as he gripped the stay, praying for salvation. A form lurched against him and other hands gripped the mainmast stay, clamping over his own.

Lightning split the sky. In the brilliance, Moultrie saw Moon Shadow looking straight into his eyes.

And when the rush of water subsided, they still held each other close, even though there was, for the moment, no immediate need. . . .

CREEK RIFLES

PETER HANSEN

A Dell/Banbury Book

Published by
Banbury Books, Inc.
37 West Avenue
Wayne, Pennsylvania 19087

Dell ® TM 681510, Dell Publishing Co., Inc.

ISBN: 0-440-01215-5

Printed in the United States of America

First printing—April 1982

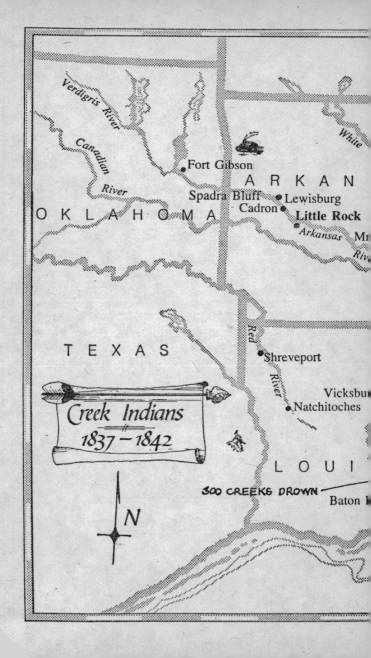

Verdigris River

Canadian River

Fort Gibson

White

A R K A N

Spadra Bluff
Cadron
Lewisburg
Little Rock

O K L A H O M A

Arkansas

Mi

Riv

T E X A S

Red

Shreveport

River

Vicksbur
Natchitoches

Creek Indians
1837 – 1842

L O U I

300 CREEKS DROWN

Baton

N

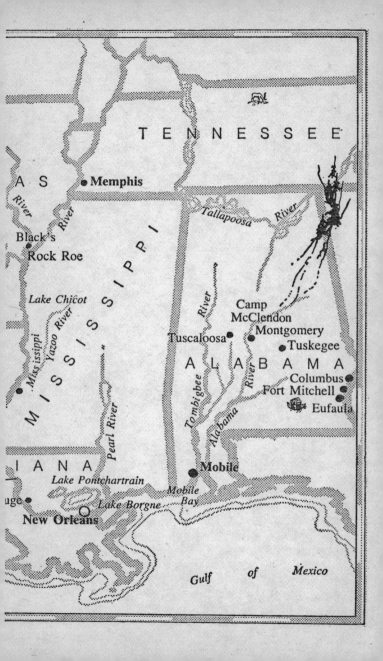

Chapter 1

The rain mingled with sleet. Even in the warm comfort of the study, with the fire crackling, Judge Leander Dupré could hear it drumming on the roof of the house two stories above him. He shook his head. He thought, this is no time for despondency. Worry about money later. You've done little else these last weeks. Besides, something will come up. It always does. Next year is bound to be better than this 1835, soon ending.

Shaking his head again, the judge looked up from the fire. Somehow he had to show an interest in his daughter's young man. "So," he smiled, "you've heard from Madden and his Indian affairs bureau people?"

The young man sitting facing the judge nodded. "There was a letter of appointment with instructions, and a covering note. I'm to proceed right away to the Yuchi reservations."

"Good. I. . . ." Before the judge could say any more, he started to cough. Leaning his head back against the chair, he closed his eyes. They were water-

1

ing. He felt phlegm rise in his throat. He gulped. At least this time he didn't taste blood, he thought, and that's a blessing.

Opening his eyes, Judge Dupré looked across again at the man sitting opposite him. He saw the youngster's look of concern and felt suddenly irritated. "Damn it, Moultrie Ravenel," he said, "I'm not dying. Don't look as if you believe me on my last legs."

"Sorry." Moultrie stood up with easy grace. Moving to the table under the window, he reached for the decanter. "Pour you a glass, Judge?"

"Hmm. Thanks." The judge watched as the boy unstoppered the crystal container. "You and Helen decided on a date yet?"

"No, sir."

The judge wasn't sure, but he thought Moultrie had suddenly stiffened. In the moment's silence the judge wondered, Is this boy trifling with my Helen?

Dupré shifted clumsily in his chair, grunting. "Did I say something wrong, boy?"

Turning, Moultrie Ravenel smiled tightly. "No, sir. It's just that I'm not ready yet. I want to get the plantation in shape before I bring a bride to live there."

"That's a noble thought, but a silly one. She can help you, boy." The judge was adamant. "And well she should."

He paused once more. After all, the boy's a handsome cuss. Stands tall. Straight and proud as an Indian. Works hard, too. The boy was handsome and promised to make money. What's more important, the judge thought, the boy comes of damned good stock.

There were no better people in South Carolina than the Ravenels. And out here in Alabama, old John

Ravenel, the boy's uncle, had made quite a name for himself before his death eight months earlier.

Old John. The judge could see him in Moultrie's stance at the bar. Not that the two were alike exactly. John had been wild. It was said he had even lived with the Indians for a couple of years, twenty-five years ago. The judge could well believe it. Even at fifty, John had spent three weeks a year with Yuchi Indian friends over on the Georgia border.

But Moultrie wasn't like that. He was steady. At least that was what Helen said. Of course, Helen's perceptions were a little suspect. After all, the judge thought, she was in love with Moultrie, and furthermore, she didn't seem to appreciate steadiness properly. She said of Moultrie's brother, Henry, the preacher, that he was dull with duty. Of course, the judge admitted, she had a point in a way. John had evidently thought so too. He had left his plantation to Moultrie. It had been Moultrie, not Henry, whom John had invited to visit Alabama after the boys' father's death. And Moultrie had returned year after year, staying for months each time. He had been quite the little man. The judge smiled at the memory.

"Here you are, Judge," Moultrie said, coming over from the table with two glasses in his hand. He gave the judge one glass, then raised his own in salute. "To your health."

Leander Dupré took the glass and returned the salute. "To you, boy, and Helen." Sipping, he cocked an eyebrow. He had good sherry, even if he did say so himself.

As Moultrie returned to the wing chair on the opposite side of the fireplace and sat down, the judge cleared his throat. "I didn't mean to pry or prod," he muttered. "I just want Helen's happiness." He paused for a moment. "And since I'm not going to be here forever, I want to see her future secured."

The young man nodded, a shock of dark brown hair falling across his forehead. Was he agreeing, being sympathetic or polite? The judge could not decide. He waited for Moultrie to speak. When the boy did not, he continued. "I think that you and Helen are suited for each other." Having said it, he winced. "That didn't come out the way I meant it to." He cleared his throat again. "What I mean is that. . . ." He banged his fist on the arm of his leather wing chair. "Damn it, you know what I mean, boy. Don't let an old man die before he gets a chance to see his grandchildren."

The judge felt the weight of the silence again as he and Moultrie looked across at each other, the fire flickering between them. He shifted uncomfortably in his chair. As he did, Moultrie put down his glass and said, "After I finish getting the Yuchis moved from Alabama across the Mississippi to the Indian Territory, I hope to come home to take Helen's hand."

To the judge, it sounded as if Moultrie was speaking with more deliberation than passion. The notion irritated him. "Lord, we're not talking about cotton futures! Maybe I was wrong when I suggested you apply to Madden for this job as Indian agent." As he spoke, he tried, with difficulty, to keep his tone light. "I didn't mean to get you a job that would keep you away from us."

Moultrie glanced quickly at the judge, then picked up his sherry glass. "I'll miss you both," he admitted, "but you were right. This job is a good way for me to make contacts both around the state and up in Washington. Besides, I want to do what I can for those poor Indians."

"Poor Indians, my eye," the judge snorted. "The

whole damned Creek Confederation, and especially the Yuchis, have been getting damned uppity lately. Hell, they've even driven the Methodist missionaries off." The judge paused, then added, chuckling, "Not that I blame them."

Leander Dupré had vivid memories of the missionaries as they had left the Indian reservations. They had come, many of them, through Montgomery, Alabama, where he had been presiding over his court at the time. For a while there, the town had been thundering holiness. The judge, listening, had thanked God that those preachers were not arguing in his court. "Montgomery," the judge had told his friends then, "has enough resident hot air as it is." Then he had added a favorite saying. "Hell, there are almost as many lawyers as cockroaches in this town, and the roaches eat better. That's why the court dockets are so full of stupid, make-work suits. The lawyers are scrambling for any, every crumb."

It had been into that confusion of litigation, right in the middle of court week, that Preacher Jones had strode. Gaunt and angry, he had cornered the judge. "Judge," he had said, his voice vibrating with the accent of the backwoods, "you have to do something. The Indians are going to suffer eternal fire and damnation if we don't save them from themselves."

The judge had had trouble controlling his laughter.

"How you going to force-feed them on God?"

Jones had sat back then. "I don't rightly know," he said finally. Then he had added, still frowning, his voice fierce in the judge's ear, "The Indians don't want to do anything but hunt, fish and drink!"

"Just like most white men," the judge had answered. As far as he could see, there wasn't much choice between a driftless savage and a shiftless squatter on the Indian lands. Both lived from hand to mouth. Both would sell their souls for a jug of corn squeezings or peach brandy. Both were worthless. Most of humanity was. That didn't bother the judge. "Except," he had remarked often, "you've got to live with the scum. At least, the white scum. I personally would never live with Indians, though, by God."

The judge banged his fist against the arm of his chair again and glared at Moultrie. "I've been digressing. But, the faster we get those bloody Indians west of the Mississippi, the better."

As he spoke, the judge felt the terrible pressure of another cough welling up. He struggled to suppress it. "Leave Alabama to white men," he gasped. "We aren't going to clothe the world and employ half of New England in cotton mills unless we can use the Indian lands to plant cotton to send to the mills."

The judge could not hold back any longer. The couch racked his body. As Moultrie started back up out of his chair, the judge waved him back angrily.

"I'll be all right," he grumbled, his chest heaving.

Moultrie studied Judge Dupré sitting by the fire with his sherry in his hand and his books around him.

"Go on, boy." The judge waved him on. "Go and find Helen. She'll be at me for weeks if I squander any more of your last day in Montgomery."

Moultrie laughed out loud. "Wild horses couldn't keep me from saying good-bye to Helen, Judge."

Out in the hall, Moultrie drew the door softly behind him, then shook his head. I'm damned, he thought, if I'm going to be stampeded into bringing Helen to Forest Hall. It's not ready. Nor am I. Maybe she is a splendid household mistress. Of course she is. Look at this town house of the judge's. Look at Hope

Chest. Helen rules that plantation for the judge. But still I'm not ready for her to rule mine.

With a shrug, Moultrie started toward the stairs. There was the sound of a piano being played in the music room up on the second floor. At the foot of the stairs, he paused to listen. He had heard occasional chords in the study. Now the music was much clearer. Moultrie smiled. "Damn, but that's nice," he said aloud. The thought surprised him. Usually music did not hold him unless it was the tonguing of dogs on a scent or the frothy stuff he had danced to the year before in Vienna.

But now, hearing Helen playing, Moultrie was listening eagerly, trying to anticipate notes and harmonic shifts. He smiled again. You're turning into a romantic fool, he thought. Serves you right. He started up the stairs, taking the steps two at a time. He covered the few yards between the head of the stairs and the music room in three more strides, then paused. The door was ajar. Moultrie saw Helen sitting erect before the keyboard, her body framed by the heavy damask of the drapes behind her. Candles in two silver candelabra burned brilliantly atop the piano. There was a fire in the grate. The flickering of the flames gave the shadows of fading daylight a gentle warmth.

Moultrie stood for a moment, bemused. Then, as Helen came to the end of a passage, he applauded, first one clap, then a second, then a flurry of claps.

Helen started, then turned. She wrinkled her nose. "Moultrie Ravenel, you're awful," she scolded. "Don't you know that ladies these days are supposed to faint when they're surprised like that?"

Moultrie grinned and mimicked her. "Helen Dupré, you're awful. Don't you know that men these days are supposed to faint when they hear music like that?"

Helen's laughter joined his. Striding into the room as she rose, he took her hands in his. "You're beautiful," he said, this time in his natural voice. "And so was your music."

"Why, Mr. Ravenel." Helen curtsied. Then her smile faded. "You've come to say good-bye. I can see good-bye in your face. You have come to say good-bye, haven't you?"

"Lord, your intuitions intimidate me," Moultrie replied. "But yes, I have come to say good-bye." He paused. "And you know I hate to say it. I hate to leave."

"Then why do you?"

"Your direct way of speech intimidates me, too." Moultrie told her, flinching at the vehemence in her voice. "It's one of your finer qualities."

"Then I'll ask directly again. Why do you?"

"I guess I have to deliver the speech again," Moultrie sighed.

"I guess you do," Helen Dupré answered, "for I still do not comprehend your reason for leaving if you really wish to stay."

Moultrie tried to lighten the presentation he was about to make. "Ahem," he began, placing one hand inside the lapels of his coat and taking a comic Napoleonic stance.

Helen was not amused. This was Moultrie's last attempt at lightness. This was not a light subject. He became serious. "You don't really want to believe I want to help the Indians. Well, believe. You must. For I do. I've come to know them over the years with a fondness I hold for my own people and my own family. Each time I've gone to live among them with my Uncle

John, on those hunting trips, the knowledge and the fondness have both grown. I've come to learn their language almost as well as my own. It's a strong, expressive language, not just grunts without syntax, as so many prefer to believe. I've learned it by studying with whoever had the patience to tutor me. And I can now speak in the Creek dialect as well as any Creek." Moultrie smiled once more. "Except perhaps for some weakness with prepositions."

He grew serious again. "I fear that sometimes you believe I'm caught up in some silly, boyish spirit of adventure. Believe me, I'm not. I am very serious about doing something for them. So many of our people have done so much *to* them."

He saw that Helen was barely breathing as she listened. He continued. "But worse for me is the fear that you truly believe I'm taking this assignment as Indian agent to avoid you."

Once more, for emphasis, he started to say, "I'm not."

And he found he could not.

This blockage of speech disturbed him. He was forced to admit to himself in the following silence that Helen Dupré might be correct in her intuition after all.

And he did not want to concede the possibility that he might indeed really wish to get away.

Moultrie studied her eyes again. Seeing pain in them, he reached to caress her cheek. "And that's the Moultrie-goes-west speech once more," he finished. "I hope you do believe me this time."

"I have always believed you," she claimed. "But I still do not really comprehend. I do not believe you do, either." She pressed his hand hard against her cheek. "But never mind. You're going. Done is done. Goodbye, Moultrie."

"Only for a while, Helen."

"No. For a long time, I think. Good-bye, Moultrie."

Unhitching his horse outside the Dupré house, Moultrie had a thought which made him smile. He did not know why it did, precisely.

Then it hit him. Helen Dupré was always so direct with him in speech that her directness conveyed a sexual quality to him.

Would she be as direct with him in bed when they were married? He prayed she would be. He liked a woman who knew what she wanted a man to do with her, and knew how to tell him.

Chapter 2

The federal road ran in a straight line from Columbus, Georgia, just across the Chattahoochee River from Alabama in the east, all the way west to Mississippi. To Moultrie, the road had always seemed on the map to be a belt holding up the pants of Alabama. Near the center, at the belt buckle, was Montgomery. Montgomery's centralized geographic location made it inevitable that she would one day supersede Tuscaloosa as the state capital of Alabama.

It was to Montgomery that the roads came. It was from Montgomery that the steamboats paddled south along the Alabama River to Mobile on the Gulf of Mexico. Montgomery's growing influence was felt in every direction.

In one of these directions was Fort Mitchell.

A carriage, drawn by two horses, carried Moultrie and the black man named Cicero to Fort Mitchell on a cold, gritty winter's day. They huddled shoulder to shoulder beneath a canvas sheet against the chill and

11

the dust clouds of the Fort Mitchell road. Moultrie was impatient to be there. Fort Mitchell was where his mission among the Creek Indians was to begin.

Moultrie had another reason for wishing to be at Fort Mitchell on this afternoon. The road grit lifted by hooves and carriage wheels was everywhere, and it was unforgiving in its abrasiveness. "Curse all dust, Cicero," he exclaimed. "The man who invents something to prevent animals and wagons from throwing up dust on roads will become a millionaire."

"Someone already has, Ravenel," the black man returned. "It's called pavement."

Moultrie chuckled.

"You shouldn't laugh," Cicero said. "You move and shake more dust down on us."

"Rider coming about a hundred yards ahead."

Cicero grunted. He moved apart from Moultrie and sat erect, staring straight ahead as if he were alone. He held the canvas sheet across Moultrie's shoulders and head, giving all of its dustproofing to Moultrie and none to himself.

The oncoming horseman did not even look up as he passed on his way to Montgomery.

Cicero covered both Moultrie and himself with the canvas sheet once more for protection from the dust. They huddled together against the cold once more without speaking.

As we have always huddled together, Moultrie thought, since my daddy gave Cicero to me for my very own, when we were both eight years old.

Daddy wanted us to grow up together. He wanted me to learn my responsibilities to blacks early on.

Grow up together we did. And together we still remain.

To men passing us on a highway on a rotten, cold

afternoon, we are master and darky in a carriage, each in his proper place. We play our expected roles well. To ourselves we are still Ravenel and Cicero, long-time friends as we share a canvas against the dust, as we have shared things throughout our lives. Moultrie had often pondered this aspect of the relationship with the black man riding beside him. His thoughts along the Fort Mitchell road held no new insights that afternoon.

Helen Dupré was one of the few who perceived the dual roles they played. She had questioned Moultrie about it once, earlier. Moultrie remembered the incident well. It had occurred in the stables in his own home, Forest Hall:

"Moultrie, I don't really understand your relationship with that black man any more than I understand your running off among the Creeks."

"You mean Cicero."

"Cicero."

"I didn't realize it showed."

"It does."

"And you find it mongrelization?"

"No. You're not marrying one of them and siring children. But I believe your closeness to him may help explain the closeness you feel with your Creeks. Whether your father knew what he was doing or not in your upbringing, I think he raised you to care for other people, no matter who they might be. Certainly you get closer to more kinds of people than most of us ever could. It's difficult to understand, sometimes, the liberties you allow Cicero."

"You mean slave-lover and Indian-lover."

"Must you be so vulgar, Moultrie?"

"Those are the preferred words. So use them." Moultrie drummed his fingers along the stall of the

mare he had chosen for Helen to ride, waiting until he
was less angry before he spoke again.

"True," he said. "It is not your typical relationship between black man and white man in our South.
But it's not so unusual, either, as you know. I am not
surprised when I sense friendships between other pairs
of white and black men. They are pretty common
among our breed of people, the plantation aristocracy,
as some call us. There is no sin against our system in
the relationship itself, only in openly admitting that it
exists. And worse, in demonstrating it. As long as you
do not flagrantly demonstrate it, no one really cares.

Helen seemed to have stopped breathing, as she
often seemed to do when concentrating. Moultrie continued. "You've seen such friendships a hundred times,
Helen. When you're raised as close as Cicero and I
were raised, you cannot help but become special to
each other, no matter what society tells you about doing otherwise. Cicero and I grew up eating the same
bowl of grits between us in his folks' cabin. The two of
us using his mother's stomach for a pillow while we
napped. Passing the same single-barrel shotgun back
and forth because we did not have two guns for hunting."

"My father says you should never let them even
hold guns," Helen scoffed.

Moultrie waved impatiently. "A lot of the rules
that govern other whites and blacks no longer apply to
ourselves. You know as well as I do that the black man
a white man grows up with is the black man the white
man seldom sells. You can't have forgotten these things
even though you've been away where the ways aren't
the same as ours here. You're still born and bred a
southern woman."

"You permit him to call you by your last name

when you're alone, without addressing you as mister or sir."

"But never in public."

"And never by your first name."

"No. Last name basis is about as familiar as even we can permit things to be between us."

"But the rules which govern others do not govern you and Cicero," Helen said. "I swear my poor ears just heard you say those very words. Why, Moultrie Ravenel. If this friendship is really, truly as special as you claim it is, your black friend would have the privilege of addressing you by your first name now and then."

"Well, he doesn't. And he addresses me as 'Marse Moultrie,' his master, in public. No matter what else we may be, I'm still owner and he's still slave, and neither of us can ever afford to forget it."

The gentle, chiding sarcasm of Helen Dupré had been painful to Moultrie. The memory of it still hurt a little now, much later, on the road to Fort Mitchell. Moultrie flicked the buggy whip at the horses' ears.

Cicero began singing softly:

> I look down the road,
> And the road looks so lonesome.
> Lord, I got to go
> Down that long, lonesome road.

The grey bleakness of the sky seemed to sharpen the dark edges of barren winter woods. The air was becoming chillier than it had been. The wind was up. It was bitter.

"You might let me have the horses, Ravenel," Cicero suggested. "I drive animals a little harder than you do. I sure do want to get to Fort Mitchell and out of this cold."

Fort Mitchell. As he approached, Moultrie remembered it from seven years before, when he'd last visited with Uncle John. The two of them had taken the steamboat south from Columbus in Georgia along the Chattahoochee. About ten miles downriver they had come to the fort's landing on the Alabama side. From there they had walked up to the fort itself.

Thinking back, Moultrie wondered if the way he had described Fort Mitchell then in a letter to his brother Henry was still accurate.

> There's a square which they call a parade ground. To me it looks more like a corral, dusty in the sun, a sea of mud in the rain, with horses and cattle as well as soldiers milling about among the pigs, chickens, and stray Indians.
>
> Uncle John tells me the fort is important. He calls it the chief outpost of the federal government in the Creek Confederation, a symbol of the United States' might to the Eufaulas, Yuchis, Cheahas, Muskogeans and other tribes of the Creek Confederation. But to my way of thinking, it's a pretty poor symbol. A few cannons, a few acres of stumps where soldiers have cut timber for buildings and firewood, a few troops standing about doing little. If I were an Indian I wouldn't think much of Uncle Sam's might on the basis of what I see at Fort Mitchell.

Moultrie's description was still accurate, but for

one detail. Now there were no soldiers garrisoned there. The fort no longer stood as a threat or warning to the Indians. Rather, it was meant to be a symbol of the United States government's commitment to the treaty President Andrew Jackson had entered with the Creek Confederation three years earlier.

This was the treaty which was supposed to guarantee reservations under federal jurisdiction and protection to all Creeks who remained in Alabama.

How quickly the treaty had been broken, Moultrie recalled bitterly.

Once he had told Helen Dupré, "Speculators and out-and-out thieves are stealing the Indians blind. They cheat them of their lands. They sell them shoddy goods. They give them whiskey, and then when they're drunk, deceive them into signing over everything they own."

More and more, as they grew to know one another, Moultrie had turned to Helen as a confidante and sounding board. He trusted her to be honest. On this occasion, her honesty had not pleased him.

"That's horrible," she had said. "Who would do such things?"

"Bill Hobson in Columbus, for one. A man who is no good, truly no good."

Helen flinched. She did not speak for a moment. Then she said, "I am startled. I am also outraged, Moultrie Ravenel. I know Bill Hobson. My father regards him highly, and my father is not a poor judge of character. Bill Hobson is polite, considerate and charming. And he is honest. You should not speak ill of people on the basis of malicious gossip." She paused again. "You surprise me, Moultrie. You are usually fair in your judgments.

Moultrie had been speechless against Helen's vigorous defense of a man he believed to be so evil. Even now, as he saw Fort Mitchell again that day, he could not understand Helen's reaction. Hobson, he thought. So transparent. So greedy. So rotten and ruthless. How can Helen not see these qualities in the man?

Fueling Moultrie's anger was the conviction that the chilly, dark hills he and Cicero had just traveled through would soon be bloodied by war if Hobson and his kind were not controlled.

Moultrie also recalled a conversation with Judge Dupré on the possibility of the Creeks going to war over the broken treaty and the U.S. government's plans to move them west.

"But," Judge Dupré had insisted, "the Creeks lost one war already, against Andy Jackson in 1814. Broken treaty or no broken treaty, they won't fight again. They don't have the heart. They know what will happen to them again. Another defeat. The odds are ten times greater against them now. No, a hundred times greater."

"The Indians will fight," Moultrie had argued. "They know they'll lose, but there will be nothing else they can do but fight."

Dupré had clapped him on the back, saying, "Not if you do your work properly, boy."

The gesture and the confidence it expressed had been flattering, even though somewhat patronizing. Moultrie himself did not share the confidence. How was he supposed to defuse this situation alone in the face of such federal treachery and Indian mistrust? Tell people like Hobson to stop robbing and raping and cheating the Indians? Tell the Indians that the Office of Indian Affairs is acting for their own good in making them give up the lands of their fathers and moving them into a strange wilderness west of Arkansas?

Neither the Hobsons nor the Indians will listen, Moultrie thought. Frustration welled up inside him.

After so many months which had passed since those two conversations, Moultrie Ravenel still had no answers.

Chapter 3

Major Jeremiah Dent looked up at the sound of the knock on the door. "Come in," he sighed.

It was Sergeant McCoy. Even now, busy as he was, the major had trouble not smiling at the sergeant's bowlegs. He restrained himself. The sergeant was sensitive on the subject. He had once left a man half dead after overhearing him comment, "Those aren't legs, they're a barn door."

"What is it, Sergeant?"

Sergeant Terence McCoy saluted, bringing his heels together. Even standing at attention, he was bent. Hunched over himself like that, he wasn't much of a figure of a man. A big man had told him that once. He'd just barely lived to regret it, or so the major had heard.

The sergeant shifted a quid of chewing tobacco in his mouth. "Major," he drawled, "there's somebody here to see you. Says he's the new Indian agent."

"Says so?" The major was amused. "Isn't he?"

The sergeant nodded. "Guess so," he said. Then he hesitated. "Seems to me," he added finally, "like he's too fancy to be much of one."

"I see." Major Dent grimaced. "Well, show the gentleman in."

McCoy saluted and turned. As he closed the door behind him, the major thought savagely, The last thing we need here is some smooth, get-rich-quick type from Washington working with the Indians. Wrenching open the top left drawer of his desk, the major reached in, took out a cigar, clipped it, then pushed it into his mouth. "Isn't that just like Charles Madden?" he asked aloud. "The shriveled up excuse for Indian Affairs chief. Sending me some politico's useless son." The major grew so furious that he had trouble finding the end of his cigar to light it.

Finally, with the tip glowing and the rich tobacco smell filling his nostrils, he calmed down. If I'm going to have to work with this gift from Washington, he decided, he's going to understand a few things. The major smiled.

As Moultrie came in, ushered by Sergeant McCoy, the major nodded curtly. "Take a seat," he said.

Moultrie did, putting his commission on the major's desk.

The major read the document, then sat back. "Well, Ravenel, you've got your work cut out for you." Reaching into the upper left drawer of his desk again, he took out another cigar and passed it to Moultrie. Watching the man methodically clip and light it, the major had to admit that Moultrie was cool. Drawing on his own cigar, the major wreathed himself in smoke. "The Yuchis you're going to be dealing with," he explained, "are the most intractable of all these Indians."

Moultrie's gaze was even and unchanging.

"And if you do your job and actually get these Indians to go west, then your problems really begin."

Still there was no reaction from Moultrie. Well, the major thought, that can be fixed. Grunting, he leaned over and pulled open the bottom left drawer of the scarred desk.

Taking out a bottle and two tumblers, he poured three fingers of whiskey into each glass. He passed one glass to Moultrie. He raised his own tumbler in a salute, then tossed off the contents.

The whiskey was horrible—rough and raw. It spread like molten lava through the major's system, each swallow wrenching his insides.

Moultrie Ravenel didn't even blink. He simply downed his glass.

"Captain John Page," the major started again, gasping because of the whiskey, "has just finished taking a group west." He coughed, then shifted his bulk about in his chair. "His reports to me about the trip make it sound like he's been on the road to hell."

A knock interrupted the major before he could say more. Sergeant McCoy stepped in and saluted. "Trouble, sir," he announced. "Another Indian family complaining about having been driven off their land."

"All right, Sergeant." The major stood up. He said to Moultrie, "Look in on me next time you're here. Let me know how things are going."

"Count on it." Moultrie rose. "Thanks for the smoke and the drink."

The Creek village was quiet in the late afternoon sun. Sitting in front of his one-room log cabin, a cabin like the one his father, grandfather, and great-grandfather had lived in, Crazy Wolf felt at peace for a change. It was a good feeling. In past years, when he looked over the straggling lines of cabins around the village square, he worried. Not just about encounters with surly whites, though that was a growing problem. Not just about smallpox and yellow fever, though these diseases of the white man had ravaged many villages. But about getting enough to eat.

The whites had slashed and burned and ploughed for crops. And white hunters had killed game in incredible numbers.

Of course, there were some white men who didn't kill just for the pleasure of killing. John Ravenel, friend of Crazy Wolf's father, had been one.

Still, game animals were being destroyed. Crazy Wolf and his hunters had increasing trouble finding enough wild meat to supplement the village's diet of beef. This came from the cattle ranging in the open savannahs past the canebrake just west of their village. Corn came from the fields by the Chattahoochee.

This morning, however, the hunting had been good. Crazy Wolf and his elder son, Little Hawk, had shot two deer. Crazy Wolf smiled at the memory. Little Hawk would make a fine warrior.

Hearing shouts, Crazy Wolf looked up. The old men were sitting on logs in front of their cabins in the last rays of the sun. The women were pounding corn into flour by the outdoor cooking fires. The young warriors were charging after a ball on the playing field next to the village meeting ground. From beyond all this, children were running toward him. Their shouts swelled and mingled with the sudden barking of the village dogs.

Crazy Wolf shielded his eyes against the glare of

the western sun. He saw two men, one white and one black, riding behind the children. The white man looked vaguely familiar.

Suddenly his heart leaped. It was Little Hunting Brother. He got up and strode forward to meet the two horsemen, his arms wide.

"Crazy Wolf." As the white man spoke, he jumped off his horse.

Crazy Wolf embraced the man, laughing, then stood back and looked at him. Moultrie Ravenel was not dressed as a Yuchi brave. Instead of buckskin leggings and a breechcloth, he wore dark woolen trousers. Instead of a calico, a linen shirt. Instead of a buckskin, a woolen jacket and a greatcoat with a short cape. Instead of moccasins, high leather boots. And instead of a feathered turban, a broadbrimmed beaver skin hat.

"You're a man now, Little Hunting Brother," Crazy Wolf said to Moultrie. "It has been many summers," he added. "Too many."

"You are right, Big Hunting Brother." Moultrie smiled as he spoke. He recalled how it had all begun.

The trip to the Yuchi country on the Chattahoochee had been an annual ritual with Uncle John. Moultrie was not certain how or why, but Uncle John and Crazy Wolf's father, Big Bear, had been fast friends even as far back as the Creek War, when Uncle John had been in General Andrew Jackson's army and had fought Big Bear. It had been because of that warforged friendship that Moultrie and Crazy Wolf had been thrust at each other. They, too, had become friends, even though Crazy Wolf was ten years older and, at first, Moultrie had spoken no Yuchi. The friendship had ripened until the boy and the warrior had begun to call each other brother.

Now, sitting next to Crazy Wolf on one of the beds which lined the walls of his cabin, Moultrie felt almost as if he had not been away at Harvard and in Europe for six years. The dirt floor, the heavy scent of bear grease, the acrid sting of the smoke as it eddied in the draft around the fire pit in the middle of the room, the bedbugs; Moultrie remembered them all. He remembered the tastes, too: the fresh venison, the corn soup, the squaw bread, the sassafras tea. And afterwards there was tobacco, mellow in a cool clay pipe.

In the silence, as he and Crazy Wolf drew on their pipes, Moultrie watched Crazy Wolf's two wives. They were ladling out food for three children. Without turning his head, Moultrie said, "You are a rich man to have such squaws and such children as these, Big Hunting Brother."

Grunting, the Indian shifted his seat slightly, reached for his cup and took a swallow of the bright red tea. He nodded.

"Does your Little Hunting Brother have squaws?" This was Running Water, Crazy Wolf's first wife, asking.

Crazy Wolf grinned.

Moultrie grinned back. The son of a bitch remembers, he thought.

So did Moultrie, of course. Every detail. The seven years since had sharpened his recollection. The girl, as he'd told Crazy Wolf, had been all fire and laughter. She had wrestled with him and rolled with him on the ground and then, when the time had come, had gripped him eagerly around his waist. "She was like a steamboat in a storm," he had said to Crazy Wolf. She had been, too, pitching and rolling, puffing and blowing. His first time with a woman. Moultrie had not even minded the chigger bites or the smile on Crazy Wolf's face when he had told the story.

Crazy Wolf smiled the same smile now. "A man like Little Hunting Brother has to have a squaw. A man has to have a family. It is his nature."

Moultrie nodded. "My father used to say the same thing. 'A man's not fully a man until he's no longer just himself.' " He smirked. "Maybe the woman I am about to marry will make a man of me." Listening to himself, he wondered if Crazy Wolf had noted the sarcasm.

"Tell me about her," Crazy Wolf said.

"She is beautiful."

"Can she work?"

"Yes."

"Ah. Then it is good."

Cicero and another black man sat in silence on the bank of the river, each staring at the current. They had been arguing.

Cicero saw a snakebird swimming across the moon streak on the water. The bird's head and neck cut the surface. Then the bird shattered the reflection of moonlight into spray and lifted off, seemingly toward the stars. Drops trailing from its wings glistened against the darkness. It flew to a dead tree leaning over the river. There, swallowed in shadow, it spread its wings to dry. Shivering slightly, Cicero turned to the man beside him. "Let's go back to the village, Scipio. It's cold just sitting here. And besides, it's the only sensible thing for you to do. You know it."

The man called Scipio grunted in acknowledgment, but he did not move. He watched the snakebird.

Cicero grew impatient. "I tell you, Scipio, you must not worry." Cicero stomped as he spoke. The raw cold touched his body everywhere. My master, Ravenel, doesn't have to know you are a runaway. And even if he does know, so long as you don't announce it, he won't care. Ravenel believes a man who cannot hold his own slaves by earning their trust doesn't deserve to have them. Tell him you're Chief Crazy Wolf's slave. It's not uncommon for Indians to own slaves. After all, they are free men, in name anyway." Cicero laughed without mirth. "Yes, tell him you belong to Chief Crazy Wolf. I'll say, 'Yes, that's right.' He won't believe a word of it, but it's a story we can all live with."

"Huh. And next I'll be dancing around a fire like some Indian and going woo-woo-woo." He shook his head. "Cicero, ain't your master Ravenel know my master? And ain't my master tell your Ravenel about me?"

"Yes. But that's what I'm telling you. It will be all right. Marse Moultrie isn't like your Marse Hobson, nohow."

"Shoot," Scipio sighed. "They are both white men."

Branches soughed in the breeze, seeming to brush the stars. To Cicero, people sighing sounded like that. Shivering once more, he turned from the river. The village was a cluster of dark shapes at the foot of the hill. He and Scipio had come to the place by the river only a half-hour before to decide how best to conceal Scipio's runaway status and flight from William Hobson. They had accomplished nothing.

Now Cicero decided it himself. "It is this simple, Scipio. You must try to understand. If you insist upon telling Marse Moultrie you are a runaway, or if you insist upon telling Marse Moultrie by acting like a runaway, then he is bound by rules and codes to turn you back to Marse Hobson. But if you don't, he is not, no matter how much he suspects. And he won't."

"I guess." Scipio stood unhappily.

"Let's go see Marse Ravenel, then."

A wolf howled in the distance.

Chapter 4

One morning a few days later there was a letter for Moultrie Ravenel from Miss Helen Dupré. Parts of it deeply touched Moultrie.

> Papa says he's feeling fine. But I do not believe it for a minute. I hear him coughing late at night. And Jenny says there is blood on his handkerchiefs. . . .
>
> The governor stayed with us here at home in Montgomery last week. He assures one and all that you are doing such a wonderful job, and that a Major Dent at Fort Mitchell admires you so much. We are proud of you.
>
> I love you. My heart warms to hear others sing your praises. By extension I feel they also sing mine, for I am part of you, Moultrie, my darling.
>
> We also miss you. The ball at Milford's

Tuesday evening last was not nearly as much fun as it would have been had you been present to demonstrate those naughty new waltz steps you learned when you were in Vienna last year. The waltz is such a wicked dance, my Moultrie. To behold men and women actually holding each other close while dancing, why, it boggles the mind. Everyone asked about you. . . .

"I miss you, too," Moultrie whispered. Standing, he stretched, then stopped and picked up a log and pushed it onto the fire. Sparks splashed upward into the chimney. Helen and her dances. Moultrie smiled.

It was sad news about the Judge. It sounded as if he had consumption, though he certainly didn't look it. Or, Moultrie corrected himself, he hadn't looked it six weeks ago. Then he had been florid, not pale, beefy, not wasted.

Moultrie turned from the fire and pulled out his watch. Six o'clock. John Page would be there any minute. He'd only just met the lanky, sad-faced captain the day before. He had been returning to Fort Mitchell from a manhunt with a couple of Crazy Wolf's warriors. Page had impressed him. The man had obviously known what he was doing.

Moultrie closed the watchcase and put the watch back in his fob. His brother, Henry, had given him the timepiece as a graduation present three years earlier. Henry. His God-loving, fun-fearing older brother, the holiest man in St. John's Parish, South Carolina. "Dear Henry," Moultrie whispered. "He tries so hard not to disapprove, to like Helen. They both want me to be the man they think Father was, a man devoted to his home, his family, his land, his crops, his neighbors and his God. Lord, but he was none of those."

Get out of here, Moultrie thought. Get some air. Do something. He strode to the door of his room and yanked it open.

John Page was standing there, almost blocking the view of the parade ground empty in the darkness behind him. "Damn, Ravenel," he laughed, "don't tell me you sensed me coming?"

"Come in." Moultrie stepped back. "You're just in time for a drink."

"Some of the major's private stock?"

"Good Lord, no." Moultrie chuckled. "That stuff will dissolve your teeth."

"I know." Page's angular grin filled and transformed his face. "I took the liquor test, too. Only I failed."

"The major thinks well of you now." As he spoke, Moultrie filled two glasses from the decanter on the table by the window. "Here you are." Handing Page his glass, he raised his own. "Cheers."

Moultrie then told John Page, "I suppose you're wondering why I called you here to my lodge."

Page nodded, sipped and waited.

"There's been an atrocity, and I can't just let it pass," Moultrie began. He gave a straightforward account of the things a white man had done to an Indian woman. Page listened patiently.

When Moultrie sipped his own whiskey, ending the account, John Page said, "So you're saying the man had raped the Indian woman in this vicious way."

Moultrie nodded. "That's right."

"And you and two braves delivered the man to the sheriff?"

"That's right."

Page noted the slight flush in Moultrie's face. "That's not drink," he declared. "It's anger." He took another sip of his whiskey. "You're right," he nodded. "This beats the hell out of the major's swill." He glanced again from his glass to Moultrie's face. "Well, what did the sheriff say?"

Moultrie leaned forward, his eyes fixed on the fire. "He said, 'I can't.' "

"I can't, what?"

" 'I can't fill my jail with men that're just out having a little fun. If the man wants to roll in filth, that's his business. It ain't like it was a white woman, now. Besides, it's a free country.' " Moultrie paused, then said, "That's a direct quote."

Page had heard other stories in the same vein. He could complete this one. "Let me guess the rest of it," he requested.

"Guess." Moultrie leaned back slowly and closed his eyes. Suddenly he felt infinitely weary. "What else do you think the sheriff said?"

Page took a last swallow of his whiskey and put the glass down carefully on the table. "That he wasn't going to do anything for any Indians and an Indian-loving, long-nosed, hotty-totty aristocrat."

Moultrie did not open his eyes. "He wasn't quite so eloquent, but that's the gist of the first part."

"And the second part went like this." Page thought for a moment. "I'm a white man and a plain man, and let no one mistake it. No one tells me what to do. I know my own mind, and by God, I'm going to follow it without so much as a 'by your leave.' Let any man tell me different and I'll teach him a thing or two about respect."

"That's right," Moultrie answered. "And then there wasn't much more said."

"Except for you then advising the sheriff he had better sleep with loaded weapons and one eye open in the future, if he plans to stay in Creek Indian country."

"Something like that."

"You're just everybody's friend, aren't you?"

Moultrie smiled faintly.

Later. Dusk. Bitter wind, and stars that looked brittle.

Cicero squatted before the fire. It filled the hearth with eye-burning light and heat. Lights danced like live things on the mortared log walls of the lodge Moultrie had been given at Fort Mitchell. Cicero studied Moultrie closely. It was not often that Ravenel fell into dark moods. He appeared to be falling into one now. Violence and hurt were a possibility. He took up one of Moultrie's boots to shine it.

"Two things are bothering you," he professed. "One, you want to see Miss Dupré and two, you are mad as hell about how your own white folks are treating—and mistreating—the Indians."

Moultrie did not answer.

Cicero rocked back on his heels, squatting before the fire. The warmth was precious to him. "Thank God I'm not out there in the cold, marching around with all those soldiers on that parade ground."

He could hear the drill sergeant braying commands. Marching feet pounded the gritted ground rhythmically. Cicero cocked his head, listened for a moment, then said, "What are you thinking about, Ravenel?"

"Nothing." Moultrie's voice sounded as though it was far away.

Cicero shook his head. Moultrie's apprehension annoyed him. It seemed so self-pitying. "There is no use fretting over either of those two things, particularly the second, for there is nothing you can do. Any more than you can do anything to stop white men from doing what they do to blacks."

Moultrie held his silence. Cicero started polishing the boot again, rubbing with more vigor than before.

"Cicero," Moultrie finally said, "you'll wear out that leather."

Cicero saw Moultrie was sitting up, feet swinging over the side of the bed. Cicero felt better. He grinned. "If I wear out the leather, you will have to stay here, indoors, and you will not be able to insist we scout the swamps so often."

"Quit complaining." Moultrie was grinning now, too. "No matter how bad the swamps may be to you, you're not being shot at as those soldiers drilling out there are."

"Ravenel, I surely will be shot if you keep up this foolishness about saving Indians."

"No one is going to shoot us, Cicero. You know as well as I do that Uncle Sam would run all over them if they shot an Indian agent."

"But not if they only shoot the Indian agent's black man."

"Oh, yes, Uncle would, if the black is worth as much as you are."

Cicero hooted in laughter. He placed the boot next to the other one on the pine board floor.

"And what would my woman say if I come to her full of holes. She is not interested in a man full of holes."

Moultrie laughed. Standing, he stretched. "So you have a woman here already, do you?"

"As if you didn't know, Ravenel," he teased. "I've got a squaw. She doesn't speak any English as yet, and

I speak little Creek. But Lord, we understand each other fine when it's dark."

Moultrie stretched again. "What do you want with an Indian girl, Cicero? I thought you had better sense." He spoke casually.

"Like your Uncle John?"

Moultrie sighed. "Cicero, Cicero. Even among Indians who do not matter to most white men, a white man can still do things no black man can. So, no playing around with Indian wenches. I've got enough problems without having to make sure some jealous Indian doesn't split your fool head open and show the world how empty it is." He turned, grabbed his coat, wrenched open the door and slammed it behind him.

Still standing in front of the fire, Cicero stared after Moultrie, his face hot with the sudden rush of blood to his cheeks. They seldom spoke sharply to each other.

When they did, the words stung.

It had been two days since Cicero had mentioned Uncle John's affair with a squaw back twenty-five years before. The two days had done nothing, so far as Moultrie could see, to lessen Cicero's resentment over Moultrie's interference in his Indian affairs. It still weighed down the atmosphere like a heavy cloud, but now Moultrie ignored it. He had other things on his mind. For one, he was wondering about the trip he and Cicero were making back to Crazy Wolf's village, two days south of the fort and just north of Eufaula. Moultrie had determined that he was going to start pressuring Crazy Wolf to convince his people to leave their reservation lands and move back to the Indian Territory over the summer.

Moultrie had several reasons for his decision.

Chief of these was the war, which he was afraid was getting perceivably closer every day. More and more outrages were being perpetrated against Indians. More and more Indians were reacting in anger instead of with sense.

That was why Moultrie had told the sheriff to sleep armed in the future: so he wouldn't wake up dead at the hands of Indians who were angry that he had let go the rapist that Moultrie and the braves had brought him.

The other reason Moultrie was more anxious than ever to get Crazy Wolf's village and other Yuchi villages moving westward was that John Page had told him of the horrors of moving in the winter.

"Moving the Indians," Page had explained, "is a horrible business at any time. You can't clothe them. You can't buy them enough food. You can't get them enough transport. People try to cheat you at every turn.

"It is mostly the weather, though," Page had continued, "which is most devastating." As he had spoken, he had become agitated. He was jumping up and pacing, stopping to bang his right fist against his left palm for emphasis. "I started out with six hundred thirty Indians last fall. By the time we got to Fort Gibson, just over the Arkansas line in the Indian Territory, there were only four hundred sixty-nine left. One out of every four died. That's almost a death a day. Those Indians were sick, half-naked, and half-starved. They nearly froze in the rain and sleet and snow. Some did. They just couldn't withstand it."

Chapter 5

The trail curved with the bend in the Chattahoochee. Pulling up the reins of his horse, Moultrie watched a flight of swallows cross the water. The birds are early, he thought, but spring can't be too far away. He shivered as a gust of wind struck. The middays were still cold. In a month they won't be, though, he reflected. All the more reason to convince Crazy Wolf now to go west. It'll be harder to make him move after he's started spring planting.

He heard a distant shout. "Hiyee!"

Moultrie turned back from the water and looked down the trail. "Hiyee!" It rang out again.

Crazy Wolf's older son, Little Hawk, was whipping his pony up the trail.

"He's in a hurry," Moultrie said aloud. "I wonder what's the matter."

Cicero grunted. He did not know.

The boy reined up. He was panting and heaving. His mount was lathered at the mouth. They had obviously been pushing hard. Gradually the boy's agitated breathing subsided.

"Brother to my father," he said to Moultrie, "Mother says you must come quickly."

"What's happened?" Seeing Little Hawk's strained look, Moultrie felt a sudden, wrenching fear. The skin over the boy's face was drawn taut. Cheeks which were usually round with life and laughter were now etched with weariness and worry. The boy shook his head. He was unable to talk for a moment. "What's happened?" Moultrie asked again.

Little Hawk took a deep, ragged breath. "A band of whites attacked our village at dawn," he finally let out. His voice was small, barely above a whisper. His lips were trembling. "Fire," he added, his voice stronger, more urgent. "Shooting."

"Your father? Where is he?"

"Not there. Off hunting."

"Many killed?"

"Yes." The boy bit his lip. The husky ten-year-old that Moultrie remembered suddenly appeared frail and small. Moultrie felt his facial muscles tighten. "Lord, it's happened!"

He turned to Cicero and translated for Little Hawk.

"Sweet Jesus." Cicero, his anger gone, looked stricken.

"Go back to the fort. Tell Page. Tell him to bring a company. Fast." Moultrie clipped his words in his haste.

Cicero wheeled his horse around, lashed it and set off at a gallop.

The black man had raced off northward. Then the

white man had started off to the south. Little Hawk had been left behind.

"Come on at your own pace," the white man had urged, "or you will kill your pony."

The white friend of Little Hawk's father had been right. Little Hawk had ridden him hard, harder than he had ever ridden a horse before. Even so, the pony had seemed to move slowly. To Little Hawk's anxious eyes, it had been an eternity between one landmark and the next on the trail north from his village toward Fort Mitchell.

The forest on one side and the river on the other had bordered his path, their strength and majesty seemingly taunting him and retarding his progress. He had ridden on regardlessly, leaning forward almost to his pony's ear. He urged his mount on, pleading, praising the pony's strength and endurance, calling on its love.

"Find Ravenel, find Ravenel, find Ravenel."

The galloping hooves had pounded an incessant accompaniment. Now, his mission accomplished, Little Hawk wanted only to sleep. Sleep. His head nodded forward.

He found no sleep. His memory tortured him. Little Hawk heard the shots, saw the fire. Screams rose up with the smoke. Brutal men laughed. A dog howled, then yelped. Jerking himself upright, Little Hawk opened his eyes. "Mother!" he screamed. "Mother!"

The village was ashes and smoke when Moultrie got there late that afternoon. Overhead, vultures circled. A dog whimpered. Otherwise, nothing was moving. Even the air was still, the stench of burnt flesh and charred wood stagnating. Bending over one body, Moultrie stiffened.

It was Running Water, Little Hawk's mother. Her clothes were torn, and her limbs were spread at odd angles on the ground. He touched an arm. It was cold with death.

Suddenly, Moultrie felt sick. He had never seen death such as this. Turning quickly from the body, he retched. He stumbled to the edge of the village and sat down on the ground. He rested his head between his knees.

It was there that Crazy Wolf found Moultrie at dusk. "So, Little Hunting Brother," he addressed him, "you have seen."

Moultrie had stood when he heard the Indian coming and was leaning against a tree when he arrived. Crazy Wolf, his face a stone mask and his voice even, continued. "If I had not recognized you, Little Hunting Brother, you would have been a dead man. You should have remembered what I taught you. You should not have ridden straight here. We could have been other white men. Murderers."

The Indian stopped. Moultrie could think of nothing to say, other than, "I am sorry, Crazy Wolf."

"You know this is war." The Indian's tone was almost conversational.

"It's suicide, Big Hunting Brother." Moultrie shared the helpless feeling. He had worked so hard to prevent this. Now, what could he say? In Crazy Wolf's place, he too would fight. But damn it, Moultrie thought, that's wrong. He had to tell Crazy Wolf so.

"Your children will die," he cautioned, his voice sounding thin in his own ears.

Crazy Wolf turned away to look out over the desolation, mercifully shrouded now in gloom. "The whites will not be satisfied until we are dead or gone." His voice sounded fierce. "And we would rather die like men in the land of our ancestors, beside the ashes of our sacred fires, than drop like cattle on the road to where the sun sleeps."

Moultrie said nothing.

Turning back to him, Crazy Wolf added, "We did not know. We arrived here just in time to hear you coming." Behind the stony mask, Moultrie saw his pain. Crazy Wolf spoke again. "We do not even have time to gather our dead. As soon as the moon rises, we must go to find the women and children who survived."

"There is one you do not have to look for, Big Hunting Brother." Moultrie's heart was aching for his friend. "Little Hawk is alive. Running Water sent him to find me. His pony could not keep up. I told him to come on at his own pace. He should get here sometime after sunup."

Moultrie thought Crazy Wolf had not heard. Then the Indian put a hand on his shoulder. "Thank you, Little Hunting Brother. You will keep him safe for me. When he comes tomorrow you will tell him I have said that he should stay with you. I may not see him again. Keep my son alive."

An hour later the Indians were gone.

Little Hawk did not fear the night. The moon was high and full. Pools of light spread along the path, lapping at the shadows, rippling around clumps of trees swaying gently in the breeze. Beyond the pale light, the darkness massed over the secret rustlings of possums, raccoons and squirrels. A fox barked. A sudden cry floated shrilly over the gentle passing of the river. An owl flapped heavily upward, a rabbit kicking feebly in its claws.

Shrugging, Little Hawk turned back to studying the trail. White men—men on shod horses—had ridden north as far as this point, driving cattle before them. Probably our own cattle, Little Hawk decided.

A branch snapped. Startled, his heart pounding, Little Hawk looked about. A doe, swollen with child, stepped into the path, glanced to the left and then the right, then crossed over, heading toward the water. Little Hawk let out his breath, slowly, softly. A warrior would not jump as I just did, he thought. But it is not stupid to fear that some white men may have stayed behind in ambush. Dismounting, Little Hawk knelt and looked more closely at the tracks.

All the cattle and men, he decided, took the fork to the ferry at Barnham's plantation. That means they're crossing the Chattahoochee to Georgia. I'll tell Father.

Little Hawk turned to mount, then hesitated. No, he thought, I'd better circle through the woods and come into the village from the south. That is what Father would do.

Leaving the trail, he angled southwest through a break in the undergrowth, leading his pony.

Little Hawk studied his burned village.

A horse nickered. But he was fairly confident that there was no one in the village except the white friend of his father, Little Hunting Brother.

It was probably Little Hunting Brother's horse nickering in greeting.

Still, Little Hawk was not going to take any chances. His breath billowy white before him in the cold night, he moved forward slowly, crouching in the shelter of piles of burnt rubble, darting to one pile, then waiting. Suddenly he stopped still. He wanted to cry out.

He had just touched a hand. It was cold and

dead. He bent in the darkness. There it was. An arm stretched out from under a log as if to touch something, but it just hung in the air.

Little Hawk had not come home unobserved.

Moultrie Ravenel followed him by the sights of his pistol. He released the hammer and thumbed it back to safety position.

He sighed. That boy has a lot to learn about stealth, even as I myself do. Lord spare both of us, but I almost blew his head to junk before I recognized him, didn't I?

Wouldn't that have been something to tell Crazy Wolf? I say, Big Hunting Brother, I sure have taken good care of your son, all right. I've shot him dead for you.

I would like to spank the boy. We came too close.

Holstering his weapon, he stepped from the shadows into the glow of the moon. Little Hawk took no notice. At that moment, there was nothing else in the world but the dead arm.

Moultrie walked forward softly. Five feet from Little Hawk, he stopped.

"Little Hawk." Moultrie called his name softly. "Little Hawk?"

The boy turned his head slowly. "Where is Mother?"

"Dead."

His face sunk. Tears filled his eyes. "How many others are like this?" The boy gestured at the gnarled hand of the dead man under the timbers.

Moultrie's heart was wrenched by the lifelessness in Little Hawk's voice. "Many. But your sister and brother, I think, got away. Come. Let me feed you." Moultrie gestured for him to follow.

Later, as he ate, Little Hawk described the raid. The dawn, like the one on this day, had been clear and cold. That, Little Hawk said, was when the attack had started. "I was just waking up. I heard a scream. It was Spring Swallow." The boy fell silent for a moment. "There was a shot," he said finally. "I looked out from my father's lodge to see Spring Swallow fall, her arms like this." Little Hawk spread his own arms wide.

Moultrie visualized it all with horror as Little Hawk spoke. The troop galloped in on horseback, shouting and shooting. Women gathered up children. The few warriors left in the village grabbed rifles and fired, often at no specific target. New screams sounded. Another troop broke from the cover of the forest on foot. Three warriors were killed before they had fired a shot. The battle lasted five minutes at most. All the other six warriors were killed as well.

Little Hawk and his brother and sister ran toward the river with their mother, Running Water. Their father's second wife followed. Just before they left sight of the village, Little Hawk looked back. Not a warrior was standing. White men were everywhere. They were lighting torches at cooking fires and throwing them on the lodges. Several were on fire already.

Drawing up on the bluff, Running Water told Little Hawk to ride to Moultrie Ravenel at the fort and get help as quickly as possible. Little Hawk circled the village and found his pony. Leading it through the swamp, he had no pursuers.

Five hours later he found Moultrie on the road from the fort. And that was Little Hawk's narrative.

"You didn't know that your mother had been killed?" Moultrie asked.

"No." Little Hawk wore the same expression

Moultrie had seen on the boy's father's face the night before. "I thought Mother and the others were safe. I can't understand. What could have happened?" The question was a cry of anguish.

Moultrie did not tell Little Hawk his own thoughts. It was his guess, however, that while putting the children into boats, Running Water heard the raiders approaching. As a bird diverts a snake or hawk from its nest, she ran off then, hoping to distract the men. Apparently, the plan had succeeded all too well. As Moultrie pictured it, they chased her, hopped and skipped in circles about her until she fell exhausted and then kicked her back to the village. There they had abused her again and again until she had died. That much was plain, judging by the condition of her body. The raping may well have been the least of the things they did.

Moultrie slammed his right fist into his left palm. "We'll one day destroy the men who did those things to your mother," he told Little Hawk.

"Column, whoa."

Holding up his right hand, Captain John Page signaled his men to stop.

Ahead was the village of Crazy Wolf. In the bright day, the burned lodges were distinct jagged black shapes. Some smoked still, and persistent little flames flickered here and there. Scattered lumps on the ground interested the buzzards. Small animals plucked at them. Page knew they were corpses and felt nauseous.

The column of horses stilled except for their heavy breathing and the sound of hooves occasionally kicking the earth. Everyone stared.

Page did not want to ride in. And he knew no one else did, either.

Sergeant Terence McCoy, sitting stiff in the saddle beside him, said, "God be good to them."

Yes. To Page, to McCoy, and to the others, the picture was too much to take in all at once, especially after a peaceful morning ride through the forest.

John Page suddenly came alert. Two figures were moving there in the village. A voice to his rear called, "It's Marse Moultrie and Little Hawk."

Page was startled. He had not heard Cicero come up beside him. Looking to where the black man pointed, Page saw Moultrie Ravenel and an Indian boy carrying a corpse between them. They took it from the burnt ruins of a log cabin to a clear spot where other bodies had been laid out. Animals and birds fled as they came. "That's the boy who came and got you?" Page asked.

"Yes, sir. His pappy is the chief of this here village."

"He isn't chief of much anymore." McCoy's voice was filled with disgust.

"There'll be a reckoning on that score soon, Sergeant."

"There never is, sir. Why this time?"

Page bristled. "Sergeant."

"Sorry, sir. I didn't mean disrespect. I was thinking aloud. I've seen how we've gotten justice for the Indians before."

"The sergeant is absolutely correct," Page agreed. "But if anyone ever questions me on it, I never said so." Page stood in the saddle and slashed downward with his arm. "Forward," he yelled.

The troop moved ahead, twenty strong.

* * *

Page and Moultrie faced each other. "Where are the rest of them?" Page asked, gesturing toward the bodies on the ground.

Moultrie shrugged. He was weary and angry. "Half are hiding. The men who were hunting at the time of the attack are looking for them."

"They're not going to do anything stupid, are they, Ravenel?" Page frowned. "We can't have them charging after the men who did this. There'd be unholy hell to pay."

"Would you blame them?" It was Sergeant McCoy, standing next to Page, who spoke. There was fury in his voice. "It seems to me that if the Creeks are going to get justice, they have to go for it themselves."

Moultrie studied Page. He did not know many officers who would take talk like that from a sergeant.

Page smiled grimly. "We're going to be there, McCoy, before the Indians. Mount your men." Then, turning to Moultrie as McCoy went off, he asked, "You coming?"

Moultrie, watching the retreating figure of McCoy, did not answer right away. He cupped his hands over his face and blew on them. The white of his breath hardly showed against the sunlight. It was a bright day, but cold. He clapped his hands together a couple of times. When he had been moving bodies, he had been warm. "You're damned right I'm coming," he answered at last. "But, first, you and I are going to have a word."

"All right." Page strolled toward a large elm. Moultrie followed. "Now," Page grunted when they were away from the soldiers. "Let's have it."

Moultrie picked up a charred stick and hurled it at the surrounding trees.

"Does that make you feel better?" Page asked.

"No. It's war now. You know that. After this, it's war."

Page hissed. "Christ Almighty." He paused for a moment, then said, "Damn it, Ravenel. You were here and aware this had happened? And you didn't say a thing in warning?" His voice was low. His tone was angry.

"*You* weren't here, John, so don't ask *me* why *I* didn't say anything. None of us have ever wanted to say anything about incidents such as this, hoping that if we said nothing, it would be as though they never happened." Moultrie was hoarse and weary in his rage. "What the bloody hell would you have said with the man's wife out there, used as a football, raped by God knows how many, dead, and now the whole place burned?"

John Page did not answer. Finally he murmured, "Nothing." He looked at Moultrie for a long while, then squatted and fingered the soil.

"You really think so. War."

Moultrie squatted beside him. "You think so, too."

"Maybe Crazy Wolf and the rest of his Creeks can still be reasoned with. Maybe they can be convinced this was just one isolated thing." Page swept his hand toward the smoking lodges.

Buzzards soared on the heated air rising from them.

"You know it's not just one isolated thing. If you believe that, you believe the men who handed Christ His Cross were not bent upon mischief."

"But maybe the Creeks *can* be convinced to hold off, that they'll be destroyed if they don't."

"Maybe that's wishful thinking, too. What would you do at this point if you were Crazy Wolf, or any other Creek?"

Page sighed. "Go to war."

"No matter what the price?"

"No matter what."

Moultrie stood. "Then face it. And others higher up in the command and administration had better face it, too. The Creeks are going to war, and it's our own doing. We finally forced them."

Page threw down a piece of straw he had been chewing. "Well, we knew it had to happen." His voice was bitter. "Hitchitis and Cheahas are rampaging. So why not the Yuchis? Poor devils. Their revenge is going to cost them."

Moultrie stepped out from under the elm's shadow. "I became an agent because I hoped to forestall this. Some help I've been." The village's ruins seemed to mock him. "No wonder the Indians are on the warpath."

Page stirred restlessly. "Even if it is hopeless, we have to try to defuse it."

"Captain." McCoy's voice rang out across the debris of the village. "The troop's ready."

"Right. Thank you, Sergeant." Page turned to Moultrie. "Anything else before we go?"

"Do you know who the raiders were?"

"It's obvious, isn't it?" Page spat out the word.

Moultrie nodded. Sixty or eighty men together like that, maybe a hundred. It could only have been a state militia company. No other group would have turned out a band of that size with the discipline and command this group must have had to have performed as it did.

"Georgia or Alabama militia?"

"Georgia. You saw the trail."

"Yes." Page turned on his heel. Over his shoulder, he called back. "Let's go."

"To fight the militia?"

Page paused. "No, we're investigating the reason for the raid." Suddenly slapping his leg with a gloved hand, Page started toward his mount again. Moultrie, watching him go, heard him mutter, "Damn, damn, damn!"

Moultrie stepped from the shadows and strode through the light and ruins toward Cicero and Little Hawk. The Indian boy and the black man were standing together, mute and forlorn, away from the soldiers. "I've got to get the boy to stay with us," Moultrie said aloud. "But how?"

Moultrie came up to the boy and put a hand on his shoulder. "Your father wants you to come with me." Plunging on, intent on stopping Little Hawk's protest before he had had a chance to utter it, Moultrie said, "Crazy Wolf wants you to come with me to help me. You can point out men you saw here yesterday."

Moultrie was anxious. Was he pushing too hard? He rushed on. "Crazy Wolf," he continued, "told me you were man enough to help me."

Little Hawk nodded. Though he was a very small boy, he tried to speak as a man. "I will come with you."

"Good." Moultrie tried to be matter-of-fact. "You will ride with `Cicero." Turning to Cicero, he translated.

"I don't know what to say to him," Cicero warned, "but I can watch him."

Leaving them, Moultrie mounted and spurred his

mare and cantered over to Page. "Let's go. I'll ride with you."

They started off trotting two abreast, through the swamp, past the cornfield, along the savannahs where the village cattle had grazed until yesterday.

Chapter 6

Page and Moultrie rode in silence for three hours through the cold brightness of the midday sun. Finally Page called a halt at a small, sluggish stream. Horses were watered and kindling gathered for fires to heat coffee.

All around the troop were signs of the raiders: hoofprints in the mud of the riverbank, droppings, broken branches. Sergeant Terence McCoy shook his head. "Captain," he said, "I'd say from these prints that our chasing this party is a little like a squirrel chasing a bear." McCoy spit out a stream of tobacco juice. "We've got to be following a hundred men."

Page turned to Moultrie. "Ravenel, you want to tell him?"

Moultrie knocked his pipe clean on his boot heel and put it in his pocket. "Even if we had a thousand men," he told McCoy, "we wouldn't fight them."

"Not fight." McCoy's face was twisted in disbelief.

"You mean we're going to do nothing? We're going to let those men get away with murder?"

Page, his hands in his pockets and his breath white before him in the cold, nodded. "That's right, McCoy. We can't go fighting our own militia, and that's what these men must be. What's worse, they've just started a war. We're going to have to help them fight it, and there isn't a damned thing we can do about it."

"Well, Captain, all I can say is it makes a man a little ashamed to have a white skin. Damned if it doesn't."

"You're an unusual man for your times, Sergeant, and sometimes the things you say amaze me," Page said. "I basically share your sense of injustice, but we have a job to do in spite of it. Mount your men. You know your duty."

McCoy drew himself up to attention, saluted smartly and turned on his heel and marched off.

"Oh, and Sergeant!" Page's voice rang through the cold. "Shake out some scouts. We're not fighting anybody yet, but I don't want to be surprised by someone who doesn't know that."

Saluting again, McCoy shouted his commands. As he did, Page turned back to Moultrie. "Well, Ravenel, here we go."

Moving back along the column, Moultrie found Cicero talking with gesture and dance to Little Hawk. Three mounted troopers watched, smiling as Cicero tried to communicate English with the help of pantomime to a boy who spoke only Creek.

"Don't you worry none," Cicero was saying. "Old Cicero going to be there with his sword. Yes, sir. Just like the Good Book say. I going to hack them and chop them and turn them every which way but loose."

As he spoke, he slashed about with an imaginary sword, his face fierce. "Yes, sir! Them low-down, no-count poor buckra going to think the devil's done come for them when they see Cicero charging after them."

The troopers watching laughed aloud.

Looking up at Moultrie, Cicero grinned. "Marse Moultrie, you tell this boy. Ain't I one mean warrior? Ain't I tree raccoon better than a dog, catch fish better than a 'gator, and wrestle better than Jacob in the Good Book? Tell him."

Later, as Moultrie and Cicero talked in low tones over the head of the boy trotting along on his pony between them, Cicero stopped playing the buffoon role and spoke comfortably. "Maybe the boy doesn't understand a thing I say yet, but he will. I'll learn his tongue and teach him ours. For now I did bring him to laughter. And that's important. Poor lost boy. I can show him how to forget his troubles for a while, anyhow."

Moultrie was touched. Cicero just shrugged. "Children need to laugh. It doesn't take much to make them. Although God knows there isn't much to laugh about right now."

As Cicero spoke, quail started up in a whir of flapping wings from a cover ahead of the column. Startled soldiers, slumped half asleep in their saddles after two days of hard riding, jerked upright and reached for their weapons. Holding up his hand, Page halted the column. Anything could have driven those birds up, he knew. Probably a skunk or a bobcat.

But it could also have been a man.

"Hold fire!" Page yelled.

The column came to a halt just as one of the scouts Sergeant McCoy had sent ahead broke through the cover. He was coming at a dead gallop between the barren trees, ducking and swerving to avoid branches. Pulling up in front of Page, he saluted.

"What is it, Jaeger?" The tenseness in Page's voice made the words electric.

Corporal Jaeger had been in the U.S. eighteen months and in the army a year, but he still had trouble being understood in English. Stammering between his gasps for breath, Jaeger tried to report. Words, though, wouldn't come out. Page and McCoy were impatient.

"Come on, man, out with it."

"Damn it, Dutchman, use your tongue."

Jaeger managed two words: "*Soldaten*. Soldiers!" Then he pointed in the direction from which he had come.

Mounted men were spurring horses toward them, turning easily among the trees, their horses flattening underbrush with their hooves. They formed up in order of charge and came onward slowly. They bore sabers at rest upon their shoulders.

Page's grin was mirthless. "There's our brave Georgia light horse militia, Moultrie. Here we go. God, how I hate this."

"Captain," McCoy pointed, "they're coming in on our flanks, too."

Page slapped a hand on the sergeant's arm. "Easy, McCoy. There won't be a fight. They're just flexing their muscles for us. There's no worry."

"We could take them, Captain," McCoy said confidently. "We're professional soldiers. They're not. We could break their charge line on the first rush."

"We're not going to take such brutal advantage, Sergeant."

McCoy saluted without expression. But it was plain to see that Page's acknowledgment pleased him.

Moultrie made a quick count of the oncoming riders. "Page, there are at least fifty of them."

Page nodded. "A ragtag crew, if ever there was one," he noted under his breath. "Jaeger was giving them credit, calling them soldiers. There isn't a uniform among them."

"Maybe not, but they're armed and they're approaching with some semblance of discipline." Moultrie saw the front line of the militia troop stop ten yards away. Behind the thirty or so in that line, back roughly another twenty yards, he could see men among the trees in a second line. All of these men had rifles cradled in their arms.

"Welcome to Georgia, gentlemen." The man who called out was burly. "Bill McElveen's my name," he announced with a slight bow of his head, "Colonel Bill McElveen, Georgia Militia. These are some of my troopers."

"What's the meaning of your *boys* surrounding us like this, McElveen?" Page's voice was angry.

Sergeant McCoy grinned at the slur.

"Don't get so heated up, Captain." The Georgian grinned. "Just practicing precautions. That's all. You've got no reason to fret none."

"Is yours the troop that raided Crazy Wolf's village yesterday?" Moultrie asked, making no attempt to conceal his hostility.

McElveen turned to look at the Indian agent. "What if it was?"

"I'm curious to know why you decided to begin a major war," Moultrie said. His voice was tight. "Without reason or authorization."

"Retaliation."

"For what?"

"Plenty."

Moultrie snorted. "Plenty of nothing." He inhaled deeply to control his anger. "That village hasn't been involved in any raids on whites."

"Oh no?"

"No."

"That's what you say."

One of the militiamen behind McElveen spoke up. "Colonel, the man's calling you a liar to your face. Aren't you going to say anything about it?"

Moultrie looked him over. He sat easily in his saddle, blocky, thick-necked and fit. He had a tendency to smile crookedly, as Moultrie had seen southern men with sure contempt for others often smile.

McElveen was obviously enjoying his demonstration of power. "Oh, now Peters, we're just having an honest gentleman's disagreement, that's all," McElveen answered, not looking back at the man, keeping his eyes on Moultrie. "I don't think this man is really calling me a liar."

"But I am," Moultrie insisted.

McElveen laughed. "Any man is to be forgiven one childish error in judgment."

"I don't know." Peters shook his head. He, too, was enjoying the confrontation and the advantage of a larger number of men on his side. "I think it's pretty poor when a white man starts defending worthless savages like that against his own kind. I sure do." Then, looking beyond Ravenel, he finally noticed Little Hawk, concealed by Cicero and some of Page's men.

Peters grinned. "We'll take your prisoner off your hands for you, Captain," he told Page. "He belongs to the State of Georgia, not to Washington or to you."

"You so much as touch that boy, Peters," Page warned, "and I'll personally turn your skin into your shroud."

Peters laughed. "Look around you, Captain. We've got two guns to every one of yours."

"I won't repeat my sergeant's recent estimate of the worth of your two guns, mister," Page responded.

McElveen interrupted. "You're being foolish, Peters. These troopers are going to help us fight the Indians. We've got no cause to rile them up. So shut it. And forget the boy for now."

"Colonel, we can't." Then, looking at McElveen's face, Peters apparently thought better of continuing to differ.

Moultrie himself saw the hardness there and understood that a man could be hurt arguing with McElveen for too long.

Peters finally gave in. "All right, Colonel. If you say so."

"I say so."

Moultrie noted that the two men, McElveen the older and Peters the younger, were much alike in physical makeup. Their temperaments were also similar. They were hard men. Their apparent gentleness was deceptive. In most ways each could have been a copy of the other, but there was one basic difference.

McElveen was all fire.

Peters was all wind.

Some days later at Fort Mitchell, Major Jeremiah Dent, Captain John Page and Indian Agent Moultrie Ravenel sat together drinking a bottle of the major's tear-inducing whiskey.

Thinking together, they were trying to make some sense of the building events, to determine their causes, and to develop ways of reversing them.

All still agreed that the last was unlikely.

They focused on various men who would personally profit by an open war between the Creek Confederation and the United States government.

The name of William Hobson surfaced again and again.

The major looked from Page to Moultrie Ravenel and back again. "Why would a Columbus merchant like Hobson be behind this raid on Crazy Wolf's town? It doesn't make sense."

Moultrie shifted in his chair, then leaned forward and said, "It does. McElveen has been acting as agent for Hobson, tricking, forcing, sometimes even legitimately buying some lands from Indians for the speculating company Hobson's put together."

"Hmm." The major drew on his cigar, showering ash over the front of his shirt. "So there's a connection between Hobson and McElveen. That doesn't explain anything." He paused. "Not unless, of course, Hobson's real goal is all that land of Crazy Wolf's people, too."

"Could be." Page, his lanky frame half lounging in the wooden armchair, spoke deliberately. "Moultrie and I, though, think there's more to the story."

"You mean about those new directives from Secretary of War Cass to put a stop to speculators like Hobson and company?"

"That's right." Page pulled himself upright as he spoke. "If there's an Indian War, the government will have to come to the defense of the whites. What the speculators have done to grab all the Indian land will be forgotten."

"And," Major Dent nodded ruminatively, "the Indians may then be forced to give up *all* their lands here and go west to the Indian Territory."

Moultrie, who had sat back in his chair, now

leaned forward again and nodded. "Exactly. But there is just a chance that these men can be stopped."

"How?" Dent was skeptical.

"I'm going to see Governor Clay in Tuscaloosa, then go to Montgomery, talk to the newspaper editors there. If we can convince influential people like the governor and the newspapermen that the State of Alabama is being tricked into a war unnecessarily and for damned fishy reasons, maybe we can do something to blunt this war after all. I personally don't think so. But I say, try."

The major was still skeptical. "It might help," he added, "if you point out that it was the Georgia Militia, making an unauthorized crossing into Alabama, that carried out this raid."

Moultrie smiled. "Good point." He stood up. "I should be gone about three weeks. I want to spend a couple of days at home on the way to Tuscaloosa. I've only been there once in the last two months."

Page grinned. "More importantly, Ravenel here's not been in Montgomery at all in two months, and there's a young lady there—"

"Who will never see Captain John Page alive unless he learns discretion." Moultrie's voice was serious, but his eyes twinkled.

That night, Moultrie wrote to Helen.

I should arrive in Montgomery on the 25th. As I will be travel-worn and will have both Cicero and the Indian boy, Little Hawk, about whom I've written, with me, I shall plan to put up at Falkner's Inn and not trouble you and your father on that score.

I am looking forward to seeing you

very, very much. Here at Fort Mitchell, the absence of your grace and beauty is painful. In the field, it is doubly so. I hope you will play for me the Schubert piece I heard you play the day I left Montgomery two months ago. (Was it *The Trout*? Whatever.) I want to have it firmly in my memory, not teasing me with fragments of half-recalled motifs.

Tell Judge Dupré the war news is perhaps not as grim as it first seemed. I shall be going to see the governor in Tuscaloosa now to give just that message.

You were right: this is a stinking business—a "skunk-drunk mess," as Sergeant Terence McCoy would say. What a character he is. . . .

The letter went on for several pages. As Moultrie sealed it, there was a knock on the door to his quarters. "Come in," he called.

Page stuck his head in. "Don't have time to stop," he said. "Just wanted to let you know that Hobson is reported to have started a drive to petition the federal government to protect honest men such as himself from the disreputable elements hereabouts cheating the Indians."

Moultrie pushed away from the writing table and stood. "That son of a bitch. Thanks, John. You've just given me a case of heartburn."

"You're welcome. Have a good trip. I've got to go inspect the guard."

"Can't give you a drink?"

"No, thanks." Page grinned. "I've got enough heartburn of my own."

"More than enough." Moultrie tried to respond

with a grin. It was no good. "I'll have a drink to your sobriety. Maybe two."

"Right." Page turned, pulling the door shut behind him.

Moultrie walked to the table under the window opposite the fire. The decanter was half full. "Just enough," he decided. He picked up a glass and the crystal bottle and took them with him to his chair by the fire. Having put a fresh log on, he sat down, poured himself three fingers' measure of whiskey, and raised his glass in a mock toast.

He did not drink. He felt as though he had been suddenly attacked by two hounds named Insecurity and Depression. What the hell am I doing here? he asked himself.

Here, at Fort Mitchell, his home was a box of logs with only gritty mud and mortar between them to keep out cold and summer rain. A box with floors and ceilings of planks which had probably been warped when new. A box in which snakes and field rodents roomed with him for the winter.

This is not Forest Hall, Moultrie thought. This is not home.

There was one consolation. The rest of Fort Mitchell wasn't much better, and no one was more comfortable than he himself was; not officer, not enlisted man, not civilian.

He had once described Fort Mitchell in a letter to his brother: "It's a series of boxes inside the larger box which is our stockade. It was once a fairly formidable place, I imagine. Now, I believe our local ladies' watch and ward society could take it by assault any Sunday afternoon they chose. As we both know, having managed a fairly large establishment at Forest Hall, disrepair is an enemy more terrible than siege artillery for breaking a place apart."

Moultrie suddenly wanted a hot bath in his own porcelain tub, with soft linen to put on afterward, more than any thing. And he wanted Helen Dupré more than anyone.

He shook his head to pry himself back to reality. To the devil with self-pity, he thought. He drank, finally, shuddering as the whiskey went down his throat. He poured and drank again. The third and fourth glasses he sipped.

Gradually, the hot anger he had experienced when Page told him the news about Hobson subsided to a simmer of discontent.

And then, as the whiskey took hold, there was a welcome spreading numbness. He slept deeply.

No dreams tonight, he prayed.

They will only be unhappy ones.

Cicero, Little Hawk and Moultrie set out at dawn. There was a two-day ride ahead to Forest Hall.

Moultrie rode stiffly ahead of the other two. The whiskey was still with him. He imagined himself the castaway offspring of some loathsome creature. His muscles felt as though McElveen and Peters and five more of the Georgia Militia's biggest had used him for close-order combat demonstration. He wished he had a bottle of Jeremiah Dent's terrible whiskey so he could kill himself. Moultrie had a headache. He would have gladly contemplated blindness to relieve the pain in his eyes. There was not enough water in the world to quench his burning thirst.

Cicero watched Moultrie lurch about in his saddle and decided upon an act of mercy. He would leave Moultrie alone and not speak until spoken to this day.

And, during the trailside lunch of cold corn soup, fatback and hardtack, Cicero performed another act of mercy for Moultrie. He did not offer him any of the food.

There was neither censure nor pity in Cicero's reaction. He honestly wished an end to Moultrie's hangover. And to a degree, Cicero shared his unhappiness. Cicero knew Moultrie wished desperately for an end to the oppression of Indians, for a way out of the coming war, and for punishment of the men causing these events. Cicero also wished for similar things for his own people.

During the afternoon, Cicero gave Little Hawk his first instructions in English. He matched up specific things with their proper names. This is a horse. This is a pistol. That is a tree. There goes a rabbit. That up there is the sun.

Little Hawk clearly was not interested in learning at the time. He wore the worried look of a little old man. Cicero guessed he was too concerned about his people and his father to care about a new language.

After spending the day riding with a man and a boy who would not communicate, Cicero finally became bored and lonely. After dinner that evening, he began to hum, softly at first, then louder, not caring whether Moultrie and Little Hawk objected or not. He began singing in a rich baritone, swaying with a rhythm he beat softly on his knees, his eyes closed:

> I look down the road,
> And the road so lonesome.
> Lord, I got to walk
> Down that lonesome road.
> Ain't nobody else going to walk it for me.
> I got to walk it by myself.

The fire before him rose and fell, flaring up in sparkling intensity, then subsiding to a rich glow.

As Cicero finished, he glanced at the boy beside him. Little Hawk was sitting quietly, looking into the fire, tears brimming in his eyes. Cicero reached over and patted Little Hawk on the back, then started another song.

> In my time o' dying,
> I don't want nobody to moan.
> All I want my friend to do
> Is to close my dying eye.
> Well, well, well,
> So I can die easy,
> Well, well, well.

Moultrie's voice joined Cicero's on the second chorus. He sang so softly that it was almost as if he were whispering to himself, not wanting to be heard.

Cicero heard him. "Why, Marse Moultrie is feeling a little better," he said, teasing. Then he sang on:

> Well, well, well,
> Lord, let me die easy.

Cicero smiled at Moultrie and nodded, encouraging him to keep singing.

> Well, well, well,
> Jesus going to make up my dying bed.

Another verse, another chorus and then they ended their song softly. For some time afterward, there was only the flaring of the fire. Then another voice sounded. Little Hawk began some songs of his own Creek people, his voice pure and clear in the cold of the night as he sang of the wolf clan, the bear clan, of the fire's message and the moon's promise.

And when he was done, Cicero said, "Whether he ever learns English or not, the boy knows how to pay back favors in kind to his friends."

Forest Hall.

The whitewashed office of the plantation manager held a desk, three chairs, a bookcase, and under the window a small table. Looking in through the front door at Moultrie Ravenel at work, Soames twisted his hat in his hands. He scraped his feet on the tattered mat at the front door, then cleared his throat loudly. Still Moultrie did not look up. Peter Soames knocked and entered, stooping as he did so to avoid hitting his head on the door frame.

Moultrie looked up at last. "What is it, Soames?" He was preoccupied and irritated by the interruption.

"Nothing. I . . ." Soames could not finish. Suddenly angry with himself, Soames wondered, why does he always make me so nervous? He ain't scarcely more than a boy. Besides, it's me what knows how to run this plantation, not him.

"Damn it, Soames. What is it?" Moultrie barked.

Soames gulped. I am going to tell him, he thought. Yes, I am. I don't care. It ain't right.

Twisting his hat in his hands, Soames cleared his throat again. "It's that Indian boy, sir," he said finally. "He oughtn't to be up there to the big house."

"Why not?"

Soames felt the blood rush to his face. It ain't fair, he thought. I have no reason to be ashamed. I'm right on this. But then, I always was one to blush like a damned girl. He clenched his fists, crushing the brim of his floppy, black felt hat. "Indians ain't supposed to be mixing with white folks like that. They's savages."

"Soames," Moultrie began quietly, "I pay you to run Forest Hall. That's your business. Nothing else. What I do here is my business."

Soames looked away and nodded his head. "I just didn't want people to talk. You know how some are."

"You've taught me."

"Well, unless you've got something you want me to do, I'll just get back to work."

"Good idea. We can go over these accounts later." As he spoke, Moultrie turned back to the desk. He did not say good-bye.

Ain't that like a damn rich man? Soames thought. Just turns his back on you like you weren't there.

"Well?"

"Yes, sir. I going." Peter Soames turned on his heel and strode out, putting on his hat as he went, pulling it way down over his forehead, almost to his eyes.

Inevitably, Moultrie had to leave Forest Hall and return to Fort Mitchell. And, one bright, frosty morning, Moultrie, Cicero and Little Hawk saddled up and rode out as they had come in.

On the eighth day of their journey, Moultrie was riding ahead as usual. Behind him, Cicero and Little Hawk were riding together, talking in the strange mixed language they had developed in common. Suddenly, Cicero raised his voice. "Ravenel," he called, "how can I say strawberry in Yuchi?"

"What?" Moultrie looked back.

"How can I say strawberry in Yuchi?"

"*Dedzu.*"

Cicero grinned. "Little Hawk," he said to the boy

beside him, "I shall call you Dedzu!" He chuckled. "You are my little strawberry."

The boy looked back and smiled for the first time on the return trip. "And you," he answered, "are *Daca.*"

"Daca?" Raising his voice, Cicero called out again to Moultrie. "What does Daca mean?"

"Loudmouth."

"Loudmouth!" Cicero tried to appear outraged. He could not stop grinning. He clapped Little Hawk on the back. "You are Dedzu," he said, "and I am Daca."

"One more day, and we'll be in Tuscaloosa. Thank God!"

Dismounting, Moultrie patted his mare, then turned to go.

"See you in the morning, Ravenel."

"Good night, Cicero." Moultrie strode from the stable toward the public house. God, what a foul place, he thought. He had almost forgotten. There were more fleas there, Uncle John had told him once, than on any dog in the world.

Seven years later, there were fleas still. No matter. Moultrie was tired enough to sleep anywhere. But first, he decided to get a drink or two.

The taproom was nearly empty. Good, he thought. There was just one drunk leaning on the bar. A teamster? Maybe.

Whatever he might be, Moultrie decided to leave him alone. Moultrie wanted only some drink, then bed.

"What'll it be, mister?" the barkeep asked.

"Whiskey."

The man served the drink and went back to the teamster. "Right, George. You were saying?"

"There were five thousand savages in the attack. That's what I was saying."

"And that's some mouthful, all right. Five thousand."

"What attack?" Moultrie looked at the teamster down the bar. He suddenly felt wide awake.

"Why, ain't you heard? Where have you been, mister?" The man took another sip of his beer, put it down and smacked his lips.

"I've been traveling, same as you," Moultrie said.

"Yeah?" The teamster belched. Looking up, he squinted at Moultrie. "Those're mighty fine clothes for traveling." Taking another swallow, he continued. "I guess you're a gentleman." He grinned. "And I guess that was your man in the stable with that damned Indian boy."

The man's drunk, Moultrie thought. "Where were there five thousand Indians?"

The teamster belched again. "I can't believe you haven't heard."

"Well, believe." Moultrie was becoming impatient.

"All right. No cause to get riled. Hold your horses, I'm going to tell you." The teamster emptied his mug and shoved it toward the bartender. "Give me another one, Harry. This fine gentleman here's buying. He wants to hear my story."

The bartender glanced at Moultrie. Moultrie nodded. The man drew the beer and took it back to the teamster.

"Cheers." The teamster drained half the mug and banged it back down on the bar, splashing some of the beer. Wiping his mouth on his sleeve, he said, "Reckon I ought to tell you about the Indians."

Ravenel nodded.

"Well, it's like this, mister. Opthleyaholo. You

know, he's the president or head or whatever he is of the Creeks. Well, he and a mess of his savages burned Columbus and killed maybe a thousand militia doing it, too."

"You've just cheated me out of a beer." Moultrie tossed down his whiskey. "You take me for a fool? Opthleyaholo is on the side of the whites and has most of the Muskogeans in the Creek Confederation behind him."

"That's what you think. That's cause you don't know nothing." The teamster started towards Moultrie, then stopped, swaying and leaning back against the bar again. Turning his back to Moultrie, the man muttered to himself, "Nobody but a fool calls George Washington Smith a liar. No, sir." The man drained his glass.

He turned again to Moultrie. "So that makes you a fool."

Moultrie saw the punch coming. The drunken teamster leaned far backward as if to pick something up. He lofted his fist from the floor in a high overhand arc.

Moultrie ducked easily, deflected the punch across his back, bent and slammed his shoulder into the man's middle. He lifted him up and then dumped him head-first onto the floor.

The man's head was caught between the metal footrest and the bar. He groaned, then collapsed and did not move.

The barkeeper had a pick handle resting on top of the bar.

"Put it away. That's all the fighting I want to do tonight," Moultrie told him. "Do I have to worry about him?"

The bartender shook his head. "He does it all the

time. He won't barely remember it or you when he wakes up tomorrow."

Moultrie said good night.

He noticed that the barkeeper left the pick handle on top of the bar until he was through the door.

Moultrie, Cicero and Little Hawk reached Tuscaloosa. When they had left, it had been winter. Now, spring was starting. The dogwoods, willows and elms were all beginning to bud.

Governor Clay received Moultrie and Little Hawk in the study of his house. It was almost a replica of the judge's study in Montgomery. "Now I know," he smiled, "why the judge thinks you to be such a fine man. You have the same taste in books." Moultrie took a sip of the sherry the butler had offered him, then raised his eyebrows. "The same taste in sherry, too."

"I take that as a compliment," the governor said. He was standing with plump dignity, his back to the fire, his hands clasped behind him. "When you see Judge Dupré, tell him I asked to be remembered to one of the best men and one of my closest friends in the state."

Moultrie nodded.

"Now, tell me about this fine-looking lad." The governor looked at Little Hawk, who was standing stiffly beside Moultrie.

Moultrie told the story of Little Hawk.

"I see." The governor pursed his lips. "Let me make sure I understand you. Georgia militiamen crossed over to Alabama without justifiable reason, and without prior permission, to attack this lad's village. The Georgia crackers then took these Yuchis' cattle, having killed a number of Indians. In so doing, they heightened the chances of war. And then they had the effrontery to threaten a troop of U.S. Cavalry when the troops came to investigate."

"That's right."

"Damn." Clay's composure slipped, but only for an instant. "I just wrote Charles Madden at Indian Affairs in Washington last week telling him he should look to the whites to find the reasons for the sudden rash of Indian troubles. I didn't know how right I was." The governor turned to Little Hawk. "Lad, I wish I spoke Yuchi, so I could tell you how sorry I am. And how angry. Moultrie Ravenel will have to tell his friend, your father, for me."

"I shall. But that's not going to help matters. What are we going to do?" As he spoke, Moultrie squeezed Little Hawk's shoulder. The boy looked up in surprise, his eyes questioning. Moultrie smiled. "I'll tell you what the governor said later," he whispered. Little Hawk nodded.

"There's not a damn thing that we can do, Ravenel." The governor shrugged. "When you get on a bucking horse, you don't expect to rein it. You just pray you can stay on."

Later, as Moultrie and Little Hawk were leaving, Governor Clay pulled Moultrie aside. "I know it's hard for you and the boy to see it this way, Ravenel, but this bloody business is a blessing in disguise. Instead of staying here to be cheated and robbed and assaulted, the Indians will be forced now to move to the Indian Territory, where they'll be free from interference. That's what the wisest of their leaders want. That's what we should want. It's your job to help the removal. The faster it is, the less trouble there'll be."

Moultrie nodded. "I know. But I don't like it, sir."

Governor Clay continued. "We shouldn't worry about the Indian removal too much. After all, you, me, the judge, we are all immigrants, too, in a sense, and we're doing all right. People go where they have a future. It can be the same for this lad's tribe in the Indian Territory. Mark my words. That's where the future is."

The governor became reflective. "And even farther west. To the Pacific Ocean, even. That's where young men such as yourself should be thinking of going. There's Oregon in the Northwest. I'm told there are riches enough for any man there. And for now and for some time to come, no politics and politicians to bother you. The Northwest is just too big to be governed as yet. Mark my words. The Indian move is good."

Moultrie did not believe him.

Chapter 7

All the way back to Montgomery with Cicero and
Little Hawk, Moultrie thought of the governor's words.
He tried again and again to find something positive in
them, but he could not. The benefits the governor
claimed to see in the Creek removal west escaped
Moultrie. He wrestled often to put the problem from
his mind. After all, he was going to Montgomery to see
Helen, and for now, that was the important thing.

He recalled their last conversation. She had
guessed he would be away for a long time, and she had
been right. Moultrie had been gone for months.

He was going to make it up to her, by God. And
in these times of anticipation, he did not think about
the Creek Indian problem.

The fantasies were nice.

Helen. Dark blonde hair netting candlelight at
dinner. . . . The competitive edge between them as
they spurred their horses side by side across streams
and fallen trees, and the breathless laughter after the

hard gallop. . . . In the evenings . . . her hands conjuring the magic of Schubert from the keyboard of a piano. . . . Helen. In bed, pulling him to her, whispering, "Make love to me, slow and sweet." Moultrie still waited impatiently for the first time they would make love.

But the Creek problem was always waiting in ambush, never allowing him to concentrate on fine days ahead with Helen for long.

The more Moultrie contemplated what was happening, the angrier he became. He could see only perfidy and betrayal ahead for the Creeks, and slaughter in the bloody war that was almost certain to come. For his own part in it, he felt shame.

He was in a volcanic mood by the time they reached Montgomery. And in Montgomery it brought him grief.

Little Hawk was at the center of it.

Moultrie took lodgings for all three at the Montgomery Hotel; a room for himself and separate quarters for Cicero and Little Hawk in the lodgings for slaves. This was custom.

Some time later, a troubled Cicero informed Moultrie to look into the place where Ames Falkner, the owner, had lodged Little Hawk. Cicero did not like it. He was certain Moultrie was not going to like it either.

And when Moultrie saw the place Ames Falkner had given Little Hawk, Moultrie decided that he personally had had enough trouble over one little boy and was going to end it. He went looking for Ames Falkner.

"You will not put this boy in a stall with your horses, Ames. Get him out. Now. He is not an animal." As Moultrie spoke, he slapped his riding crop against the counter. His face was red with anger.

The hotel keeper held his ground. "I can't have Indians staying up with my slaves. They're scared stiff about the Indians now. Every black in Montgomery is. The boy's lucky he got a bed at all. Hell! There's a war going on. Or haven't you heard?"

Taking a deep breath, Moultrie struggled to control himself. "All right, Falkner. It's your place. But it's my money. I'll be damned if I'm going to pay a penny for this kind of treatment."

"This kind of treatment?" Falkner's hand clenched in a fist. Like Moultrie, he had spoken loudly. Everyone in the lobby was listening. Looking around, Falkner stopped short. Then, smiling, he bowed. When he spoke this time, his voice was just above a whisper. "The fine gentleman must accept my apologies for his friend and forgive me if I ask him to take his money somewhere else."

Moultrie's voice was calm. It was also loud enough for everyone in the room to hear. "I had a bitch once," he told Falkner. "Like most dogs, she liked to roll in her own offal. Whenever she did and I caught her, I whipped her. Finally, she learned. She doesn't do that anymore."

The silence was charged. The unfolding challenge was clear. Moultrie continued. "It's because that bitch learned, Falkner, that I'm going to bother to do what I'm about to do."

The impact of his crop on the hotel keeper's face sounded like a gunshot.

As Ames Falkner staggered backward with blood filling his eye, there was another bang, louder than the first.

Moultrie imagined he had been hit across the

chest with a plank. The pain cut and burned, and the very wind seemed squeezed from his lungs. He fell backward against the hotel bar, holding himself up on the edge with his elbows. He felt like he might pass out. He was puzzled. How did this happen? Falkner was not even close.

Then he saw the small pistol. It had been ejected into Falkner's palm by a spring-loaded holster in his sleeve.

The two men stared at one another, neither moving.

So this is how it feels to be shot, Moultrie thought. He touched the blood flooding his shirt. So this is how it feels to die.

But as the next few moments passed, he realized with elation he was not dying after all. The pain was diminishing. His breathing was better. His vision was clearing. He was merely creased by the bullet. Moultrie also noticed that during this seemingly endless time no one had moved. Everything in the room was as it had been. Silent.

He knew he was now in charge.

"Too bad your dirty little belly gun's only got one shot, Falkner," Moultrie grinned. "Because now there's nothing to stop me from beating the hell out of you. Certainly not your courage and manhood."

"I'm stopping you." Judge Leander Dupré had suddenly appeared and stepped between Moultrie and Falkner. "Now, what the hell's going on here?"

Moultrie told him. Turning to the hotel keeper, the judge looked him up and down. Falkner was a burly fellow, getting soft, but still firm. When the judge spoke, his voice rumbled through the lobby. "You could have thrashed Moultrie, and I wouldn't have anything to say about it, Falkner. But you pulled that peashooter."

Falkner glowered. "You calling me a coward, Judge? If so, come right out and say it."

"No." The judge shook his head. "I know you're not. But it's going to look like that to others."

"Nobody's going to say that to me twice." Falkner almost hissed as he spoke.

The judge smiled. It wasn't the smile his daughter's friends loved. It was a tight, cold, humorless smile. "That's right, Falkner, because you're not going to be here to hear them."

The hotel keeper appeared startled, and for the first time showed uncertainty. "What do you mean?"

The judge shook his head. "I don't mean anything. I'm only predicting." Then he turned to Moultrie. "Come on, son. Let's get you fixed up." He touched Moultrie's wound. "Every man's got to be bloodied sometime, I suppose, but you were lucky, son. Another two inches closer. Your heart. Yes, you were fortunate."

When Helen saw the two men come into the hall at the judge's house and saw the blood on Moultrie's shirt, she did not flinch. "You've called the doctor?" she asked. "Good. Then let's get the wound bathed. You can tell me what happened while I'm doing it."

"The doctor will be here any minute," Moultrie protested. "You don't need to be messing with this. Besides, the wound's just a superficial one."

Superficial. He was grateful to be able to describe it as such.

Calling for warm water, Helen ignored him. Later, in the judge's study, after she had stripped off Moultrie's shirt and begun to wash the wound, she said, "All right, now tell me." So Moultrie repeated the story with Judge Dupré interjecting from time to time.

Helen did not comment then. The doctor arrived before Moultrie finished. But she expressed her feelings later.

They were in the garden. Helen had asked Cicero to bring a chair for his master and another for herself. Pouring lemonade for them from the butler's tray the house man had brought out, she handed Moultrie his glass, brushing his cheek after he had taken it. Moultrie smiled and sighed. "It's good to be with you again, Helen. Stretching gingerly, he turned his face toward the noon sun and closed his eyes. Dinner was not due for three hours. He had time to relax. And to reflect.

Helen had been splendid that morning. Calm and competent. She was a hell of a woman as well as a lady. The judge hadn't been wanting either. Moultrie grinned as he remembered Falkner's sudden faltering when Dupré had told him he was staying in Montgomery. No. The Duprés were not the run-of-the-mill new rich out here. They had class and character.

"What are you grinning about?" Helen smiled as she spoke. It was her first smile since Moultrie had walked in with his shirt seeping blood.

Moultrie's eyes caressed her as he answered. "I was just remembering your father's handling of Ames Falkner at the hotel."

Suddenly Helen was serious again. "Father says you behaved like a hotheaded fool. Why on earth did you make such a fuss? The Indian boy had a place to sleep, after all, even if it was in a stall. And can you blame Falkner for wanting to avoid any trouble with his own people?"

"Helen." Moultrie said her name and stopped.

But the single word was eloquent. Frustration, anger, hurt, pleading, all were in it.

Did she hear? Was that why she stood up from her chair and came to stand in front of him, looking down into his troubled eyes? Moultrie took her hand and kissed it.

He looked up and suddenly wanted more. He wanted to kiss her lips, her neck, her breasts.

The fantasy began again. Helen. Himself. Sharing a bed. Making love. Kicking the sheets to shreds. He knew Helen suddenly wanted more, too.

She seized his face in both hands, bunching up his cheeks between his fingers as she might bunch up a length of cloth.

He yelped. The wound was hurting again. "Don't stop," he told her. "I want you so much sometimes that my guts ache." He pulled her face to his, saying, "The pain in my chest can go to hell."

They kissed, gently at first, simply brushing lips from side to side, then harder and harder. Her mouth parted. Her tongue tapped at his lips.

Then abruptly she pushed herself erect and backed away. Helen was now clutching her own face. She gasped when her breath began once more. "I've always wanted to kiss you that way," she said. "But I—I cannot. Not yet. Not until we are married. When I did a moment ago, I became afraid. I am afraid of what it could make me do with you." She paused again, then added, "It is always that way for me, kissing you. Is it for you, still?"

Moultrie slapped his forehead, then wished he hadn't. The quick movement of the slap pulled his chest once more. Wincing, he hissed, "Helen, if you have to ask me, you'll never know it is. I wouldn't dare tell you my fantasies."

Helen giggled. "They're probably not much different from my own."

"You know, Helen, there's something basically wrong with our codes. They make no sense."

"What do you mean?"

"Here we want to bed each other in the worst way. Right?"

Helen reddened. "Do you have to put it quite that way? But yes. We do want to bed each other."

"But we can't because supposedly we are both to the manner born. And people to the manner born do not bed each other until they are married. But I could go out tonight and bed another woman and it wouldn't matter, except maybe to her father or her husband. That's what I mean when I say there is something lunatic about rules that say no, no, to bedding someone you plan to marry anyway, but yes, yes to bedding someone you're not."

"Fine for men. Women don't generally have the option of sleeping with anyone else at all," she said, "although that doesn't stop a lot of the manner-born virgins of Montgomery."

"But the rules stop you."

"Yes. I believe in them, though I may not at this moment like them. You'll not be disappointed in me when we finally bed each other after we're married, to be vulgar about it." She smiled. "You know how good we'll be."

He knew.

Helen became serious. "But I didn't come out here to seduce you or talk about manners, Moultrie Ravenel. I'm more concerned with what happened this morning at the Montgomery Hotel. Why, Moultrie? Why?"

Moultrie shook his head. Why indeed?

Was it so awful that Little Hawk had not been given a bed with the coachmen and boys, but had been made to sleep in an unused stall?

"I guess the fact that the boy has done nothing to deserve such treatment made me mad."

"But it is his people who started this fighting." As she spoke, Moultrie involuntarily seized her hands once again. She gasped.

"That boy's village was peaceful," he said harshly. "The militia came in on whim, killed all the men who weren't out hunting, killed and probably raped the boy's mother, and burned the place. For no reason. No, the Indians didn't start this."

"I didn't know, Moultrie," she said gently. "I'm sorry."

They didn't talk any more about fighting then. But later that afternoon, they returned to the subject. It was Helen who brought it up. She was at the piano in the music room as she spoke. Her question was simple. "Why continue on as an agent when, despite your best efforts and the efforts of others, there's a war? You have to see the situation is impossible. Besides, it's cruel of you to stay away for months on end. I miss you so. You must realize that my love, any woman's love, is like your Forest Hall. Unless you regularly tend it, it can't bear fruit, only weeds and briars."

Moultrie stood silently, the sadness growing deeper and deeper in his eyes as Helen spoke. When she finished finally, he walked slowly to the window. Standing there, he looked out over the dusk enveloping the same garden where they had been so gay that morning. Even then he did not speak at once. When he did, his voice was low and husky. "Helen, I hope your love can survive and grow from the seeds I planted while you are in the care of your father, just as I hope the crops at Forest Hall will survive and grow under the eyes of Mr. Soames."

Taking a deep breath, Moultrie turned around. "I am going back, Helen. I have to. The more hopeless the situation, the more I am needed."

Helen stared at him, her lower lip quivering. As if suddenly seeing the keyboard in front of her, she brought her hands up, playing one note, then another, then a chord. A tear fell as she began tentatively to pick out the opening bars of Schubert's *The Trout*, which she had been playing the last time Moultrie had said good-bye. He moved to her through the growing shadows in the room. She did not look up. Instead, she began to play. Not tentatively any longer, but with authority.

It was that night in the study after dinner that Judge Dupré asked Moultrie why he didn't resign. "Now, with this war," the judge told him, "there's nothing to be gained from staying on the job. Nothing. Write Madden at the Bureau of Indian Affairs telling him you quit. If you like, I'll write him too, explaining that you're not a quitter, but this business has blown up in your face despite all the really good work you've done."

"I can't."

"Can't, hell. You're just wasting yourself. You don't deal with savages as friends, Moultrie. You show them a strong arm. Make them do as whipped curs do, put their tails between their legs where their manhood is supposed to be and run."

"We have treaty obligations."

"Treaty obligations be damned." Suddenly the judge gasped. Then he coughed. Pulling out his handkerchief, he coughed into it again and again. Finally, leaning back weakly in his chair, he let the hand holding the handkerchief drop. Moultrie saw blood staining the linen.

"Are you all right, Judge? Let me get you some water."

"No!" The judge yelled the word. "Thank you." He shook his head weakly. "If I can't talk sense into you," he said, speaking more softly, "Charles Madden can put it in an order."

"I don't think," Moultrie said, standing, "that I like the implication of that."

"Damn it, boy. I don't want to make an enemy of you. I'm thinking of your own good. And Helen's. This Indian trouble is out of hand. You've got to see that. Leave it to people who know how to deal with savages, both white and red."

Chapter 8

Is this country never to enjoy a season of repose? Will interested land speculators from Alabama and Georgia continue to palm off their deception on the public? Who believes that the Creeks are about to assume a hostile attitude towards the whites? We answer, no one.

The war with the Creeks is all a humbug. It is a base and diabolical scheme, devised by interested men, to keep an innocent race of people from maintaining their just rights. . . .

Page looked up from the newspaper. "Well, Moultrie, there you have it. The Montgomery *Advertiser* still agrees with us."

"A lot of good that will do." Moultrie's voice was biting.

John Page shook his head. Moultrie's tone irritated him. Ever since the man had come back from Montgomery two months ago, it had been the same. "Of course, this kind of article is doing good," Page declared. "It helps people like General Shearer fight public hysteria. Do you think the general could have told Governor Clay last week that there was no need to prepare the militia for war if some of the newspapers weren't publishing this sort of thing? Hell, no. Clay's like any politician—an old woman. Just say boo and he jumps."

It was said that Clay did jump at shadows, even at high noon, when there weren't any. According to Charles Madden, at Indian Affairs, his letters to the secretary of war were almost hysterical. Yet, things were going well. Secretary of War Lewis Cass had appointed three commissioners to investigate the frauds against the Indians, and they were doing a good job. Many Indians were beginning to hope they might actually receive protection and justice from the government. Many were beginning, too, to prepare for removal. In the last two months, Moultrie and other removal agents had managed to gather two thousand Indians in all for the march west. That was one out of every ten or so in the state, and they were under their elected head, Chief Opthleyaholo, the most influential man in the Creek Confederation.

Of course the governor's not the only pessimist, Page thought. Just try to convince Moultrie that anything looks hopeful. The man's not bitter, exactly, and God knows he works like ten men. But he's become fatalistic, almost indifferent. He does everything mechanically. Sure he's been depressed from time to time before, but he also has laughed. Not now. Page had tried to make him laugh. So, he knew, had the man's black and that Indian boy who rode around with him all the time. No one had managed to arouse him in the last couple of months, though. It was like talking to an intelligent stone wall.

Page stood up. This business frustrated him. It wasn't only Moultrie or Governor Clay, but the whole bloody mess. Oh, he tried to look on the bright side of things, and there *were* hopeful signs. There were lots of countersigns, however. That rotten Columbus merchant and speculator, Hobson, and some others, had just had Opthleyaholo thrown in jail as surety for tribal debts for which the chief was not responsible. And as a result, two thousand Indians mustered earlier for the removal now refused to go.

That situation was annoying and stupid, but it could be taken care of in time. Other signs were more worrisome, particularly the sudden increase in the number of raids by Yuchis, Hitchitis and Cheahas around Columbus in the last couple of weeks. Some raids had been pretty spectacular. The burning of the bridge across the Chattahoochee and the capturing of two steamboats just below Columbus were only two instances. Page shrugged. Dropping the newspaper on the table, he jammed his hat on his head and said, "See you at mess tonight, Moultrie."

The war finally began the following week.

It broke out over a little thing. Indians, led by an unidentified white man, attacked the mail coach out of Columbus, Georgia.

But as little as it was, it was provocation enough for Secretary of War Lewis Cass. Nullifying the treaty, only three years old, allowing the Creek Indians to remain in Alabama if they chose to, he ordered the forced removal of all Creeks to the Indian Territory. On May 19th, General Winfield Scott arrived in

Columbus to oversee their removal and the suppression of resistance to it. Moultrie went on orders to see Scott a week later.

Moultrie did not look forward to the meeting. He tried to stay away from Columbus as much as possible. He called it Hobsonville when talking to people such as John Page. "No general in Hobsonville can know what's going on. He's going to see events the way the land speculators want him to. It's inevitable."

Of course, Sanford, the militia leader there, was sometimes at odds with Hobson and the others. He was no dupe. In fact, he was pretty sharp, in Moultrie's opinion. He had told Hobson, Moultrie had heard, that Opthleyaholo was no more responsible for his tribe's debt than he was for the national debt of Great Britain. Moultrie, on hearing the story, had wanted to cheer. But Sanford, even so, was still fighting Hobson's war. The Georgia Militia under William McElveen and others had made some of the first attacks on Indian settlements.

And now Moultrie was going to meet with Sanford *and* Hobson *and* Scott.

Riding into Columbus at any time was like riding into a madhouse. The place always was packed solid, choking with immigrants. Now it was worse. Refugee settlers and their cattle, soldiers and militia had doubled the population and quadrupled the confusion, it seemed to Moultrie. The noise was incredible.

And the dust and the smell were the worst of it. Every squad that marched by, tramping through the offal and the splotches of tobacco juice in the road, kicked up more. The dust billowed up in clouds between the rows of unpainted frame buildings and rained down again under shirt collars. The smell, on the other hand, just hung there. Riding into it was like riding into a quilt. It wrapped around one, filling one's nostrils, even one's mouth.

What would Cicero say about this? Moultrie grinned at the thought. Plenty. Too bad old Cicero had had to stay behind with Little Hawk, but I just couldn't have brought the boy. Even dressed now more or less like a white boy and speaking some English, it's obvious that he's an Indian. If he'd ridden into Columbus alongside me and Cicero today, with all these refugees here thinking the only way they want to see Indians is dead, some drunk would have made trouble sure as shootin'.

"Hey, Indian-lover." Moultrie looked down from his mount. It was Peters, of the Georgia Militia—McElveen's man. Peters grabbed the bridle of Moultrie's horse.

"Let go." Moultrie's voice was sharp.

Looking up at the Indian agent, Peters grinned. "Damned if your manners aren't bad," he chuckled, "and you a gentleman, too. Didn't your mammy teach you how to say please?"

Moultrie smiled. "Let go the reins, Peters, or I'll kick your damned head in." He spoke in the same tone of voice he would have used to tell an old lady the time of day.

Peters flushed slightly, but kept smiling. "Try it, Indian-lover, and I'll shoot you so full of lead, you'll sink plumb to China. I've been looking forward to doing that to you for so long I can most taste it."

"Shut it, Peters." It was Colonel McElveen. He had just come out of the large brick house, one of the few in Columbus, which was serving as Winfield Scott's headquarters. "I told you to lay off. I mean it."

"Colonel, I was just trying to teach this gentleman

a few manners. When I spoke to him, he didn't answer me civil-like and this got me riled. He knows I meant nothing by it. Right, Ravenel?"

"That's right, McElveen. Peters here never means anything by what he says." Moultrie now spoke in a voice loud enough for everyone in the block to hear. A couple of militiamen guffawed.

Moultrie grinned as he continued. "Seems you spend more time fighting your men, Colonel, than you do fighting the Indians."

McElveen said, "Keep it up, Ravenel. Keep it up." Then he called to one of the laughers lounging against the wall. "Take Mr. Ravenel's horse, Sergeant. We'll be awhile."

Dismounting, Moultrie handed the reins to the man, winking as he did so, and then followed McElveen up the steps of the headquarters building. As the two men came up on the porch, Moultrie saw a face, well-barbered and strong, smiling at them through the window. It was William Hobson. The swine, Moultrie thought. He watched the whole show and enjoyed it.

There was only one man in the room besides Hobson: General Scott's aide-de-camp, a major. Hearing voices in the next room, Moultrie gathered that Scott and Sanford were there. He hoped they would not take long. He wanted to get out as quickly as he could. "An hour in that place," he had told Cicero before leaving Fort Mitchell, "will be more than I can stand."

As Moultrie took off his hat and coat, Hobson inclined his head from his stand by the window and said, "It's good to see you again, Ravenel."

McElveen snorted. "You can stomach more than I can. Damned if you can't. It'll be a rainy day in hell before Bill McElveen ever says he's happy to see

Moultrie Ravenel. The devil will be spitting embers that day. He sure will."

Moultrie's bow to Hobson was as exaggerated as Hobson's had been restrained. So was the cordiality in Moultrie's voice. "Hobson, glad to see you're still smiling." He could not keep the anger from his voice for long. "But, then, why shouldn't you be? Your war's going splendidly. Washington, Tuscaloosa, Milledgeville. They're all dancing to your tune."

"Oh, I smile whenever I have something to smile about." Hobson seemed entirely at ease and was either unaware of or indifferent to Moultrie's sarcasm. "Don't think I'm not glad for an excuse. Thank you, incidentally, for the little scene you and Peters just played." Hobson chuckled before continuing. "For some reason, Peters dislikes eastern aristocrats with Harvard educations. I've tried to wean him of the prejudice, but as you can see, I've not had much success. That's all right. I don't despair." Hobson's voice was smooth and easy. "If people like Peters or McElveen here don't believe me when I say we need Carolina gentlemen such as you, Ravenel, to give this society we're making some tone, well, I'm not too disappointed. I console myself by thinking that your day will come. In hell."

McElveen's grin transformed his face. Dark, heavy, sullen, it suddenly lit up. The major coughed uncomfortably.

Moultrie turned to the major and shrugged his shoulders. "You know, Major, I'm having the same difficulty with my family back in South Carolina that Hobson here is having with Peters and McElveen." The major looked as though he wanted desperately to change the subject, but Moultrie continued.

"I keep telling them back in South Carolina that men like Peters and McElveen are the salt of the earth.

But my family somehow doesn't believe me. As far as they're concerned, Alabama's just the place for the Peterses and McElveens of the world." Glancing at McElveen, he added, "I think they're wrong myself. Don't you, Hobson?"

Moultrie did not turn when he asked the question. He didn't expect an answer. He just kept talking, looking all the while at Winfield Scott's aide, who seemed to be trying hard not to fidget in his discomfort. "It's as I keep telling my family," Moultrie said, keeping his tone like Hobson's earlier—easy, conversational. "Alabama is soon going to be too civilized for our friends here. Without any Indians to rob and rape and murder, Peters and McElveen are going to have to change professions. Or leave. White people aren't going to stand for that sort of thing."

Moultrie heard the major draw in his breath and turned. McElveen, his face red, had his pistol halfway from its holster.

"Gentlemen." General Scott's voice was commanding. Apparently startled, McElveen let his pistol drop back into its holster. The general stood in the doorway to the next room.

Scott was scowling. He spoke firmly. "We're here to take care of the Indian removal, gentlemen. We're not here to fight amongst ourselves."

"There isn't anyone but ourselves to fight, General." Moultrie's tone was direct and firm. "You've got nearly ten thousand soldiers and militia arrayed against a few hundred half-starved, half-naked Indians. Unless we fight each other, there won't be any war to speak of."

The frown on Scott's face was not reflected in his voice. Stepping into the room, he nodded to everyone, then turned to Moultrie. "You're Moultrie Ravenel," he said. "That makes you kin to John Ravenel. I knew him in the old days. If you've got a quarter of John's sense, you should know then that ten-to-one odds are pretty poor when you're fighting Indians. Look at the campaign I've been waging against the Seminoles in Florida. Besides, the secretary of war—your boss and mine—says we're at war, so we're at war. By attacking the Columbus mail, the Creeks have finally forced Washington to nullify Andrew Jackson's old treaty and retaliate. And you know that, Ravenel."

"Sir, I know the attack on the mail finally gave Washington the excuse to do what it's wanted to do all along."

"That's enough, Ravenel," the general said.

McElveen brayed in laughter. This time Hobson snapped at him. "I do not see anything funny, McElveen."

"Neither do I." General Sanford, of the Georgia Militia, spoke from the doorway to the inner room. Then, turning to Scott, he said, "General, I told you you'd invited a menagerie. You ever see cats and dogs in a cage together? Well, now's your chance."

Scott ignored the comment. "Major, we're going into my office. I think these men would agree with me. The faster we get this business over, the better we'll all like it." Just before closing the door, he added, "Unless General Jesup, Cass, President Jackson or God comes through that door, I don't want to be disturbed by anyone else. Understood?"

The aide sat down behind his desk with a sigh. He looked as if he was thinking about turning to drink or volunteering for line duty against the Seminoles in Florida.

Inside his richly paneled office, Scott motioned everyone to chairs. He remained standing. Clearing his throat, he looked at the four men in front of him. Sanford, an active man getting a little portly now. McElveen, built like a log. Hobson, of middling height, middling build, middling everything. And Moultrie.

The general had met the others before, but not the Indian agent. The boy even looked like John Ravenel. The resemblance was uncanny. Though it was years now since Scott had seen John Ravenel, he still remembered him.

He told Moultrie, "One of the best damned woodsmen and horsemen you'd ever want to meet. The man knew the woods like an Indian. What was it John's sister-in-law, your mother, once called him? Oh, yes. Her civilized savage. That was about right, too. And now it looks as if you, Moultrie, are cast in the same mold. Pity for the girl you marry. At least John had had the good sense not to marry."

While the general surveyed them and formed his judgments, Hobson sat with his legs crossed and his face creased with his half smile.

Shifting his bulk back and forth uneasily in his chair, McElveen glowered at his feet.

Across from him Sanford looked first at one and then another of the men seated with him.

Only Moultrie relaxed and frankly returned the general's gaze.

Scott cleared his throat again. "I asked you here," he began, "to help me decide some things." Even McElveen looked up as the general spoke. "What I want to decide is how we can, and should, use friendly Indians in this campaign against the hostiles." His words were measured. "Opthleyaholo—despite that ridiculous suit of yours against him, Hobson—has raised about three hundred warriors who'll fight for us, and they've done a damned good job thus far. But now they're quitting. Apparently, McElveen, they're tired of your boys hiding behind them. Frankly, I don't blame them."

McElveen colored, but said nothing. Hobson remained as bland-looking as ever. Let the man talk, his face seemed to say. He'll be gone soon. But come hell or high water, Bill Hobson is going to get the money he claims the Creeks owe him, just as McElveen is going to use Indians to do this fighting, no matter what some general says.

Scott saw defiance in McElveen's eyes, too. So that's it. The reports are true, he thought. He shook his head in irritation. It would not do to show that he had noticed. But, by God, it was useful to know. This is a hell of a business, Scott decided. Not the fighting, though the devil knows that's bad enough in those swamps and woods where you're fighting snakes and mosquitos more than you are Indians. No. What makes this war hell is the politics. You can't do your job as a soldier unless you're a bootlicking politician besides. Old Andy Jackson had learned that. Now look at him. He's president and giving the orders instead of taking them, something he always had trouble doing.

Shaking his head again, Scott continued as if there had been no awkward pause at all. "As I see it, we've got two options. We either use the Indians a little or we use them a lot. We have to have Indian guides. Do we want Indian troops? I would say so, seeing the hell those warriors of Opthleyaholo have raised. They're superb fighters. I wish I had two divisions of them. What do you say, gentlemen?"

McElveen, Hobson and Sanford voiced agreement. "Recruit them by all means," Sanford urged.

Scott turned to Moultrie. "Yours is the only opinion we don't have."

"Sir, no disrespect meant, but you already have three opinions. Do you really need mine?"

"I want to know it, Moultrie. So, if you please."

"You know my answer is no."

"I do," Scott said. "I would like to know why."

"We're pitting brother against brother, as we're fond of doing here in the South when northern abolitionists try to drive the wedge between the South and slavery. We're dividing a people by telling some of them they are right and others they are wrong, when at the bottom of it, it is ourselves who have broken a trust and nullified a treaty with the Creeks. We are deceiving Opthleyaholo and his troops into fighting for us because they believe they will have something left here when the warring is done. Everyone in this room knows they will not."

"Is that all, Moultrie?"

"No, General Scott, it's not. If any one of us here tried to persuade even one state to secede from the Union and fight the others, he would be charged with sedition and treason. I see little difference between advocating secession and what we propose to do here to the Creeks."

"Yet, you remain involved," Winfield Scott noted. "I understand you've been offered the chance to resign as Indian agent with honor and have refused."

"I stay, sir, only to salvage what I can from men like the three I now sit with."

The anger in the room was almost palpable. He knew he should not have spoken. Yet he was glad he had. Moultrie now felt better than he had in days.

It was William Hobson who spoke first. "I may take you to court for that speech, Ravenel. You have called me a traitor before witnesses. That's slander."

"I may take him behind a tree and shoot him,"

McElveen bellowed in anger. He was stroking his pistol, not even realizing he was doing so. Moultrie tensed. Was he angry enough to draw and fire?

Scott said quietly, "You will all come to order. And I will take it personally if anyone acts later against Mr. Ravenel because of his remarks. I asked for them. I appreciate his candor. Is that understood?"

McElveen, Hobson and Sanford all nodded and became quiet.

Scott continued. "So. Three votes against one for using Opthleyaholo and his Creeks. We're decided." Scott did not wait for affirmation. How do we get Opthleyaholo and other chiefs to promise us warriors?"

"We get Ravenel," Hobson stated, "to talk to his cousin." The merchant's smile was almost angelic.

Moultrie's face was suddenly white.

Seeing Hobson's smile, watching Moultrie's reaction and hearing McElveen's barking laugh again, Scott masked his anger. What is it now? Can't these men get on for five minutes without digging at each other? Well, the ball's been played, he thought. I'll have to carry it. "Who's your cousin, Ravenel?"

It was a long time before Moultrie said, "Little Johnnie." As he spoke, Moultrie's color returned to normal. He even managed a sort of smile around the lips, though his eyes didn't brighten. "Little Johnnie," he continued, "is Uncle John's boy by an Indian woman."

The general snorted. Just like John Ravenel, too, he thought. The old goat. He always did have an eye for the ladies. "Well, what about this Little Johnnie?" he asked. Scott was beginning to lose patience. "It's getting closer and closer to lunch time, and if things don't speed up, we're going to be here all day."

"The half-breed's done work for me," Hobson

said. "Knows the whites." He was still smiling as he spoke. "He's also pretty highly thought of by Bear Chief, whose village is over on the Tallapoosa River. Ravenel, I'm sure, could get him to rouse the Indians, tell them how grateful Uncle Sam will be and how an end to this war is in their interest."

"Why don't you talk to Little Johnnie yourself, since you know him so well?"

"I can't leave Columbus with the influx of refugees forcing me to be at my store," Hobson answered.

Moultrie's response to the comment was startling. "You mean," he said, "that you've got too much sense to leave town for someplace where you might run into your old clerk, Jim Henry?"

"What?" Scott was taken aback. He had heard that the half-breed, Jim Henry, now leading the Yuchi renegades, had once worked in Columbus. He did not know that the man had been Hobson's clerk. *Why the hell didn't Hobson tell me? Damn.*

Hobson smiled again. The man had control. "No, I don't mean that, Ravenel. I *do* have to be in my store. But you have a good point there. It's not particularly healthy for me outside of town just now. You see, I'm not an Indian-lover like you and your Uncle John."

Moultrie was halfway across the room before the general could speak. "Ravenel!" he shouted. It was enough to stop him.

Moultrie came to a standstill and took a deep breath. "I know what you want, General," he said. "I'll talk to Bear Chief and Little Johnnie, while John Page and whoever else you want talks to Opthleyaholo and some of the others." Turning toward the door, Moultrie started to open it. "I'm going to say good-bye now, with your permission, General Scott. I've had enough of some of your company."

Scott came forward and extended his hand. "Thanks," he said, smiling. Then he patted Moultrie on the back and added, "John Ravenel was a good man. I'm glad to see so much of him in his nephew."

Chapter 9

Back outside in the brawling street, Moultrie thought, It still stinks, but not as much as it stinks in there.

The mare was across the street in front of Hobson's Mercantile Emporium. Seeing the store, Moultrie grinned. "What a name."

He crossed over, dodging a pig and two little boys chasing each other on the way. The man McElveen had told to hold the mare was still there, leaning against the wall of the store. As Moultrie came up, the man spat into the street. The Indian agent nodded to him. He did not respond. But when Moultrie started to swing into the saddle, the man said, "If I were you, mister, I'd check the cinch kind of close. Peters was fooling with it a while back."

Moultrie raised an eyebrow. "You don't say?"

"I say." The man shifted his chaw. "And, if I were you, I'd look around a bit on the way out of town, too. Wouldn't surprise me at all if Peters was somewhere out there with his fingers itching around a trigger."

"Why are you telling me this?" The thought that Peters was gunning for him was no surprise, but why on earth would Peters' man say so?

The man flipped the sliver he had been whittling into the air, spat and hit it dead on. Then he took a tobacco plug out of his shirt pocket and bit off another chaw. "Could say, I guess, that I love Indians, but I don't." His words were muffled by the tobacco. "Guess I just think Peters is a skunk. I don't hold with bushwhacking a man. If a man don't fight like a man, I figure he's no better than an Indian or a varmint."

"Thanks." Moultrie extended his hand.

The man looked at him for a moment and then said, "Thanks just the same. I maybe don't hold no truck with Peters, but that don't make me a friend of yours." Then he spat again.

Shrugging, Moultrie mounted.

Once across the Chattahoochee, Moultrie turned northwest toward the mountains. He had three or four days of riding ahead of him. That gave Peters a lot of chances. The question was where he would strike. And now that Moultrie thought about it, how could he defend himself? The first question was unanswerable, so far as Moultrie could see.

As for the second, he figured that he had three choices. He could go off the trail and try to lose Peters. He could ride along as if he suspected nothing and hope Peters' first shot missed. Or he could join other travelers and try to stay among them, so Peters would have a harder time getting a clean shot.

None of the choices were very good. Peters was probably a bully, but he was also probably a good shot. A man made his way in this country by shooting well, after all.

So much for hoping to draw Peters' fire on the trail and survive, Moultrie decided. So much, too, for the idea of riding with others. Peters won't mind shooting into the middle of a group, hoping to get me, even though he might hit someone else.

No, as far as I can tell, Moultrie reasoned, I've only one choice really. I'll have to strike out into the woods and hope to shake Peters long enough so that I can set up a bushwhack myself. Moultrie shrugged. Of course, if Peters manages to get ahead of me, I'm dead.

Riding along as nonchalantly as possible, Moultrie tried to give the impression that he didn't expect or suspect anything. With luck, he thought, Peters will wait until we're a little farther out from the settled area to attack. So the best place to break out is on the trail just ahead.

The trail there took a couple of sudden turns and if he could get around the first without Peters suspecting anything, it would be possible to lose the man. Unless, of course, Peters had chosen that place for a bushwhack himself.

It wasn't until after the second bend that Moultrie pulled up. Dismounting, he led his mare up the ridge, keeping her between himself and the rhododendron thicket to the right. If Peters was there, he was going to have to shoot past the horse.

At the top of the ridge, Moultrie found just the place he wanted: a clump of trees which would obscure him from the path, but still give him a view not only of the path but of the entire ridge. Now all he had to do was wait and watch the mare's ears.

Ten minutes. Fifteen minutes. Eighteen minutes.

Where is Peters? Moultrie wondered. Won't it be fine, he thought, if Peters isn't hunting for me at all, if the sergeant was just trying to make me sweat? Maybe that's what's happened. If not, Peters is trailing a long way back.

Watching the mare's ears, Moultrie saw them suddenly move forward. He put his hand over her nostrils. He did not want her nickering. The rider was Peters, but he wasn't alone. There were two others with him.

A jay called overhead. It was the same bird that had scolded Moultrie when he had turned the second bend. Peters looked up at the sound and saw Moultrie standing on the slope, his rifle aimed at the three of them. Instinctively, the militiaman started to swing his rifle up. He hadn't gotten it halfway when a shot boomed.

Peters howled a sound that was not like anything human. He was looking at his left hand, the one that had held the weapon. One finger was shot off entirely, another was shreds. As for his rifle, it was shattered.

"Peters." Moultrie's voice seemed far away, even to himself, after the loudness of the rifle shot. "Why don't you and your boys dismount? Slow and easy. That's right." Moultrie started down the slope. One of Peters' men lifted his rifle to take a shot at Moultrie. Suddenly Moultrie dropped to one knee and fired. One of the horses reared, throwing its rider. As the man got up, Moultrie called to him, "That wasn't very smart, mister. You saw what happened to Peters when he raised his rifle."

Peters was doubled over, leaning on his mount, pushing the remains of his wounded fingers against his gut to try to stop the bleeding. His face was blue and he was perspiring.

As Moultrie walked from the slope, he held his

rifle ready to shoot again. Peters, he saw, was on the threshold of shock. He was biting so hard on his lips that blood was showing. Then he convulsed and started to vomit.

To the other men, Moultrie said, "Damn it, you don't want him to pass out and bleed to death. You. Get your bandanna around his arm. Make a tourniquet. Squeeze the knot down on the vessels on his forearm. Stop the flow."

Later, Peters' bleeding stopped. His color was back and his breathing was close to normal. "Thanks for making them save me," Peters said. "It doesn't mean I'm not going to try for you again."

"I know that. But not for now, because I'm going to strip you and take your horses and weapons, so you can't."

One of the other men protested. "Hey, not the clothes." Peters swatted him with his able hand and told him to start stripping.

Moultrie left them naked on the road.

He stopped after he had ridden about a hundred yards. He turned and cantered back to the three. He looped the strap of his own full canteen of water around Peters' neck. "Don't share it," he told Peters. "Drink it all. You're going to need it."

As he rode off once more, Moultrie cursed himself for a damned fool for caring about the man.

Moultrie took the clothes, weapons and horses of Peters and the two others with him on his ride toward Cheaha Mountain. He knew the path well. He had ridden it with Uncle John a dozen times at least. It was only the last time, however, that they had gone to Bear Chief's village on the Tallapoosa, south of the mountain.

That was the time Moultrie had met Little Johnnie.

The meeting had been strained. Maybe Little Johnnie had sensed Moultrie's embarrassment, or maybe Johnnie was just defensive concerning his mixed origins. Whatever the reason, he had been sarcastic and belligerent toward both his father and his cousin. He had told his father, in fact, that there was no point in bringing Moultrie to the Tallapoosa because, no matter how hard he tried, he could not turn a white man into an Indian any more than he could turn an Indian into a white man.

That had been seven years ago. A lot had happened since then, but not enough to change Little Johnnie's point of view, if Moultrie's guess was right. Of course, the Indian agent could have read his cousin's character all wrong. Little Johnnie might have left Hobson's employment as Jim Henry had, to embrace and defend the heritage of his mother's people. Moultrie did not think so. Bear Chief had said of Little Johnnie during that visit seven years ago, "His home is with us, but his eyes see your horizons."

Bear Chief had impressed Moultrie. The man seemed extraordinarily clear-sighted. He also had had an obvious love for the land Moultrie was going to take from him. The poor bastard, Moultrie thought. Not that he blamed the chief for loving his land. Just seeing the mountains now rising before him had sent Moultrie's heart soaring. This was the first time he had felt like this since arriving in Montgomery ten weeks ago. No wonder Uncle John had come up here. Every man here was a visionary, looking for mile upon mile at summer green and winter barrenness.

The village, when Moultrie first saw it, looked much as he remembered it. Typical Creek log houses sprawled across a shelf of land, twenty feet above the river. Downstream, corn and squash fields straggled across some bottomland. Through his spyglass, it looked to Moultrie as if there were maybe as many as a dozen blacks working there. Bear Chief apparently had bought a few more slaves. The man had always had business sense.

Riding down the last ridge, Moultrie looked left toward the river. The Tallapoosa still looked calm here. The sound of rapids above and below the village, though, filled the air with the same dull roar he had remembered. Uncle John had said the Indians called the sound God-talk, and Bear Chief had said no one in his village wanted to die while they were away from the noise. "It is the breath of our land, the heartbeat of our village," he had added, his eyes looking far away into the distance.

"Hello, cousin."

Moultrie jumped. It was Little Johnnie, as lithe and graceful in his stance as ever. They looked at each other for a minute.

"Hello, Little Johnnie," Moultrie beamed. "You look more like your father than you used to."

"So they tell me," Little Johnnie said, now speaking Muskogean. "I can't help it. Old age is bringing the worst out in me." He grinned.

Dismounting, Moultrie walked along beside his cousin. The man did look like Uncle John. He even had the same springy step and the same off-again, on-again smile. See him one minute, and you'd swear his life was a deadly serious business. The next minute he would smile and the world looked all sunshine and play.

"What you cut your eye at me like that for, boy?"

Little Johnnie's mimicking of the Gullah accent low-country blacks used was perfect.

Moultrie laughed. "I ain't study about you," he answered.

Little Johnnie clapped Moultrie on the back. "It's good to see you, cousin," he said, speaking again in surprisingly precise English, "even if you are here to tell us we've got to leave the thunder waters for the Indian Territory." His face was suddenly serious again.

"So you know?" Moultrie was not really surprised.

"We all do." As he spoke, Little Johnnie pointed toward Bear Chief and some warriors standing to receive them. "The chief is happy that you, the nephew of his old friend, are doing what you are for his people. He'll listen to your advice, too, though there isn't much you can tell him that he doesn't know already."

"Where do you stand?"

Little Johnnie stopped and looked at Ravenel, one of his sudden smiles flashing across his face. "On my own two feet, Cousin Moultie, on my own two feet." Then the smile was gone. "Some others here, Deer Warrior for one, are standing on the ground where they were born. Watch out for them, coz. They're not going to listen to me, you or the old chief. Their blood's up and they can't hear anything but its pounding in their ears."

Moultrie sensed Deer Warrior's hostility when he met him. Bear Chief, on the other hand, was warm and cordial. They talked and smoked and ate late into the darkness. Nothing, though, was said about Moultrie's mission. Talk of that would wait until tomorrow, when they would all go through the purification of the Black Drink Ceremony before a council meeting. Moultrie did not look forward to any of it. The black drink, cassia tea, was vile. And no doubt the council meeting would be stormy.

The warriors came to the council grounds singly and in pairs, taking seats on logs placed around the edge of the space. Bear Chief sat at the upper end of the rough circle in front of the village storehouse. Moultrie sat next to him on his right, with Little Johnnie on the other side.

Laughing and talking, the warriors waited. They look like a Saturday militia muster, Moultrie thought. Business seems to be the last thing on their minds. Only Bear Chief and Deer Warrior were somber. Their clothes, however, like the clothes of the other warriors, belied their seriousness. Brightly colored turbans, bold calico shirts, brilliant sashes, gleaming ornaments. The Creeks were noted for their love of ornamentation.

Bear Chief was passed a large pottery bowl. Taking it in both hands, he drank deeply. Then he lowered it and passed it to Moultrie. Moultrie caught his breath as he inhaled the odor of the bitter spice tea. Only once before had he drunk the emetic. It had been at Uncle John's insistence. He had drunk deeply, not once, not twice, but five times. For hours after that he had felt the purifier welling back up in his throat. He had spat streams of the juice. Grimly he lifted the bowl to his lips. No wonder the Indians think this stuff will purify a man, he thought. He drank, then passed the bowl. It came around again, then again, and again. Each time he drank. In between swallows, he screamed in the ritual manner before rejoining the easy conversation around him. As the black tea rose in his throat, he belched and spat. Like the warriors around him, Moultrie aimed toward the center of the council circle, where a puddle began to form, black and stinking in the rising sun.

After each man had taken the bowl as many times as he could stand it, Bear Chief lit his pipe and passed it. Looking at the assembled warriors, then at Moultrie, Bear Chief began.

"Our white brother," he said, "has not explained why he has come. But we know. He is here to tell us we must go to the land across the great river."

Taking the pipe, Bear Chief filled it again, lit it and passed it on. The warriors who had been laughing and joking between ritual screams just a few minutes before were now silent. The cries of children and laughter of women seemed far away.

Bear Chief continued. "Many of our people have died on the trail to the land beyond the sunset. Many have returned from there to see again the land they knew, feel the rain wash them where it had washed their mothers and fathers, hear in the waters the spirit talk they learned as children."

The wind, as if applauding, suddenly gusted through the trees, filling the warriors' silence. In the distance, the Tallapoosa's roar sounded. Bear Chief's face was blank and his eyes looked into some far distance as he spoke. "When McIntosh led some of our people from their homes seven summers ago, I said we should not go. Now I say, we must. The white man crowds the spirits of our ancestors. No longer can we hunt the lands our fathers walked in the company of the Great Spirit."

"No." Deer Warrior had jumped up. "We are not women to fall down for the white man. We must fight. We cannot let the white man spit where our ancestors worshiped, laugh where our ancestors listened to the silence speak."

Standing up slowly, Little Johnnie looked across the circle at Deer Warrior. When he spoke, his voice was challenging. "I am not a woman, Deer Warrior, but I am also not a fool. The whites are too numerous to fight. If we stay, we will see blood poured over the land. And for what? No, friend, if you want so much to fight, join me and we will help the whites finish this war against our misguided brothers, before it goes further and destroys *all* our people. I am sick when I think of fighting my brothers. But fight we must. Then we can go behind the sunset together where we can fight the Indians who grow their hair long and ride on the sea of grass."

Most of the warriors murmured approval as Little Johnnie finished. Deer Warrior was angry. "*My* mother did not open herself to a white man," he barked, "and I am not a traitor."

"Am I?" Bear Chief did not stand.

Deer Warrior raised his hand as if in supplication, then dropped it. "Your eyes do not see as mine see," he said. Then he turned and made his way toward his cabin.

Bear Chief watched Deer Warrior go, then addressed the circle. When he spoke, it was not of Deer Warrior's incredible rudeness to Little Johnnie or his disregard of council etiquette by speaking so bluntly and then leaving. Rather, it was of the chief's sadness that his people were divided against each other.

"It is a sadness I share." Little Johnnie's face carried pain in it. "I worked with Jim Henry. He is a man to love. Deer Warrior is another. They will fight and I will fight and it will be against each other. I am sad in my heart."

Moultrie still had not spoken. Now he did. "It is sad," he agreed, "but you are right to fight them, Little

Johnnie. The longer the others fight against the whites, the more damage all Creeks will suffer."

"Who will fight with Little Johnnie?" Bear Chief stood as he asked the question. First five or six, then a dozen, finally all the warriors said they would. Bear Chief said he would get other chiefs to send warriors, too.

That afternoon, walking down toward the river, Moultrie told Little Johnnie how much he had admired his handling of himself at the council. "I was afraid when Deer Warrior said that bad thing about your mother, that you would do something drastic."

"Why?" Little Johnnie sounded astonished. "Deer Warrior was right about her. Given his point of view, he was also right to call me a traitor. It's not what I've done or what I'm going to do that matters to him, you see, but my attitude. Frankly, it's awful. I can't live, don't want to live with whites, but I want white things. Money, don't you know?"

Moultrie shook his head. He wanted to argue, then thought, no. Why should he? It was Little Johnnie's decision alone.

The two men came to the edge of the bluff over the river. Below, the village women were bathing. They were leaping and laughing, unaware of the men above them.

"Now there," Little Johnnie said, pointing to the nude women, "is reason enough for any white man to wish to be an Indian." His laugh was infectious. "If trees could talk."

The view was splendid. Not just the women, but the late afternoon sunlight angling across the water in streaks of gold and silver glint. And beyond was the forest, swelling up toward the mountains. Patches in the distance were dark with shadow. Others were suffused with light, almost radiant.

Gesturing as if to embrace the view, Moultrie said, "If it weren't his anger, but his love of this, I would sympathize more with Deer Warrior."

"I know." There were tears in Little Johnnie's eyes as he spoke. Then he shook his head and laughed. But the laughter rang hollow.

Suddenly he pointed to one of the young women in the river below. "See her?" he asked. "She's Deer Warrior's woman." He paused, then continued, "Now that Deer Warrior's taking off to fight with Jim Henry, she'll be fair game, too." This time Little Johnnie's laugh was convincing.

Very convincing.

Chapter 10

Bear Chief secured more than one hundred warriors to go with Little Johnnie and Ravenel to fight the rebellious Yuchis, Cheahas, Eufaulas and Hitchitis at the side of the U.S. Army. Some came from the other side of Cheaha Mountain. All were mountain men. Eight days after the council meeting and Deer Warrior's departure to join Jim Henry on the other side of the war . . . seven days after Bear Chief had set out with Moultrie to talk to other villages about their sending warriors to put an end to the war as quickly as possible . . . and three days after Little Johnnie had first made love to Water Bird, the woman Deer Warrior had been courting . . . the combined force of Creek Indians and U.S. Cavalry started south toward Fort Mitchell, center of military operations.

Normally, the march to Fort Mitchell from the Tallapoosa east to the Chattahoochee and then downriver would have taken four days. They made it in three, going hard from the first dawn until dusk.

Fort Mitchell was a free-for-all, worse even than Columbus had been two weeks before. Indians were everywhere, squatting around fires, huddling over their small piles of possessions. Some were prisoners. Some were voluntarily there waiting to go west. Most, however, were there because they had been burned out of their homes and harassed through the countryside by both Georgia and Alabama militia.

The sky around the fort was hazy with smoke from hundreds of fires. Adding to the haze was the dust from the cattle and horse pens. Two days after a rain, it was as if the land were desert.

Captain John Page was exhausted when Moultrie saw him in his office. He had been trying to help regulate and control the chaos. "It's like riding the whirlwind, Moultrie," he complained, his eyes sunken, his face haggard. "I haven't slept more than four hours at one time since you left for your meeting with General Scott."

Page got up and walked around his desk. Putting his hand on Moultrie's shoulder, he said, "I'm sorry I've got to be the one to tell you this, old man, but the Indian boy took off a week ago."

"He what?" Moultrie sunk into a chair. "Tell me about it."

Page did. He had been in the habit of taking Cicero and Little Hawk along with him on rides out past the fort. They had ridden together almost every day. The past Monday they had gone out again, this time to investigate enemy activity downriver from the fort about fifteen miles.

"Usually," Page began, "Cicero and Little Hawk chatted back and forth in that incredible mixture of Yuchi and English of theirs. This time, however, the boy fell silent about ten miles out. I didn't think much of it at the time. Looking back on it, I suppose the boy had seen signs of his father's people. Neither I nor Cicero caught them. God knows what those signs were, though. I'm not such a hot tracker, but your Cicero, Moultrie, is first class.

"Well, anyway, the squad I was leading got to the plantation where the Indians—Yuchis, by all accounts—had been sighted. It was one of the few plantations, in fact, which hadn't been deserted in the last months. The place was like an armed camp. Six or seven white families from surrounding plantations had gathered there instead of going on up to Columbus. The planters had brought their slaves with them, too. Hell, there must have been nearly two hundred and fifty people, all told.

"To hear the plantation owner tell the tale, he was awakened in the middle of the night by shots. He went down to the barnyard, where the shots had come from. He met his overseer. According to the man, some Indians had tried to steal several head of cattle by lifting the railings on the fence on the south side of the cattle pen. They almost had gotten away with it, too. But one of the men was coming back from visiting his girl. If he hadn't almost stumbled on the Indians and given a shout, the Indians would have walked off with God knows how many head of cattle.

"The owner demanded to know what I was going to do. I told him there was nothing I could do at present except report the incident. The answer wasn't good enough. The man ranted and raved at me for ten minutes. He would have gone on for another ten, too, if Cicero hadn't come up, out of breath. That was when he said his little Dedzu wasn't anywhere to be found.

"I had trouble getting Cicero to explain who Dedzu, or Strawberry, is. Cicero was too excited to talk either coherently or slowly. Finally, however, I pieced the story together. Cicero had been talking to the man who had stumbled on the Indians the night before. The man, incidentally, had been put in the plantation stockade by that stupid planter. Would you believe that planter was punishing the man for being out after hours instead of thanking him for saving his cattle? Anyway, Cicero had been talking to this man at the stockade and had decided to go look at the place where the Indians were supposed to have been the night before.

"He took Little Hawk with him. They struck me as inseparable. Cicero went to the south side of the cattle yard. Most of the signs had been trampled over, but he found enough to figure out roughly how many Indians had been involved, where they had come from and where they had gone. He turned around to tell the boy. Cicero didn't see him anywhere.

"Cicero has a head on his shoulders. Instead of running around like a chicken with its head cut off, he immediately worked out the boy's trail. It led into the woods at an angle which showed that Little Hawk had not wanted to be seen by his friend. As soon as the trail entered the woods, it led back to the Indians' escape track. The boy obviously had been running. There was no way Cicero could have caught him on foot, so Cicero came back to tell me, hoping I would send the squad after the boy on horseback.

"That planter blew up when he heard this. He said, 'What do you mean you're going to use the army to chase some damned Indian boy, when the army can't do a damned thing to help whites?' He was going to have my hide if he had to go see Old Hickory himself.

"I lost my patience then," Page explained. "I told the planter to shut his mouth before he got a saber down it. The man turned red. But he also stopped talking long enough for me to say some things.

"The first thing I said was that if he had only listened a little more closely to Cicero's story, he would have realized that by following the boy the troops would be tracking the Indians who had raided the plantation the night before.

" 'Besides,' I said, 'I never said I was going to follow the boy.' In fact, I said, 'I'm not. I can't. To lead a squad of twenty into those woods is potential suicide. Furthermore, my orders expressly forbid my going off on my own like that, and talking to Generals Jesup, Scott, Cass *and* Jackson, all four of them, can't change that.' "

Taking a deep breath, Page concluded, "That's the story, Moultrie." He stood up, went over to the window and looked out on the parade ground. "I couldn't have been sorrier, but there wasn't a damned thing I could do. Anyway, the boy was running to his father's people. That's clear enough. He'll be all right."

"As all right as any of those poor bleeders." Moultrie's jaw was tight. "What must Crazy Wolf think? That I neglected his trust?" He punched the door frame. "Crazy Wolf," he explained, "asked me to look after the boy, because he hoped that that way at least one of his children would be relatively safe." Banging his fist again, he added, "It's not your fault, John. Or Cicero's. You did all that you could, and you have my thanks."

Back at Fort Mitchell, Moultrie could not dismiss

as unimportant the stormy confrontation he had had with Judge Leander Dupré the night before he left Montgomery. Lord, Moultrie thought, it was awful. What's worse, the man carried out his threat. He wrote to Madden, not once, but three times. The Office of Indian Affairs clerk had sent copies of his answer to Moultrie. Moultrie had found the last of these on his return to Fort Mitchell with Little Johnnie and his warriors. He also found notes from Helen.

Madden's letter to Judge Leander Dupré made Moultrie chuckle. In it, Madden went to great lengths to assure the judge once again that, while Moultrie Ravenel was no doubt headstrong and certainly had angered a number of influential people by his attitude toward the Indian problem, Moultrie was nevertheless doing a remarkable job for the Office of Indian Affairs in difficult circumstances. According to General Scott, among others, he deserved praise. The judge, in short, need not worry, though Madden appreciated his concern and highly regarded his opinion. After all, Moultrie had been hired on the strength of the judge's recommendation.

The letter was typical of Madden, Moultrie thought. The judge thinks that such diplomatic phrasing is an affront to his common sense and clearness of vision. How he must have squirmed, particularly at the end. He's not used to having his actions thrown in his teeth. Neither is he used to having a government clerk dismiss his advice. Yet that is what Madden did.

Madden had obviously had a shrewd idea of what the judge's reaction would be. In the cover note he had sent to Moultrie with the copy of this last letter to Judge Dupré, Madden wrote, "While I meant what I said about your performance, that does not mean that I am not also displeased with the way you are beginning to alienate influential people like the judge, a man not easily put off." With a bluntness that Moultrie had come to expect, a bluntness very different from what Madden had once called his "baby-the-politico" style, the clerk had added, "Learn diplomacy or you will become more of a liability to us than an asset, no matter how good a job you do."

Moultrie showed the note to Captain John Page. "Here," he said, "is advance notice of my decease."

Page's smile was wry. "The man makes sense, you know." He handed the note back. "You could do worse than follow his advice."

"And deprive Madden of the privilege and pleasure of dismissing me with suitable expressions of thanks, regret and irritation some day?"

"That's brave talk." Page grinned. "You know the ritual saying of the gladiators as they entered the arena in Rome, don't you?"

"Hail, Caesar," Moultrie quoted, "we who are about to die, salute you." He returned Page's grin. "At least," he said, "I don't have to worry about my future."

In fact, though, he worried a lot about the future, or more precisely, Helen. Her notes saddened him. It wasn't what they had said. Rather, what saddened Moultrie was the tone of the letters. There was no word or phrase, no single sentiment or thought which defined for him Helen's melancholy. Nonetheless, he felt it. He felt it most in her last note, in which she wrote, "I hope you have not forgotten the way to Montgomery and that we shall see you here before long."

The note read like an invitation. Somehow, though, it seemed to Moultrie to be a good-bye. The phrasing, the subjects, everything had been neutral.

There had been no recriminations, no explanations, no pleadings, no protestations of love. These things had all been written in earlier letters. It was as if Helen had retreated from the painfulness of emotion into an exhausted state and, looking back along the route of her retreat, was filled with a vague sadness.

La belle Helene. The beautiful Helen. A gulf has opened between us, Moultrie thought, and the more I look, the more impossible leaping the gulf seems. Yet she's so close. If we both stretched, leaning into the void between us, could we touch? Moultrie jumped up from where he had been sitting in his room at the fort and began to pace. "Sometimes," he said suddenly to Cicero, who had been watching him, "I want to say to hell with all this Indian business and go back to Montgomery. At other times I wonder if I'll ever go back there."

"You're not really serious about going back to Montgomery before this Indian transfer is done."

Moultrie sighed. No. He was not really serious.

"No one could blame you if you were," Cicero allowed. Something about Cicero's straightforward manner showed he really shared the concerns of Moultrie's dilemma.

"It would be better for you, Cicero, if we went home. More comfortable. Besides, this is no war of yours."

"The kind of white men causing it all are no good for my people, either, any more than they are for the Indians. That makes it my war too, in a way."

"You could stay then, if I went, Cicero."

The two faced each other.

"You're talking about those freedom papers for me again," Cicero noted.

Moultrie nodded.

"I get the sweats every time I think about it. The possibilities are so beautiful. But the risks are so fearful, Ravenel. You treat me more as friend than slave, in every way, but I have never been anything but slave. Nor have my parents and my ancestors, whoever they may be. I fear I would not know what to do with freedom. I have heard that some men in prison a long time grow afraid to get out. I have heard they will stab others over mere tobacco. What they really want is to lose their release." Cicero made a gesture, as if stabbing with a knife. "I understand that fear, Ravenel. Hold on to your papers for a while." He smiled. "Every time we have this discussion, my answer is the same, isn't it?"

"I'll not draw them up until you want them," Moultrie said. "But you'd do fine."

"I sometimes wish you hadn't taught me to know there could maybe be another way of life besides being a slave. I'm not content knowing too much. I'd probably have been happy if you'd let me be, just a darky. It's not easy being an educated darky. You see too many things you know you shouldn't want. Like being your own man."

"You're still missing a major point."

Cicero waited for his answer.

"You'd better take the papers some day soon and be your own man," Moultrie advised. "Because if anything ever happened to me, you're not fit to be anyone else's. Whoever tried to make you would probably have to kill you."

Chapter 11

"Haven't you heard?" Page was grinning at Moultrie.

"Heard what?"

"General Jesup, with the help of Jim Boy and his warriors, took Eneah Mathla and his son."

Moultrie sat up. "If they've got Eneah Mathla, that's one quarter of the resistance right there."

"I know." Page filled Moultrie's glass, then his own. Sitting back, he took a puff on his cigar. "Damn, but it's good to have you back. And your old self again, too. Not that cynical bastard who came back from Montgomery back in the spring." He shook his head. "Jim Henry, Eneah Micco and a half dozen others are still on the loose."

"True." Moultrie picked up his glass. "What are Scott's plans?"

"I'll show you on the map." Page stood up and walked over to the wall. He pointed out the line of march: first to Roanoke via Fort McCrary, halfway, then across the river to the Cowikee country.

Moultrie grunted. "The plan's solid. Don't fight the Indians. Just keep pushing them through the swamps until they drop from fatigue. Six weeks ought to see the end of this business. Maybe less."

"I agree."

On the march Moultrie first saw the quality of the new troops in the command and retracted his optimistic estimate of a six-week war. He refused to make further predictions. "Soldiers as green as these could not even win at marbles, let alone war," Moultrie told Page. "We shall be out here forever."

A sentry posted on the first night's bivouac was typical of all. He fired into the dark forest each time he heard a sound. In the night, a forest is full of sounds.

"They're only owls and other small things, mister," Moultrie told him.

There came the noise of a larger animal. The soldier fired. The animal screeched after the shot and continued to screech for a long time.

The soldier smiled, pleased with himself.

Then Sergeant Terence McCoy choked the new soldier by the collar and informed him he had just shot one of the company mules.

On another night, a sentry heard movement in some bushes. He called the challenge of the day. The answering yell was in a language the sentry did not understand. "Creek war cry," he called out smartly, then fired.

Corporal Wolfgang Jaeger came from the bushes as troops rushed to meet the attack. He was cursing the sentry, shaking one fist and holding up his issue trousers with his other hand. He had been relieving himself when the sentry challenged and fired. Surprised, he had fallen backwards. He now needed a bath desperately.

When asked why he had not answered the challenge properly, Corporal Jaeger replied that he had, but that the damned fool sentry did not know the difference between a Creek war cry and High German.

But the problem of skittish green troops and challenge misunderstandings ceased to be funny a few nights later.

A number of figures in the distance were moving silently between the trees and coming up on the camp perimeter.

The sentry had presence of mind not to fire. He quietly passed word of pending assault by a large enemy group.

Sergeant Terence McCoy moved a squad into place. He was about to give the order to fire by files when he realized they were aiming at Little Johnnie and his men.

McCoy later asked Little Johnnie, "Why didn't you respond to the sentry's challenge? You could have gotten yourself killed."

"McCoy, there was no challenge," Little Johnnie answered. "He was so damned scared he never opened his mouth."

Little Johnnie was restless. He and his warriors had come to fight, not just march as ordinary soldiers did.

"Maybe so," Moultrie answered. "But they look as though they like the parade, too."

The Creeks, in their fondness for flair, went to war in scarlet turbans with strips of white cloth around the center, scarlet scarfs thrown over their shoulders and ornamented bullet bags at their sides. Their shirts were the usual calico hunting shirts and their leggings were buckskin. Some also carried fans made of turkey feathers. Little Johnnie, on his cream-colored stallion, had an eagle feather in his turban.

They were a spectacular sight, moving through the pinewoods toward Roanoke and a meeting with General Scott's troop.

Army regulars marched behind in their sky-blue fatigues with white cross belts and black leather caps. There's poetry, Moultrie thought. Splendid. Forget this is war for a moment. Splendid.

There was nothing splendid, however, about the eight miles between Fort McCrary and Roanoke. The land was scarred badly with war. Not a house or barn or corncrib was standing, just heaps of ashes, a few charred logs and, occasionally, a splinter of bone or a shard of pottery. Crazy Wolf's village had looked like this. The smoke even smelled the same.

Crazy Wolf has done unto others as others had done unto him.

Moultrie was numb, almost ready to weep.

Worse, few settlers had escaped. Those who had escaped, but had not gone to the safety of Columbus, were huddled in Fort McCrary. McElveen was one. When Moultrie saw him, McElveen's face was etched with exhaustion, bitterness and anger. The man did not look at him with the mockery he once displayed. There was just hate left in his red-rimmed eyes. "He's lucky to be alive," a soldier told Moultrie. McElveen had managed to shoot his way out. Making the river, he had hidden behind a log, keeping just his nose above water. The other people in his house had not been so lucky.

"His wife and son burned to death," the soldier said.

William McElveen rode back to Roanoke from the fort with the troop. For the first four miles, he said nothing. Then he reined back so his horse was beside Moultrie's. "Well," he asked, "you satisfied, Indian-lover?" Moultrie did not answer. Reaching over, the colonel grabbed his arm.

"Damn you," McElveen said, shaking it, "when I ask you a question, I expect an answer."

Moultrie looked at him. When he spoke finally, his voice was low. "I'm sorry about your wife and boy, McElveen, but you brought some of this bloody business on yourself."

"You swine." McElveen's face was twisted with pain. "You goddamned son. . . ." He could not complete the phrase. Dry sobs racked him as he shook Moultrie's arm weakly. Suddenly shivering, he launched himself from his saddle at Moultrie.

Moultrie was not prepared. Both came crashing to the ground. Dazed and breathless, Moultrie could do nothing as McElveen, sobbing and cursing, shook him and pounded him.

It took four soldiers to pull the militiaman off. As Moultrie got to his feet, McElveen, his arms pinned, spat in the agent's face. Saying nothing, McCoy handed Moultrie a dirty handkerchief. Moultrie held it, the spit running down his face as he struggled, his chest heaving for breath.

Gradually, McElveen calmed down. "I'm all right," he declared finally. "You boys can let me go. I'm not going to try to attack Ravenel again." Then, looking at Moultrie, he added, "Why should I? Peters will kill him for me." He grinned. "There isn't a man here who doesn't know what I'm talking about," McElveen pronounced, looking around him. "The whole army, in fact, everyone in west Georgia and east Alabama knows the story. How Peters and the two men with him were found naked on the trail to Columbus by that calvalry detachment. The three of them cursed and ranted against Ravenel. They threatened to gouge the eyeballs out of any man to even think about laughing at their nakedness. 'Maybe I only have three fingers left on one hand,' Peters supposedly said, 'but there ain't a mother's son from here to the Natchez Trace to keep my thumbs from pushing his vision into perdition if he riles me.' "

One soldier, McElveen had been told, had been fool enough to ask Peters if he'd pushed in Moultrie's eyeballs. It took six men to pry Peters away from him.

The soldier was still in the military hospital in Montgomery. Doctors reportedly judged that his eyesight would eventually be normal again. His nose would always be a little crooked, however.

General Sanford's Georgia militiamen arrived the evening after Moultrie and the rest of the troops from Fort Mitchell.

There were two thousand of them. They marched into camp out of step with flags waving and the drum and bugle corps playing loudly and out of tune. General Winfield Scott and his staff followed.

Moultrie was summoned to see Scott that night. After a few minutes of innocuous chatting, Scott suddenly became all business. "Ravenel," he confessed, "you're making life difficult, not just for me, but for a lot of people. First, you shoot Peters, not that you weren't justified. Next, you fight McElveen. Not to mention the fact that Hobson, Sanford, Judge Dupré, Governor Clay and other people I could name want you locked up, sent on a vacation to Russia or hung out to dry. What on earth are you trying to do?"

Not waiting for an answer, the general grinned. "Just because you're John Ravenel's nephew doesn't mean that you have to fight the whole world. Your uncle did enough of that to last your family for an eternity." The general stood up, facing Moultrie. "I told you before that we're here to deal with the Indians, not fight each other." Then he added, "If I were you, I'd listen to good advice. Otherwise, you're going to be hurt so bad you'll be looking forward to hell as a relief."

The general was quiet. Moultrie waited.

"Well, Ravenel, I've had my say. Now let's hear yours."

"I don't have anything to add, sir. You've told it as it is. Those are the facts. Nothing I can say would alter them. And I'll do it all over again if I must. There's no point in saying anything."

"That's all, then, Mr. Ravenel," Scott concluded.

As Moultrie was leaving, Scott called him back. "There *is* one other matter."

"Sir?"

"The story about Peters and those two men of his coming down that trail dressed the way God made them was the funniest thing I'd heard in a long time."

Little Johnnie organized a pig hunt to keep his braves occupied. They caught over a dozen squealing pigs while being cheered on by soldiers.

Looking up in the middle of the butchering and seeing it was about noon, Moultrie called over to McCoy. "If you're ready to swallow some bile, Sergeant," he exclaimed, wiping the sweat from his eyes and waving halfheartedly at the flies, "join me for lunch. Cicero should have it about ready."

They started back toward Moultrie's tent. Cicero,

lurching in a drunken run, met them. He had a welt across his face as if he had been hit by a whip, and blood was oozing from a gash above his right temple.

"Cicero! What happened. Who hit you?"

"Who done it?" Cicero shook his head, then winced. "That Peters man. He come over just a little bit ago. He said he was looking for you, Marse Moultrie. And when I said I didn't know where you were, he hit me up side the head and told me not to give him sass, or he was going to make me feel his whip real good." Cicero sucked in deep gulps of wind. Playing the role of frightened black man, he nonetheless looked squarely into Moultrie's eyes. Moultrie saw the controlled anger there. And Cicero's unspoken message was clear.

All right, he thought, I'm playing my role in our ongoing act, yours and mine. I'm groveling. Now it's time for you to play yours. Defend me. "I tried to run from him, Marse Moultrie." Cicero was again the Cicero everyone expected him to be, namely, slave to Moultrie's master. "That's when he knocked me hard with his gun. Right here." Cicero gently touched the edge of the open wound on the side of his head.

"The scum." McCoy hissed the words.

"Cicero, you go to the field surgeon's tent and get that wound tended to." Moultrie turned to McCoy. "You coming for the show?"

Peters was waiting for them. So were the two men who had been with him when Moultrie had shot away half his hand on the road. Peters grinned as Moultrie and McCoy came up. "You ought to teach your boy respect for white folks or he's going to get hurt bad some day," he called.

"He showed respect. I wouldn't have him if he didn't. I'm going to hurt you, Peters."

"Will you listen to that? The man's talking big," Peters said mockingly. "Bushwhackers like you," he scorned, "ain't going to try anything man to man."

Moultrie began unbuttoning his shirt.

Peters sneered. "Why the hell should I mess with a goddamned aristocrat?" But he too started to take off his shirt. By this time the two men were ready to square off, there was a small crowd forming a circle around them.

"Peters, you want me to tie one hand behind my back to compensate for those missing fingers?" Moultrie asked.

Peters' answer was a roar. He charged.

Moultrie backpedalled out of Peters' reach. Peters abandoned all effort at tactics and charged again. Slugging at first, Peters closed in and caught Moultrie about the middle with a bear hug. With hands locked behind Moultrie's back, Peters ground his knuckles up and down hard on Moultrie's spine.

Moultrie had not felt such pain in his entire life. The cracking pressure on spinal bones seemed to drive clear into his viscera. Moultrie felt himself being bent over backwards, farther and farther. Peters' head was battering Moultrie's chin. Moultrie knew his spine was about to snap.

Suddenly he kicked up both feet, wrapped his legs about Peters' hips and allowed his own weight to pull both Peters and himself to the ground.

Moultrie came down hard on his back. Peters fell on top of him. The sudden weight pounded the wind out of Moultrie's lungs. But the maneuver accomplished what Moultrie had desperately wanted.

Peters' lethal hold was neutralized.

Moultrie rolled over, and he had just gotten onto his feet when Peters swung and hit him so hard that the punch twisted Moultrie's head around to one side. As Moultrie staggered back, he wondered how a fist with only two fingers and a thumb could hurt so much. He felt his knees giving, but managed to hurl himself away from Peters onto the ground.

Peters leaped high, drawing his legs up and under, aiming to uncoil them and smash down on Moultrie's chest and break his ribs. Moultrie rolled and kicked hard with both feet. They caught Peters' hips and shot his legs out from beneath him.

Peters hit the earth hard. He was pushing himself erect again when Moultrie's fist split his mouth open up to the nose, knocking him over in a shower of blood.

Moultrie, sucking in wind, was sure that last punch would end it. No. Peters came back up, seemingly faster than ever. My God, Moultrie thought, the man is smiling through blood and broken teeth. Pain actually seems to fuel him.

Blood bubbled in Peters' mouth when he spoke. "You'd better hope I don't bring you down again." Crouched low, he circled Moultrie as he talked. "If I do," he continued, "you're going to lose your eyeballs." He laughed.

Moultrie shook his head to keep sweat out of his eyes as he followed the circling Peters.

Then, suddenly, the men were grappling again. Somehow, Moultrie managed to get a hammer lock on Peters' head. Peters tried to pry Moultrie loose. He could not. Bellowing in pain, he swung his fist full at Moultrie's crotch. Moultrie saw the punch coming and stepped back on one foot. Still, the blow landed hard. Moultrie groaned in pain, but he did not let go. Instead, catching Peters a little off balance after his swing, he brought his knee up straight into the man's jaw.

The cracking bone could be heard around the ring. Peters' head went back, his eyes and mouth suddenly wide, and then he toppled like a falling tree.

Moultrie himself could no longer stand. The agony in his crotch and middle buckled him like a hinge. He too hit the ground.

The men in the crowd yelled, "Up! Up!"

Moultrie tried. His arms trembled as he pushed.

He saw Peters on his side struggling to get his arm into play beneath him for leverage.

Let me be first up, Moultrie prayed. Let me be first.

He was. He had to stagger about just to hold his balance and remain erect. He shoved his hands into Peters' armpits and hauled him erect, too. Peters was soaked with sweat. He almost slipped from Moultrie's grip twice.

Moultrie turned Peters around to face him. Peters cocked his arm feebly to strike. Moultrie slapped the fist aside.

Then he coiled his own right hand around behind himself and brought it forward again from knee level. He rolled all of his body weight in behind it.

His fist broke Peters' nose. Blood spattered onto Moultrie's knuckles.

Peters went down, rolled over and looked at the sky for a few seconds before he closed his eyes.

The fight was over.

But then Moultrie saw the face of William McElveen among the whooping men. McElveen's look concentrated on Moultrie. Men moved back and forth between them, blocking their view of each other. Yet

McElveen was still there when they passed, watching Moultrie.

And Moultrie knew then that McElveen wanted another encounter with him, and wanted it to be just as rough as Moultrie's tangle with Peters.

Captain John Page was placing Moultrie's shirt across his shoulders like a cape when Cicero took it from him and arranged it. Cicero's own cut was still bleeding.

"You didn't go to the hospital after all," Moultrie noted.

"I thought you might need help."

"You couldn't have given me any even if I did."

"Ravenel, that Peters almost had you. I don't think I could have let him. I'd have brought him down with something. And to hell with whatever they all might have done to me for it."

Page glanced quickly from Cicero to Moultrie when he heard Cicero call him Ravenel.

Page, to his surprise, saw that Moultrie apparently accepted the familiarity as a natural thing. He smiled and said nothing.

Chapter 12

That night the rains came.

Moultrie and Cicero sat on separate boxes in Moultrie's tent. They held their knees up beneath their chins to keep their feet clear of the water flowing across the earth inside the tent. They said little to each other. Each suffered the pain of his particular injury in silence.

Captain John Page lifted the tent flap and ducked in, trailing feathers of water from his glistening oilskin.

"I didn't hear you knock," Moultrie carped.

Page slapped the tent canvas several times, making splashy thuds. "A punch below the belt sure makes you touchy."

"Enter, friend," Moultrie said, grinning. "It's important that we remember our manners." He was rubbing his groin, wincing because of its extreme tenderness.

Page sympathized. "Don't worry. You'll be servicing the ladies again in no time. Although, if I were you, I might go easy the first few times."

They enjoyed their verbal fencing. "You didn't come out in this rain just to tell me that," Moultrie remarked.

"No. You're not worth it. I came because General Scott sends you his compliments and says that he hopes you cleared your head and the air both in that fracas this morning. That nice Mr. Hobson was there with the general." Page stressed the word "nice" with sarcasm. "He said he was pleased to hear you were bearing up. He hopes you're on your feet tomorrow and fit again when we move across the river."

"Seems to me we're in the middle of that river now. Someday somebody's going to design an army tent with a waterproof basement."

Page enjoyed the comment.

Cicero removed his shoes and stood, settling ankle-deep into mud inside the tent. "With your permission, Marse Moultrie, I'd sure like to go see if I can rustle up some grub. The army mess is open twenty-four hours and sometimes they give something to the darkies."

Moultrie nodded. "Sure."

"Can I bring you something, Marse Moultrie?"

Moultrie shook his head. "No thanks, Cicero."

"Okay, Marse Moultrie."

When Cicero went out into the night rain, Moultrie told Page, "I don't wonder he's hungry. Neither of us have eaten since before the athletic demonstrations this morning."

With Cicero gone, Page said, "He just called you Marse Moultrie."

"Yes."

"And he's your ordinary garden-variety subservient black."

"Yes again." He suddenly felt alert. "What's the point?"

"This morning he called you Ravenel. No mister or anything. Just Ravenel. As though you were equals."

"White men and their blacks often become so close in the South," Moultrie explained, "that to the outsider it often seems as though they are more intimate than they really are and that the recognized bounds are overstepped. Especially when - they've grown up together since they were boys, as Cicero and I have. I assure you, you overheard nothing improper."

"I'd have thought his calling you Ravenel that way would be considered improper."

"I didn't notice it, I confess. If he did, it was a slip of the tongue in the stress of the moment."

"Moultrie, I'm not trying to make something gothic of it, and if he calls you Ravenel instead of Marse Moultrie, and you let him, it's no skin off my nose," Page said. "But as someone who is not a Southerner, it struck me as odd. You people are so tight about your divisions between black and white. It just seemed like a form of insubordination to me—or perhaps intimacy—and I'm asking because I'm curious."

"Even if it was," Moultrie laughed, "it shouldn't surprise you. I could make a similar observation about you and your Sergeant McCoy."

Page was puzzled.

"Your Sergeant McCoy talks back to you and the major every day of the week."

"Touché." Page tilted back his head and laughed.

"So. Cicero talks back to me. Your Sergeant McCoy talks back to you. It's something you allow good people to do when you have authority and you care about them."

"Well, I'll never tell," Page teased. "But I sometimes suspect you *are* a different sort of southern gentleman than most, Moultrie."

Moultrie pretended not to hear. After a moment, he asked, "You wouldn't happen to have a dry cigar, would you now, Page?"

The morning brought more rain. The "general" was sounded throughout the camp at eight a.m. At the drumroll, men pitched out into the mud and water, cursing and straining. Striking the tents, they packed and loaded the wagons for the march. Then, wheeling a six-pounder into place, they aimed it across the river to cover the crossing. "It might not be more than a peashooter," McCoy admitted, "but it'll scare Indians."

For all they knew, there were Indians over on the other side just waiting to catch a bunch of soldier boys crossing the river on their newly built raft. "Sitting out there, the boys would be goner than a goose at Christmas," McCoy said. "There ain't nothing like a clear shot at a target coming straight at you slow and easylike. It might not be sporting exactly, but it plumb makes sense to a fighting man who wants to win or a hunting man who's hungry."

With rain pelting down, McCoy stripped to his underdrawers and called Jaeger. "Dutchman, get over here. We're going to let you have another wash. You need it." The men laughed. McCoy grinned. There wasn't a soldier in the camp who had not heard of the incident involving Jaeger and the sentry that night on the march to Roanoke.

"Take this rope," McCoy instructed, "and tie it to your saddle. We're going to swim over there and hook up a couple of ropes so we can haul this flatboat back and forth." McCoy boarded his saddle and spurred his horse into the river. Jaeger was just behind him. When the horses reached the place where they had to swim, McCoy swung over into the water on the upstream side, grabbed his saddle and let the horses pull him toward the other side. Jaeger followed suit.

There were no Indians, just lots of trails and tracks. McCoy was relieved. "But it just isn't neighborly of Indians to watch us and then leave without staying to get properly introduced," he joked.

"*Ja*. It is terrible," Jaeger agreed. "In my fatherland enemies do not do that. They stay and shoot you dead."

Laughing, McCoy slapped the German on the back. "No question about it, Dutchman," he grinned. "Your people over there plumb have the Indians beat for civilized murder."

Moultrie and Cicero stood apart from the others, silently bearing the soaking rain as they held their horses' bridles. Water drained from their hats in lines resembling beaded curtains. It found a fresh creek bed down Moultrie's spine. He no longer cared about staying dry. He could be no wetter and colder than he was.

Watching Sergeant McCoy and Corporal Jaeger fight the stream with their horses, Cicero finally spoke. "John Page is a good man."

"Now what the hell brings that up at this moment?"

Cicero chuckled. "I heard you explaining what my calling you by the name Ravenel was all about. He didn't believe that stress-of-the-moment excuse for a second."

Moultrie smiled. "You're going to get us both

oiled and feathered by making a slip like that in public sometime. The wrong people are going to hear. I'll have a hell of a job saving your neck."

"My neck."

"It won't be my neck in trouble for sassing the white boss. I'll probably have to give you a public whipping."

"Real loyalty I hear from you."

The smile slipped from Moultrie's face. "Cicero, damn it, you know as well as I do, in public you can't slip and be familiar and call me Ravenel. I know it's hard to have two codes of conduct."

"I know that, Marse Moultrie," Cicero admitted, rolling his eyes heavenward and bowing just a bit. "Forgive me, boss, Marse Moultrie, but I sure do know. Yes, sir."

"Some joke. Funny, you are."

"Some people think we're pretty funny already, you and me. Funny strange."

Both chuckled once more. "But Page doesn't," Cicero said. "He's a good man. I liked his reaction fine. Like he said, he'll never tell."

"You mean you were listening to Page and me talk? Out in the rain?"

Cicero did not answer.

"You were supposed to be getting something to eat."

"I did. After I listened."

"Was it good?"

"How can four eggs, side meat, hot bread and coffee not be good? The mess sergeant's a good man, too."

"Why didn't you bring me some? Real loyalty I hear from *you*."

"You said you didn't want any."

"You know I lie."

It was noon when Little Johnnie and some of his braves rode in with a captive. Stopping at the abandoned farmhouse that General Winfield Scott had taken over for use as temporary headquarters, he asked whether General Scott or General Sanford wanted to interrogate the captured slave. Scott asked that the man be brought in.

General Scott, General John Sanford, William Hobson, William McElveen and Moultrie were there. Looking up from the map they were studying, they saw a man of medium height with a barrel chest, thin but muscular legs and arms and a face horribly disfigured by a series of welts.

"My God." Hobson stepped back, knocking over a chair. Then he laughed. It was a short, mirthless sound. Coming forward, he stopped in front of the black man. "It is you, isn't it, Scipio?" he asked.

The black man did not answer. Hobson's slap rang out like a shot. Sanford jumped at the sound. Moultrie got up out of his chair. "When I speak to you, boy," Hobson said evenly, his hand still raised, "I expect an answer. Now, your name *is* Scipio, right?"

The black man nodded.

"I said answer, not nod your head!"

Scipio started to answer. He spoke, fell silent, spoke again, then bellowed, "No. No more." He lunged, locking his arms around William Hobson's middle. The momentum of his rush almost sent both to the floor.

The others in the room began yelling.

Scipio lifted Hobson easily. Hobson kicked and flailed with his arms, trying to wriggle loose. Scipio boosted Hobson shoulder-high. "No!" he yelled one more time.

Then he hurled Hobson to the floor as though he were tossing out the trash.

Hobson was hurt, but he was not disabled. He rolled out from under Scipio's stomping foot, which had repeatedly landed on his back.

Hobson came up on one knee. A small, black pistol was in his hand.

Scipio stopped as though frozen, poised above him.

Hobson had time to consider and hold fire. He did not.

Moultrie did not anticipate the loud boom that now rang in his ears. The noise filled the room, momentarily stunning everyone inside. He had a flashing recollection of one other time he had heard a weapon fired indoors, though Falkner's pistol had not reverberated quite like Hobson's.

The impact of the ball bent Scipio over and pushed him backward across the room. He clutched at the hole in his stomach as though this could have stopped the bleeding. The wall stopped Scipio. He was dead before he reached the floor. He fell to one side and rolled over, facedown.

Moultrie realized that it had all taken place in seconds. He himself had begun to move to intercept Scipio the moment he had attacked Hobson. Moultrie realized that thus far, he had only risen from his chair and taken one or two steps.

The door to General Scott's office swung open so hard that it vibrated on its hinges. Scott's aide had kicked it open. The man leaped into the room, pistol in hand, saying, "Hold it, or the first man who moves will be shot."

Scott thanked the aide for his concern and told him to put away his weapon. He suggested that the aide call the medical corpsmen with a stretcher and a sheet to cover the body. He concluded, "And relieve Mr. Hobson of his firearm for now, before he shoots someone else in his temper." Seeing Hobson prepare to protest, Scott said, "And if he resists, Major, break your own weapon across the top of his head."

Hobson did not like Scott's order. He nonetheless handed over his pistol to the general's aide, saying he would expect it returned when he left.

It was plain there would be no further productive strategy-planning on that day. Scott addressed the men. "Gentlemen, in light of this tragic circumstance, I think it best we adjourn for today and collect ourselves. Speaking for myself, as often as I've seen men die in battle, I have never been able to view violent death as so much ho hum. Thank you gentlemen, we can discuss the war another time. For the moment, I think we've all had enough drama."

The men filed from the room. Moultrie heard Scott call to Hobson, "Be so good as to return here this afternoon at about three p.m. I realize that normally you would not be inconvenienced by civilian authorities too much to explain your shooting your own slave in cold blood. Since this is a U.S. Army facility, however, there will have to be an inquiry." Scott paused. "I'm certain it will be but a formality and you will not be put out." The sarcasm in his voice rang out.

On the farmhouse porch, Moultrie pulled his green slicker around himself. He marveled at the ease with which a white man could kill a black one. He had seen it happen before, with such ease, but nonetheless, he marveled each time.

"You will not be put out by the inquiry," Scott had told Hobson.

He was correct.

Scipio was dead. For Hobson, the only price was the inconvenience of an explanation, and not too great an inconvenience at that.

The others regrouped with him on the porch. Sanford. McElveen. Little Johnnie. Hobson.

No one was anxious to step into the rain for a drenching.

It might have been better if they had gotten drenched; Little Johnnie and Hobson might not have quarreled.

Hobson touched Little Johnnie's rifle, slung from his shoulder, muzzle down, to keep rain from the barrel. "You just stood by in there," Hobson said angrily, "while a black man attacked me. You didn't even raise your weapon to stop him." He tapped Little Johnnie's rifle with his fingers. "I had to kill him myself. I shouldn't have. We're paying you to fight for us. You didn't in there. Now I want you to pay me the price of that slave. He was a prime hand. I'm out eight hundred dollars."

"All you're out, white man, is the luxury of beating your own man to death when you got him alone. You're good at beating black men. I saw the scars on that one. No wonder he went for you. The only thing I regret is that I just didn't leave him out there."

John Sanford raised his hand for quiet and order. He asked Little Johnnie, "Did the man tell you anything useful out there before you brought him in?"

"No," Little Johnnie replied, "but his dress says he's been with the Yuchis."

"That's right," Moultrie said. "He was in Crazy

Wolf's village when McElveen here attacked it for no good reason."

McElveen leaned toward Moultrie. Hobson flatened his hand against McElveen's chest to stop him, then turned to Moultrie. "You knew he was a runaway and didn't do anything about it," Hobson said. "And you a planter holding slaves yourself."

"I pledged to Crazy Wolf I would not tell of his kindness, sheltering the man."

"And you felt honor-bound to keep your word to a stinking Indian."

As Hobson spoke, Little Johnnie moved behind him and put his hands on Hobson's shoulders. Moultrie realized he was going to throw Hobson off the porch into the mud. Do it, Moultrie thought. Do it.

Wrenching around, Hobson snarled, "Get your pig hands off me, half-breed."

Moultrie had never heard Hobson speak so viciously. Moultrie also realized that even though Hobson was a vicious man, he was not a cowardly one. His manner was clearly a challenge to Little Johnnie.

"What's the matter, white man? You don't like my smell? Maybe you don't like the smell of my warriors, either. Maybe we should just leave you all here to wade around in the Cowikee swamps all by yourselves. Would you like that, white man?"

"That's enough, you two," Sanford interjected. "Johnnie, why don't you leave first and put some distance between yourself and Hobson?"

Little Johnnie thought that was a fine idea. He bounded from the porch.

Moultrie called to his cousin. He blinked at the slanting raindrops striking his face and stepped from the porch.

The two dragged their feet through the mud toward Moultrie's tent.

Cicero mourned Scipio's death.

He sat for a long time at the entrance to the tent, looking at the rain. When he finally spoke, his lips were pulled tight in a trembling snarl. "You say Hobson could have put his pistol down, but he shot him anyway?"

Moultrie nodded.

"May Hobson die with blood in his throat." Cicero stood. "There's something I have to do." He stumbled out of the tent into the rain.

Head bowed against the downpour, he started after two men carrying a stretcher bearing a body draped in white.

The rain finally stopped at nine o'clock. Cicero came into the tent soon after. He was muddy and dripping wet. One look told Moultrie his guess had been right. "The general let you have Scipio's body?"

"Uh huh. I buried him in that cornfield." Cicero's voice was listless. Sitting down, he stared at the ground.

"Want a preacher to say a few words?"

"I can provide the words, Ravenel." As he spoke, Cicero began to rock back and forth, humming almost tonelessly. Then he began to sing.

> I look 'cross the Jordan,
> And guess what I see,
> Coming for to carry me home,
> A band of angels
> Coming after me,
> Coming for to carry me home.

Later, Cicero got up and washed himself. When he came back to his blanket, the lines were gone from his face. "My mind's easy now, Ravenel. Easy."

The next day saw six columns march from Camp Sanford, as they'd named the old Indian Field on the Chattahoochee River opposite Roanoke. Moultrie rode with McCoy and Jaeger.

McCoy was indignant. "You can't sneak up on a turkey," he beefed, "if you're going to crash through the woods like a damned ox, now can you?"

Moultrie laughed. "We don't want to sneak up on the Indians, just drive them out of hiding."

"It makes no sense," he said, "to tell them we're coming. This here's a war. Not no game of tag."

"All we do besides drink dust," Cicero complained, "is slap skeeters."

Moultrie shook his head morosely. "Three days we've been at it, and we haven't caught one Indian. Well, tomorrow we're going back to Camp Sanford for mail. Maybe there'll be something to cheer us up there. Even a note from McCoy." Moultrie grinned. The little sergeant had hated going back to Fort Mitchell when Scott had briefly been recalled two days earlier. He had threatened to transfer to the navy.

"First," he'd said, "they have me playing tag in the woods. Now, they're going to let me sit in a lousy fort."

The steamboat brought more bacon and bread and a large mail sack. Two letters were for Moultrie.

One was from Helen, saying that she had just learned about her father's correspondence with Charles Madden about Moultrie's job.

I told Papa that I was shocked and sorry. Oh, I knew he was thinking of what was best for both of us, but he was wrong. He can't run your life. No one can. He still doesn't see that. He wants, he says, to have you benefit from his experience. It seems to me his experience is getting in the way of his judgment. Young men never live by other people's rules, do they?

Moultrie was pleased by Helen's letter. True, she had not said anything about love or marriage, but she had shown that she understood his motivations and accepted his situation in a way she had not demonstrated before.

The other envelope was postmarked Charleston and dated a month earlier. The handwriting was his brother's. It had been months since he had received a letter from Henry. What was the old goat up to?

He tore open the envelope. When he read, he almost wished he had not. He read again and then the first sob convulsed him.

Henry's letter began, "Our mother has died. . . ."

Chapter 13

There was not much Moultrie could do. His mother had died a month ago. Henry, he was sure, had taken care of everything that had needed taking care of back in South Carolina. Furthermore, Moultrie had a job to do. He could not leave, not when there would be no purpose served. Write to Henry and go back to chasing Indians, he decided. That was all he could do.

That afternoon the steamboat sailed. It carried a sack full of mail from the soldiers and Moultrie's own scribbled note to his brother.

That night Moultrie lay in his makeshift bed, too numb to feel loss. What hurt was the vision of that strong woman, his mother, her frail frame lying there as cancer ate at her, draining her energy, changing the laughter lines in her face into lines of pain. The picture was clear, clearer maybe than if he had been there over the weeks and gotten used to the idea of her being crippled at first, then consumed.

When he finally fell asleep, he was emotionally

drained. He did not remember having dreamed at all when the bugle sounded the next morning. For that matter, he did not remember having even slept. When he woke up, it was to see the same vision of his mother again.

God, he had loved her. She had been beautiful, delicate. He had always felt clumsy beside her.

"It's time, coz."

Moultrie shook himself. He had not seen Little Johnnie come in. "Right, let's go see Crazy Wolf."

No one had the energy to talk. Ten minutes out of camp, all were sticky with sweat. Every forty-five minutes, the troop stopped to drink and rest. The sweat in their clothes gave off a sour smell. There was no wind to remove it. It just clung to them.

During the third rest stop, Moultrie heard a challenge at one of the pickets. Making his way there with Little Johnnie, he saw Crazy Wolf carrying a white flag. The man's cheeks were sunken, his eyes red with fatigue. Moultrie experienced a rush of relief. The white flag could mean only one thing. Crazy Wolf wanted to end the fighting.

"Hello, Little Hunting Brother."

"Hello, Crazy Wolf."

"I have come to surrender my people."

"I am glad."

"You will come with me. We return in the morning."

Moultrie turned to Little Johnnie. Little Johnnie shook his head. "It could be a trap, coz," he pointed out. "That's an old trick."

"It's no trap. I know Crazy Wolf. Besides, what would they gain?"

"It's your hide. We'll wait for you until this time tomorrow."

Moultrie and Cicero mounted and joined Crazy Wolf. Heading in the direction of the north fork of the Cowikee River, they rode without speaking. At one point they dismounted and pushed through a cane-brake ahead of their horses. On the other side, they mounted again. They rode trails Moultrie had never seen seven years before when he had hunted the very same savannahs, swamps and woods. No soldiers had found them, that was certain.

"You are well hidden, Big Hunting Brother," Moultrie said.

Crazy Wolf grunted.

It was hard for Moultrie to estimate, but the whole trip could not have taken them more than fifteen miles. They must have covered close to twice that much ground, however. The sun was low when they rode into the Yuchi camp.

The silence was eerie. There were no dogs fighting over bones, no women laughing over cooking fires, no children shouting as they played tag, no boys cheering each other on in games.

"Lord," Cicero exclaimed, "look here. Isn't this something? These people are walking round almost dead."

Then Cicero saw Little Hawk. He grinned and started toward the boy, then stopped. There was not even a flicker of recognition in Little Hawk's eyes.

"Dedzu, don't you know me?"

The boy stared at the ground.

Watching the scene, Moultrie's heart wrenched. God, what had happened to these people? How they had suffered!

Cicero came over, shaking his head. "I don't know what to do, Ravenel, I just don't know."

Moultrie tried to comfort him. "He's not forgotten

you, Cicero. It's these weeks of hiding here. We're the enemy now. That will change." It was poor comfort, Moultrie knew. Crazy Wolf's stubborn silence had hurt Moultrie, too.

That night the council drank its last black drink in freedom. Only seven shared it with Crazy Wolf. Moultrie was not one.

After drinking and then smoking the pipe, Crazy Wolf stood. His face was without expression, as it had been that night months earlier when he had carried Running Water's body. "The summer has come," he announced. "Our fields are not planted. Instead of deer and bear, our hunting grounds run with soldiers. In the day, we hide our sacred fire, so that we will not be found. We move now only at night. Never do we sleep in one place more times than there are fingers on a hand or toes on a foot. Our babies are dead. We have had to strangle them to keep them from crying out when the soldiers are near, and to make it easier for the women to fight. Our women and children are thin with hunger. And there is nothing we can do."

As he continued, Crazy Wolf told how they had attacked the whites again and again. He told, too, of the daring of the dead and the bravery of the living. "But," he added, "it was for nothing. We must surrender. The warriors must put down their guns and put on chains like those who are already captured or have surrendered. Our sacred fire will never burn again in the land of our mothers. When our grandchildren see the sun rise, it will not be the same sun that our grandparents saw. All that our grandchildren will know of the home of our youth is our sorrow. It must be so."

"It must be so," every brave repeated in agreement.

After the council, Moultrie ate with Crazy Wolf

and his three children. His youngest daughter served. Moultrie thought this was odd.

"Where is your second wife, Big Hunting Brother?" Moultrie asked.

"Dead. Childbirth."

Moultrie knew better than to ask about the baby. He tried to apologize for not having been able to keep hold of Little Hawk.

Crazy Wolf cut him short. "It is not your fault. I owe you thanks. Little Hawk told me how well he was treated by you and the slave."

The boy still did not say anything. Later, Moultrie reminded himself. Later.

Four hours of sleep.

After that, the camp was dismantled. The women took the sacred fire. They refused to be chained and herded as the men were to be. With the first light of dawn, the band was ready. This time Crazy Wolf led them along a different path.

The only men riding with the women and children were Moultrie and Cicero. All the others were in positions well ahead of the band, off the flanks and in the rear. Where the path went between swamp pools that flankers could not pass, the warriors took up temporary positions in the column. Crazy Wolf risked nothing.

For the first couple of miles, Cicero did not speak.

"That scene with Little Hawk still troubling you?" Moultrie put his hand on Cicero's arm as he spoke.

"Oh, Ravenel, it's not only Little Hawk. It's Red Wing, too. Do you know she won't even barely look at me? She tells me I belong to a white man. And to her, that's no kinda man at all."

As Cicero finished speaking, Little Hawk reined back beside him. "Daca," he said, "don't talk on the trail. It's dangerous." Then Little Hawk spurred forward again, leaving Cicero smiling for the first time all morning.

"He knows my name," he beamed.

It was four hours later when Crazy Wolf trotted back to where Moultrie and Cicero were. "Are you ready, Little Hunting Brother?" he asked.

Moultrie nodded. Crazy Wolf broke off a small branch, stripped the leaves and tied a white cloth to the stem. Then he and Moultrie cantered forward along the line of Indians. Once down the trail, they slowed to a walk. It was not a good idea to startle a guard by bursting into his view at a run. The man would shoot first and ask questions later.

About a half mile from Little Johnnie's camp, Moultrie told Crazy Wolf to wait while he rode forward.

Fifteen minutes later, he was back with Little Johnnie and ten warriors. Crazy Wolf surrendered his weapons to Little Johnnie, then led the warriors back to the place where his band had stopped.

That afternoon the captives and fifty guards, better than one for every Yuchi, reached camp just before dusk. While Little Johnnie took the captives to the holding pen, Moultrie went to report to Winfield Scott. John Sanford and William McElveen were outside the general's tent together when Moultrie rode up.

McElveen grinned. "Took you long enough. What's the matter? Lose your way?"

Moultrie just laughed. Turning to General Sanford, he gave a brief summary of what had happened.

"Why," the general asked, "did they catch you on the trail like that, Ravenel? Seems a funny way to do things to me."

"Their chief trusts me, General. We used to hunt together."

McElveen lost his temper, yelling, "You mean your captive is that mad dog Crazy Wolf?" He saluted quickly to Sanford and said, "This I got to see." Then he strode off in the direction of the holding pen.

"You'd better follow him, Ravenel. Crazy Wolf was in on that attack on Roanoke back at the end of May. No telling what McElveen might try."

"Right." As he went, Moultrie saw Little Johnnie leaving the pen. "Johnnie," Moultrie called, "round up your braves. Trouble."

McElveen was standing at the edge of the pen opposite Crazy Wolf. The Indian's face was impassive. "So," the colonel began, "you've had enough, have you. Well, I haven't." Reaching down to his holster, McElveen pulled out his pistol. He lifted it, then cocked it slowly.

"McElveen," Moultrie called to him.

McElveen did not look up. He smiled again. "I see your face in my dreams, Crazy Wolf," he said evenly. "I've looked forward to this for four weeks."

McElveen tried to turn to meet Moultrie head-on. But he did not turn fast enough. Moultrie pitched his body into McElveen right behind the man's knees. As McElveen fell forward, his pistol went off with a loud bang, sending a bullet straight up into the sky.

Springing to his feet, McElveen whirled around. "You damned snake, I'm going to fix you for good." He crouched, circling.

"Stop!" Little Johnnie's yell resonated in the silence. Moultrie waved his cousin back.

"Colonel." Neither McElveen nor Moultrie even glanced in the direction of the new voice. Then there was another loud boom, louder than any pistol Moultrie had ever heard.

When McElveen looked up, Sanford was standing not five feet away, a smoking rifle in his hands. "Stop it or I'll court-martial you right here and now." Sanford was red in the face as he spoke.

Straightening, McElveen saluted, then turned to march off, his facial muscles twitching.

"Colonel," Sanford boomed, "you have not been dismissed."

McElveen went rigid. He turned around in slow motion. "There isn't a man since I whipped my pa who's dismissed me, General."

Sanford was grim. "Then I'll be the first. By God, Colonel, you so much as look cross-eyed at an Indian in that pen and I'll put you in there with them. And if you ever challenge my command again, I swear to you, you'll be tied up so tight you won't be able to even blink. Now . . . you are dismissed."

With that, the general turned and strode off.

The darkness was falling fast. McElveen faced Moultrie and Little Johnnie. "That Indian murdered my family and friends," McElveen told the two shadows facing him. "And you defended him, Ravenel." He appeared to be more disbelieving and hurt than angry.

"You burned that man's village, McElveen, and raped and killed his wife. Eye for an eye, McElveen. Too bad. But you brought it on yourself." Moultrie reached down and picked up his hat. Walking over to the pen, he looked in. He could not see Crazy Wolf. There were only shapes looming in the dark. Speaking in Yuchi, he said simply, "It will not happen again, Big Hunting Brother."

There was no answer. Moultrie turned away. McElveen had wanted another fight with him, and he had gotten it.

Suddenly, a voice called to him out of the darkness, "Death would have been easy."

It was Crazy Wolf.

That evening, Moultrie answered Helen's letter.

He wrote to her of his mother's death and of Crazy Wolf's capture. The more he wrote, the more difficult it became. Starting out, his heart was full of the hope that he and she would be together again soon, the strain of her unhappiness over his work gone. As he shifted from writing about his mother's death and turned to the war, though, he began saying to himself, "She's not interested in this. Why bother?"

Why indeed? She had not wanted to listen to war talk when he had last been in Montgomery.

"I want to know about *you,* Moultrie. Us," Helen had said. "Not how many miles and mosquitos there are between Fort Mitchell and perdition, or how many ways the army and militia can figure out to be stupid, petty and brutal."

Moultrie had been taken aback. "Do I bore you?"

"No, that's not it." He recalled that Helen's tone had been one of exasperation. "You're not boring me. You're ignoring me. Me, Pappa, Forest Hall, everything but your precious Indians and this war."

"Helen, how can you think that?"

"Simple. I listen to what you say."

Maybe the fact that she had sounded so understanding in her last note did not mean that she had come to accept things, but that she was giving him up, having decided that she, her father and others could not change him against his will or nature. As his mother would have said, Helen was growing up. She was beginning to see people as they were, not as her needs dictated they should be.

But his mother also had said there was a second stage of maturity. That was when you accepted as well as understood. She had been a wise woman.

Looking down, Moultrie saw that he had snapped the writing quill in two.

Cicero came in an hour later. Moultrie did not even glance in his direction. He was on his cot, staring at the canvas top through the mosquito netting.

"Dedzu is telling everyone you saved his father's life."

Moultrie did not get up. "Maybe I didn't do him so much of a favor after all."

"Giving him life isn't a favor? Ravenel, what are you talking about?"

"In his terms, he doesn't have much to live for. Chains now. Life forever after in some foreign place where he can't hear his beloved rivers."

"He's got his family, what's left of it, and his friends. After a while they may compensate. If he was dead, he'd never have a chance to find out." Cicero smiled maliciously. "Besides, if he's alive, maybe he'll have a chance to revolt and fight again someday."

Moultrie chuckled. In a perverse way, he liked that idea. He felt that Crazy Wolf and all of the Creeks were entitled to their revenge.

For the first time in days, he did not mourn his mother. Cicero wished to talk more, but Moultrie waved him away. "I'd really just like to be alone, old toad," Moultrie groused. "Nothing personal, and no offense."

"I guess I would too at this point, old snake," Cicero returned. He roughed up Moultrie's hair and left.

Moultrie closed his eyes, but not to sleep. His mind was too full of pictures from the past piled on top of one another, sometimes even running into each other: Crazy Wolf fighting a bear that had surprised them while they were asleep early one morning; Helen bathing Moultrie's gunshot wound; Moultrie's mother smiling at him as he sat for Mr. Samuel F.B. Morse, the portrait painter, that day in Charleston, a boy just turned ten; the line of carriages in front of the church at his father's funeral; Uncle John's face the day he told Moultrie's mother he was never going to see her again; his brother Henry falling into the river from the punt right next to an alligator.

Morning seemed to come very early. Waking, Moultrie heard himself saying, "Yes, Mama," at the end of his last dream. Yawning, he stretched. It had been a bad night. He sat up slowly, swinging his feet over the edge of his cot beneath the mosquito netting. Cicero was outside humming as he brushed off clothes. Another hot day. Muggy, too. Moultrie groaned. He imagined there was sand under his eyelids. It was going to be a long day.

Breakfast. He tried to eat. He could not. Little Johnnie came over. "You look awful, coz."

"Thanks."

"Get Cicero to hit you over the head with a hammer next time you can't sleep."

Squatting down on his haunches, Little Johnnie remarked, "That was quite a show McElveen gave us yesterday, wasn't it?"

"I can't understand why the man won't see that Crazy Wolf's reactions are similar to his own."

"You know as well as I do," Little Johnnie said, "that Indians aren't human in the eyes of a McElveen." He squinted as the smoke from the fire blew his way.

"Well, he's suffered for his blindness."

Little Johnnie nodded somberly. "Tell a man he can't see and he says you're imagining things." Little Johnnie stood up. "I did not come to howl at the moon with you. I wanted to know if you're going to hunt with us today."

"I thought the whole troop was returning to Camp Sanford."

"It is, but the general's anxious for us to catch Jim Henry. Sanford's inspired. Some of the boys managed to nab most of Jim's band while we were waiting for you to bring us Crazy Wolf."

Moultrie noted unhappiness in Little Johnnie's reaction. Little Johnnie was distressed at having been excluded from the capture of Jim Henry's band. When Johnnie pledged an allegiance and a fight, he went at it professionally, with vigor, even though the fight was against his own brothers. "Maybe Jim Henry will give you more of a battle," Moultrie said with regret. "Although only God knows why you really want one. How about simply trying to bring him in peacefully, with little or no force?"

"Not much chance. They say he was wounded badly in one shoulder. He probably needs treatment, but he'd rather fight."

"You're right," Moultrie agreed. "Dead, Jim Henry could probably still whip half of this bunch."

"You know it."

Moultrie stood. "All right, if it must be this way, I do want to be there. Maybe there's still something I can do to soften things so there'll be less blood. I'll be ready in ten minutes."

Moultrie welcomed the activity. Now he would not be able to waste time wishing things could be otherwise. He knew he should talk to Crazy Wolf. That too could wait. "Let's go and see what we can do to save what's left of the world," he said to Cicero.

Cicero hesitated. "I don't want to be with you this time, Ravenel. No hard feelings."

Moultrie was surprised. "No hard feelings. But why don't you want to come?"

"I want to talk to Dedzu. I think I should watch out for him."

"Red Wing, too?"

"I would if she'd let me. She won't. I don't waste my breath trying to talk to her. She won't listen to me about this move being the best of the worst, no more than she would listen to you, Indian agent." He smiled and slapped Moultrie's arm. "No. Believe me. It's for Dedzu."

"I think you have come to love that little rascal," Moultrie declared. "All right. Stay. But keep this in mind. You're going to feel awful when I sustain a mortal wound and you're not there to save my life. Some loyalty I hear from you."

"Some attempt at cheap sympathy I hear from you. . . ."

A group of soldiers passed, noticing Moultrie and Cicero standing close and facing each other.

". . . . Marse Moultrie, sir," Cicero concluded, loud and clear, lest they had overheard.

Had they looked closer, the soldiers would have seen Moultrie and Cicero grinning at each other.

Moultrie was still grinning as he joined Little Johnnie.

Chapter 14

Two hundred men were not force enough to capture four renegade Indians.

When they returned to camp, all Little Johnnie and his men had to show for their efforts were some more scratches and mosquito bites. Moultrie was covered, too. Looking at him, Little Johnnie suddenly put on a worried expression. "Cousin, you are a white man, aren't you?" he asked.

"Last I checked."

"Well, here, look again." Little Johnnie took off the bit of mirror hanging around his neck and passed it to Moultrie.

Moultrie glanced at his reflection. He saw a hickory-brown face covered with little red bites. "Oh, my God!" he exclaimed. "It's happened. I've finally achieved greatness."

"Yes, coz, afraid so. Sun and chiggers will do it to you every time. Turn you Indian color just as sure as shooting."

Moultrie laughed. Then he looked about. "Good Lord. Where have all the prisoners gone?"

There was a new holding pen. But there were no Indians inside. "I'll be damned if I know. Let's hope the general does," Little Johnnie groused.

General John Sanford's tent was still being set up when Little Johnnie and Moultrie arrived. Turning, the general waved at them. "Just the two I wanted to see," he called. As they came up, he told them, "I decided to send the prisoners on to Fort Mitchell overland. Ravenel, I think you'll want to meet them at the fort. Can't have you gallivanting all over the country with Little Johnnie here. You can sail on the steamboat *American*, Lieutenant Johnston commanding, in the morning."

"Right. Will do."

"Little Johnnie, what do you have to report?"

"Nothing. One man snakebit. The snake will live."

"Well, tonight, if you can, start your men on another sweep. This time in the middle fork of the Cowikee northwest toward Tuskegee on the federal road. Maybe you'll catch something. If not Jim Henry, then that band of Eneah Micco's that's still on the loose. Or better still, Big Fellow and his band. I've got Jim Boy and his warriors going up the north fork and McElveen and a troop working their way up between you. Together you should manage something."

Little Johnnie raised his eyebrows. "Both those bands each have a hundred to two hundred braves. Either will be a hard catch. The two together could be a disaster." He shook his head. "Well, I wanted a fight. Now I might get it."

"That's the plan, isn't it, General?" Moultrie asked. "Let all the Indians kill each other off before your troop's enlistments run out in a couple of days and those patriots start marching back to Columbus to muster out."

Sanford's face was blank. He either hadn't heard or had not noticed Moultrie's sarcasm. "We're pretty well in the mop-up stages of this mess, anyway," he concluded. "You'll have no trouble, Little Johnnie."

Little Johnnie snorted. "When were we in any other stage? Let me get my men fed, and we'll get on the trail. This war's beginning to look more and more like work."

Moultrie found Cicero in front of their tent cleaning a shotgun. Uncle John had given Moultrie that gun on Moultrie's eighteenth birthday. He had handed it to him and said, "If you were my son, this is the gun I'd have chosen for you." That was a year before Moultrie had met Little Johnnie. The gun was a beauty. Uncle John had bought it and its mate in France. He had willed the second gun to a friend, Jim Thorn, in Montgomery. He and Thorn had been fighting companions during the War of 1812 and the First Creek War. Now Thorn was a lawyer. He had handled the probate of Uncle John's estate. Moultrie smiled. Thorn had been a real help.

Cicero put down the shotgun. He stood as Moultrie approached. Moultrie could tell by his expression that he had something to say. "Let's hear it," Moultrie requested.

"It's Little Hawk, Dedzu. I've been with him and it's no wonder the boy doesn't know what to do. His own father is in such a state over the surrender and captivity that he hardly sees the boy. Crazy Wolf doesn't show any more reaction than a dead bird. He never even cracks his mouth to speak. Not to the boy, not to anyone. But the boy doesn't understand that kind of grown-up reaction to trouble. So how else is he himself supposed to act?"

Cicero paused for breath. Moultrie said nothing. "I tried," Cicero continued. "God knows, I tried to make him laugh. But, Ravenel, every time he was ready to laugh, it seemed he would see his pa. And then he would be ashamed to laugh when his pa wasn't laughing. Dedzu is dutiful. But no boy should be asked for that much duty. Children are children. And I don't think God wants children to act like grown-ups until they're grown." Cicero was quiet again for a bit, then concluded, "What I'm saying is, Crazy Wolf may be behaving in the only way he can, but he's sure breaking up his own son doing it."

"Have you said your piece?" Moultrie asked.

"Yes."

"And you know there isn't one damned thing we can do to change Crazy Wolf or the way Little Hawk's going to take it."

"I can let Little Hawk know he's got *me*."

"You couldn't do a better thing," Moultrie encouraged.

Sitting on a camp stool, Moultrie took out a cigar and clipped it. Cicero handed him a burning stick from the fire. Drawing in slowly, Moultrie lit the cigar, wreathing himself in smoke. "Crazy Wolf does look like a corpse, doesn't he, Cicero?"

Cicero tossed sticks onto the fire. He sighed. "Yes. He's going to will himself dead, if he has his way. Dedzu knows it. He says his pa sings all the old tribal songs. Singing is the only sign that he's really alive, the boy says. Otherwise the man is like a machine. Oh, he moves around. He tells the crying children, 'Hush, hush.' He'll stand between bucks who are fighting until they stop. He'll eat. But real life is gone from his body. He's almost dead, for true."

"Damn, damn, damn." Leaping to his feet, Moultrie hurled his cigar in anger into the fire. It suddenly tasted foul. The entire business was foul. He ached to help his Big Hunting Brother. He could not. And this left Moultrie once more feeling helpless, insignificant.

Had Helen been correct all along? Had he been a foolish, blind idealist to take part in the Indian business? He had once imagined nothing was beyond his grasp. He, Moultrie, would be able to work the miracles needed to smooth over the Indian troubles which had defeated others for thirty or forty years. He was a Ravenel. And Ravenels were always able to accomplish what they set out to do.

Not this time, Moultrie thought.

"Cicero, have I been a jackass about this Indian business?" Moultrie did not wait for an answer. Cicero did not respond. He knew no answer was needed, or expected.

Moultrie answered his own question himself. "No. I am not a jackass."

Yes, he had failed his mission on some levels. But never totally. And never for lack of trying. He took stock. How many times had he stopped trouble or solved problems jeopardizing the relocation of Crazy Wolf and Bear Chief and the others? Again and again.

And the bloody war. Its excesses had been contained to a great degree entirely by his efforts. The promised massacres had not occurred. Lord, hundreds had died. Terrible. But not thousands as had been expected and accepted as the price that had to be paid.

All of that was worth something. It had to be worth something. But even had his effort been worth nothing from the start, Moultrie knew he would have done what he did anyway. Someone had to do it. And when he had looked about, he found he was the only one willing to try.

"I know what I'm doing, Cicero," he asserted at last. "But I sometimes wonder why I do it when I see the hurt it causes my family and the woman I'm to marry. At times like that, belief in some long-range good is almost not reason enough."

"You're wrong," Cicero redressed. "It is."

Cicero and Moultrie boarded the steamboat *American* for Fort Mitchell the following morning. The *American* was one of six gunboats patrolling the Cowikee River to prevent renegade Indians from crossing to Georgia or making their way to Florida to link up with the Seminole tribes who were fighting federal troops there. The *American* was top-heavy with defenses and armament. Cotton bales were her deck armor. Rifle and cannon barrels were as numerous as spokes of a wheel.

Dinner that afternoon in the officers' mess was more luxurious than anything Moultrie had eaten since his last visit to Montgomery. He ate and drank good wine with gluttonous pleasure.

As he left the mess with the others later, he stole a bottle of the wine for Cicero.

An hour later, the steamboat docked at the Fort Mitchell landing. It was a twenty-minute ride by horse from there to the fort. Stopping at the gate, Moultrie asked where he could find Captain John Page. "Over there," the guard pointed, "counting Indians to see how many more handcuffs he'll need for the march tomorrow."

Moultrie nodded. He could see the Indians lined up in rows, the men on one side, the women and children on the other. By their dress, more than half appeared to be Yuchis and Kashitas, though there were a good many Eufaulas and Cheahas mixed in. Moultrie could not see Page or Crazy Wolf. It was hard to distinguish any one person from another. The place was a mob scene. Moultrie was assailed by the smells. The stench was unbelievable. Sweat, dust, excrement, smoke, garbage. The noise, too, was an assault. Not just children crying, people shouting, dogs fighting, mules, cattle, pigs and goats clamoring, but a constant ding-ding-ding from the anvils. Twenty smiths were making chains for the prisoners. Fort Mitchell had looked nothing like this three weeks ago, Moultrie thought.

Moultrie shook his head, then kicked up his horse. Cicero followed. Five minutes later they found Page moving between ranks of new arrivals, checking their chains and taking notes. Crazy Wolf and his warriors were among them.

Page looked up at the call of his name, saw Moultrie and waved. Dismounting, Moultrie started toward him. Seeing Crazy Wolf chained to another warrior, Moultrie stopped. "I am sorry," he said, pointing to the handcuffs. Crazy Wolf glanced at Moultrie, but said nothing. "Is there anything I can do for you, Big Hunting Brother?" The Indian shrugged. Moultrie turned to go.

"You will look after my children?"

"Yes," Moultrie promised. There was nothing more to say. Moultrie's heart went out to Crazy Wolf.

Captain John Page looked up again from his note pad at the approach of his friend. "It's horrible, isn't it?"

Moultrie nodded. He didn't trust himself to speak. Yes, it was horrible.

The next morning, the prisoners started their march west along the federal road to Montgomery to board steamboats to the West. The men marched first, in double file, manacled and chained. Behind them came the women and children. And behind them followed the long wagon train carrying supplies, little children, old women and those too sick to walk. Guards marched on both flanks and front and rear. There were also guards between the groups of marchers.

Moultrie rode with Page. They did not say much. Both were exhausted. They had been up until two in the morning seeing to chains, checking supplies and working out last-minute details of the order of the march. By five, they had been up again, seeing that the Indians were fed and doing what they could to make the departure as orderly as possible. There still had been problems, of course. Children had wandered off. Fights had broken out. Thank God, Moultrie praised the saints, all that was behind them.

In addition to being exhausted, Moultrie was depressed. The imprisonment and degradation of so many good people had something to do with it. But he also knew the journey was going to be far more brutal than the Indians knew or the army would admit. Moultrie pictured the route in his memory. . . .

Ahead lay a hundred miles on foot to Montgomery. The pace would be slow. Men in chains don't exactly skip along. Then, down the Alabama River on boats and barges to Mobile. Then, through the Gulf of Mexico to New Orleans. Then, up the Mississippi to the White River. Along the White River to a place called Rock Roe. Then, from Rock Roe, another brutal overland trek of about three hundred miles to Fort Gibson. Lord, Moultrie asked, on top of all of this misery, how could you make this one of the hottest summers on record?

It was impossible for Moultrie to keep his eyes open. The gentle rocking motion of his horse and the hot sun were soporific. Besides, it felt so good to cover his lids and end the scratchy sensation on his eyeballs.

He jerked awake. Cicero was grinning at him. "Don't go and fall off the horse now, Marse Moultrie," he laughed. Moultrie mumbled something and drifted off again.

"What's the point of a man keeping his eyes open, anyway?" Page asked later, gesturing around him. The signs of war were everywhere: burned houses, upturned wagons, mounds of dirt marking hastily dug graves, flies buzzing over dead animals, buzzards flying overhead. There were coffins scattered over the road at one place, where a carter hauling a wagonload of them had been ambushed by renegades. The road was a setting for such scenes for seemingly endless stretches.

The only building Moultrie saw still standing intact was Stone's Tavern, famous as the "Creek Stand." The column made camp here.

The next day they moved out at dawn after firing a special salute to The Stars and Stripes. The date was July 4th.

The closer the column got to Camp McClendon near Tuskegee, the midpoint on the road between Fort Mitchell and Montgomery, the fewer were the signs of war. The Indians along this stretch had been, and were still, friendly. Some of their villages could be seen from the road, with smoke rising from cooking fires, children running and laughing, women standing in groups. Moultrie was at the side of the road watching the column pass by the first of these villages when he caught a glimpse of Crazy Wolf's face. The Indian's eyes had filled with sudden anguish. So had the faces of other warriors. Looking at these domestic scenes in passing, they could see that they themselves had lost.

Five miles from Camp McClendon was Echo Hadjo's village. That was where the column camped for the night. When Moultrie rode in, almost the first person he saw was Little Johnnie.

"Hello, cousin."

"Little Johnnie. What on earth are you doing here?"

The half-breed grinned. "You tell me. For three days we march sixteen or eighteen hours a day, scour the countryside from the Chattahoochee all the way here looking for Jim Henry. Guess what?"

"What?"

"The rascal turned himself, and a couple of other warriors, in to Echo Hadjo two days ago."

Moultrie laughed.

Later, he learned that Jim Henry was not the only chief held prisoner at the camp. Eneah Micco and Cheemalee had come in too, with many of their followers. They would be joining the column on the march in the morning and would be given U.S. Army safe conduct, despite Colonel William McElveen's efforts to claim them as his personal prisoners.

Moultrie met an officer who explained what had happened. Major Peter Churchill, artillery, related this account:

Colonel McElveen had ridden into Echo Hadjo's village not six hours before Little Johnnie. Since his arrival, he had been trying all day to convince Major Churchill at Tuskegee that the chief should be turned over to Georgia for trial and execution for war crimes. Churchill was not sympathetic. "What's the matter, Mc-

Elveen?" he asked. "Hobson afraid of what Jim Henry might say if he isn't hung?"

"Don't give me that, Churchill," McElveen answered, bristling. "You know as well as me how much damage this Indian has done. Just ride along the north fork the way I have these last three days. It is not a pretty sight, I tell you."

"The north fork's in Alabama." Churchill was abrupt. "Jim Henry's folks were living peacefully on the Georgia side when you and your boys drove them over here last winter." He smiled sardonically. "Maybe Alabama should arrest you for his crimes over here. I'll suggest it." McElveen turned and stormed off.

Churchill, telling the story to Page and Moultrie that night, was gleeful. "McElveen walked out of there," he beamed, "like a horse with mustard under his tail. It was splendid, particularly when he told me how he was going to talk to Governor Clay. I don't think I've ever seen anyone so mad."

That dinner with Page and Churchill was pleasant. Now that he was turning over responsibility for the prisoners to Churchill and his artillery battalion, Page relaxed and told funny stories. It was in the middle of one such story that Little Johnnie entered.

"Sorry to interrupt, gentlemen," he apologized, making an exaggerated bow. "I have come to fetch my cousin."

Moultrie stood up. "All good things must come to an end, gentlemen. See you later." Then, turning to Little Johnnie, he added, "This had better be good, Little Johnnie."

"You've finished eating. I know. I've been watching."

"I'm not finished digesting."

"You'll forgive me, coz. I'm doing you a favor."

"Oh? What?"

"I'm introducing you to my old friend, Jim Henry. Since you're going to be together awhile, I thought it would be a good thing to do."

"Thanks."

While talking, the two cousins were making their way toward the temporary holding pens where the Indians were being kept under armed guard. Little Johnnie kept up a constant stream of chatter about his friend. A half-breed with enough education to earn him a position as a store clerk, Jim Henry was, according to Little Johnnie, both moody and impulsive.

There had been no sign of that character flaw during the campaign, however. He had fought brilliantly. Now that Moultrie thought about it, the tactics Jim Henry had used were like those Francis Marion—the Swamp Fox—had employed while fighting the British on the Santee River in South Carolina during the Revolution.

No question about it: Jim Henry was remarkable. It would be interesting to meet him.

Chapter 15

As Little Johnnie escorted Moultrie to see the prisoner, Jim Henry, they saw a man squatting on the ground staring straight ahead. It was Deer Warrior. His face carried an expression like Crazy Wolf's—filled with death, suffering and humiliation. Yet, in his weary state, a certain bitterness still came through. No longer, though, the anger and defiance Moultrie and Little Johnnie had seen in May at Bear Chief's village under Cheaha Mountain about seventy-five miles northeast of Tuskegee and Camp McClendon. Little Johnnie stopped, putting his arm on Moultrie's shoulder. Nodding toward the squatting brave, he whispered, "He's been like that ever since they turned themselves in. Jim Henry says they almost had to drag Deer Warrior here. He was determined to go down in a blaze of glory. Jim Henry says the man's crazy."

"Have you tried to talk to him?" Moultrie whispered back.

"Hell, no."

"Shall I, then?"

"Good God, no." He shrugged. "If you insist, I will." He went over and squatted beside the Indian. "Hello, Deer Warrior," he said, his voice gentle.

The Indian looked up for an instant, then turned his eyes back down again. Either he didn't recognize Little Johnnie or he didn't care any longer what happened around him.

Little Johnnie tried again. "I am glad that you have survived. It would have sorrowed me to have heard that you had died."

Still, Deer Warrior said nothing. But for an instant there was a flash of something in his eyes. Hatred? Anger? Moultrie, standing off to the side, could not tell. The starlight was bright, but hardly bright enough. Maybe what he had seen had not been in his eyes at all but in a slight stiffening of the Indian's posture and tensing of his facial muscles. Whatever it had been, it made Moultrie uneasy. "Little Johnnie," he called, "perhaps we should go."

Little Johnnie nodded. Turning to leave, he said, "Good-bye, Deer Warrior. If we don't meet during your trip west, no doubt we'll meet at the end of it."

That did it. Bellowing, the Indian charged forward only to fall flat, anchored by the weight of the man to whom he was handcuffed. Little Johnnie jumped back. As Moultrie came forward he waved him away. "No. Don't heap coals on the fire." His face carried a grave expression.

"You were only trying to be kind," Moultrie said later as they walked on.

"Sure." Little Johnnie's tone was biting. "What's the old saw?" he asked. "The ways to hell are paved with good intentions. Isn't that it?"

Moultrie nodded. He was startled. "Where'd you learn that?"

"You forget, cousin. My father. He hoped I'd be a bridge between the two races. Taught me all sorts of things." He laughed bitterly. "Didn't you know? I spent three months each year for four or five years at Forest Hall. I had a cottage to myself."

"A cottage?" Moultrie stopped.

"Yes, a lovely little cottage," Little Johnnie said sarcastically. "I would have been an embarrassment up at the big house, don't you know? I think Old Sam, the butler, would have decided to work in the fields if I'd stayed there. It was bad enough that he sometimes had to serve an Indian in his master's dining room. 'Marse John ain't got no call,' he'd say, 'for bring he shame here for all the world for see!'"

Moultrie was shaken.

"When was this?"

"Before you came, coz. Before you came." Little Johnnie grinned. "You were my salvation. As soon as he had you for a nephew, he didn't need me anymore. You were the son he'd always wanted."

Moultrie groaned. No wonder Little Johnnie had been hostile when they had first met.

"Don't misunderstand me. The old man was dutiful. Brought me books. Books. In an Indian town. He took me to Columbus, too. He was quite exceptional, really, as fathers of bastards go." Little Johnnie's voice had lost its bitterness. He shook his head. "Sorry, coz. That's history. We're here to see Jim Henry. There he is over there." Little Johnnie pointed to a young man leaning casually against a tree talking to another Indian. They were chained together. The Indian was sitting on the ground, his handcuffed arm in the air.

"Jim Henry," Little Johnnie called, "I want you

to meet my cousin, Indian Agent Moultrie Ravenel." He'd spoken in English.

Jim Henry answered him in English, the only language they had in common. Their native tongues were different. One was Muskogean, and the other, Yuchi. "I can't, under the circumstances, say as I'm happy to meet you," Jim Henry said. "But if you don't mind shaking my left hand here, I'll say I'm glad to shake the hand of a man I've heard has tried to do something for us Indians."

They shook hands.

"Your cousin ain't a talker, I take it," Jim Henry commented to Little Johnnie.

Moultrie smiled. "Sorry. I'm happy to meet the Napoleon of the Chattahoochee."

Jim Henry broke into a grin. "Napoleon lost, too, if I remember my history books correct." He turned and regarded Little Johnnie. "Darned if your cousin don't talk like you and your pa. A real aristocrat."

Little Johnnie's face lit up. "That's not his fault any more than it's yours that your father was one of the closest traders this side of the Natchez Trace and, God help us, a Scotsman to boot."

Jim Henry laughed. His young face was strong and serious: a high forehead, deep-set eyes under sharp brows, a narrow jaw ending in a strong chin. The nose was straight and thin. The mouth was broad but also thin. Judging from appearance only, Moultrie decided he liked him. He also saw how, at twenty, Jim Henry had managed to lead his people so well against such odds over the last months.

"Did you see that scene with Deer Warrior?" Little Johnnie asked, looking back toward the huddled figure of his fellow townsman.

Jim Henry shook his head. "What happened?"

Moultrie told the story. Jim Henry frowned. "It hurts to see the man choking on his own gall like that. But it don't do no good to grieve. You got to live." He paused, then continued in a low tone. "I was wrong. I thought maybe we could drive the whites out or at least fight them to a standstill, so that they'd agree to leave us alone. That was stupid. And I should have known it, knowing Hobson the way I do. I guess I'm young." He looked across the field of prisoners. "It hurt so, though, to see innocent people being robbed blind, beat up and raped. It wasn't right. It made me mad. I'm still mad. And somehow I ain't sorry neither. I did what I had to do. Same as you two."

"That's right, Jim." Little Johnnie clapped his friend on the shoulder. "See you in the morning. We're all going to need sleep." He turned to Moultrie. "Coming, cousin?"

"Yes. Good night, Jim Henry. I'm glad to have met you. Even under these circumstances." They shook hands again.

Walking back toward the soldiers' encampment, Moultrie remarked, "That's one hell of a man."

"You're right, coz. And you should see his sister." Little Johnnie grinned. "As they say around here, she's a real fine filly."

It was getting late. The two men parted company.

The next morning, John Page and Little Johnnie went back to Fort Mitchell. Moultrie went on with the Indians. "I've started this business," Moultrie conceded, "and I want to finish it." It had not been easy to convince Charles Madden at Indian Affairs in Washington that that was what he should do, but finally Madden had come around.

If you are dead set on being noble, it

would be churlish of me to refuse you the
opportunity. I am agreeing to your going,
therefore, though it is against my better judgment. Just do not give me cause to regret my
foolishness. I am tired of writing letters to
soothe your numerous detractors.

Moultrie had shown the letter to John Page. The
captain had shaken his head. "Against my better judgment, too," he had insisted. "You've no business at all
going out there. I know. I've been there."

"And you're still in the business of removing Indians."

"It's my job."

"It's mine, too."

"Here, not there."

"I'm going."

"Then I'm wasting my breath."

Page *had* been wasting his breath. But that did
not make it any easier to say good-bye. Moultrie had
come to think of Captain Page as a good friend. Both
knew it would be a long time after leaving Echo
Hadjo's village before they would see each other again.
A look at the map was enough to show that. It was fifteen hundred miles or more to Fort Gibson from Fort
Mitchell, at least two months' travel with a column of
prisoners.

"We'll be writing," Page assured him.

Moultrie grimaced. "Endless reports. I'll tag on a
note or two occasionally for your eyes only."

"Right."

That had been it. One good-bye finished. Saying
good-bye to Little Johnnie did not take any longer.
The half-breed rode over to where Cicero was packing
Moultrie's things.

"Morning, Cicero. You and your Dedzu talking again?"

"Yes, sir. Some. He doesn't want to talk much, though. He's too sad about his pa."

"I know. It's a shame. Where's your master?"

"Right behind you, old son," Cicero replied.

Little Johnnie turned. "You still confusing me with the devil?" he smirked.

"Only when I look at you," Moultrie returned.

"Well, you won't have to do that for a while now. It'll be months before I get lost enough to find my way to the verdant banks of the Verdigris River and the ample shores of the Arkansas."

"My, my. A poet. I'm afraid you exaggerate."

"Don't I always?"

"I know. That's why I'll miss you. The normal isn't going to seem as big as it really is without you around to pump it up."

"Such wit. Well, Cousin Moultrie, until worse times." Little Johnnie saluted.

"Not so fast. I have something for you." Moultrie stepped over to his travel pack and picked up the shotgun Uncle John had given him. "It's rightfully yours," he said, holding it out to Little Johnnie.

Little Johnnie's grin faded. "I'm touched, but you're wrong. You're the son he had in mind. And you're the one he gave the gun to."

Moultrie shook his head. "Take it. Please."

"I can't."

"The hell you can't."

"Such profanity," Little Johnnie kidded. "Thanks, coz. It's a foolish gesture, but I appreciate it."

The good-byes were finished. Little Johnnie and John Page marched with their troops east. Major Peter

Churchill's battalion moved the prison column, now nearly two thousand strong, west toward Montgomery.

A fast coach, changing horses at regular intervals, could have made the trip in two days, even though the road was just a series of deep ruts in places. The column took nearly three times as long. The warriors, marching chained together at the head of the column, slowed the pace. Holding things up even more were the constant stops to pry overloaded wagons out of ruts. Then too, simply getting the column going in the morning took time.

The days that followed were a blur for Moultrie—until they passed Hope Chest. It was the day before the column was to enter Montgomery. Having found that the best way to avoid the marchers' dust was to stay ahead of it, Moultrie was trotting leisurely along a mile in front of the column with Major Churchill. Behind them rode Cicero. Turning a bend and seeing a new vista open up, the major stopped. "Damn, that's beautiful."

Moultrie reined up beside him. In past days he had not stopped at all to admire the view or to think of where he was. The major was right. The view was splendid. The gentle slope of the cotton fields toward the river and the forest beyond looked familiar. He and Helen had stopped here on morning rides from Hope Chest many times. The thought jolted him. It seemed incredible, but he actually had not thought of her for days, had not considered that he would be passing right by her father's plantation. And it was only a week earlier that he had been agonizing about what they would say to one another the next time they met. Damn. Looking around, Moultrie saw Cicero grinning at him.

"You're thinking about Miss Helen now," he stated without a trace of doubt.

Chruchill was curious. "Miss Helen? Who's that?"

"My fiancée. Her father's plantation is up ahead. Come on, let me introduce you."

Churchill shook his head. "You don't want me crowding the horizon if you've only an hour or two to spend with your fiancée. We'll just ride on."

"No, I don't mind at all. I would like you to meet her."

"Sure you wouldn't rather have the hour alone?"

"If they're there, I'll leave you with the judge and steal off with Helen." Moultrie wanted Churchill to come. In fact, he wanted him to come very much, because with the major there, the judge was less likely to treat him as a witness on the stand. There would be far less awkwardness all around, even with Helen. Thinking of her had opened floodgates. Doubts and questions swirled in his head. "Let's go." Moultrie kicked his horse.

The judge and Helen were not at the plantation. "No, sir, Marse Moultrie," the butler said at the front door, "they's down to Montgomery. The judge got court now."

"Look at it this way," the major offered. "You'll have several days to spend with your Helen in Montgomery instead of just a couple of hours here." That was just the point. Moultrie was not certain he wanted that now. What if things did not go well? Looking at him sharply, Churchill added, "As lovers go, old boy, you're not very enthusiastic. What's the matter? Does your intended have pockmarks along with her money?"

Cicero grinned, and answered for Moultrie, "No, sir. She sure doesn't. She's almost an angel."

"Too holy for you, Ravenel?"

Moultrie's smile was forced. "Hardly."

That night, when they were alone, Cicero bluntly told Moultrie, "You're fretting like some child. It's preventing you from doing what you want to do with Helen. And the worst thing a man can do is nothing."

"I'm not fretting."

"Excuse me, Ravenel, but you are. You've been fretting ever since the last trip to Montgomery. Listen to me. No woman is worth stewing over like that. Marry her or don't marry her. But decide, man. Decide. You're just sweating your brain in indecision."

"Seems to me you've brain-sweated plenty over someone named Red Wing," Moultrie retorted. "There. That's paying you back in your own coin. Such darky insolence I've never heard." Moultrie slapped his forehead in mock horror.

Cicero remained serious. "That's true, I did sweat over Red Wing. But I'm telling you, no more. And you should say no more, too. Life is too short to sweat over one woman. Catch the fish when they jump, as my daddy used to say, and sleep when they sleep. Beat them all at their own game, and don't set the net for any particular one." He squatted by the fire and stirred the evening soup. "You white folks get all tangled up by romance. Black men and women don't, probably 'cause we can never be sure some master will let us stay together long enough. Maybe in a way we're better off not having too much sentiment in our lives for one another."

Moultrie grinned. He enjoying teasing Cicero. "Maybe I'll forget women altogether."

"Sure. And you'll forget you have a man's need to hunt them, too. Or maybe I've been mistaken all these years." Cicero grinned back at him. "Maybe you aren't a man who beds women at all."

"That's not what they tell me."

"Then you won't have a chance to forget them, Ravenel, my foolish friend. If you're a man in bed, the women are not going to leave you alone. Unless you hide off in the woods by yourself."

"That's it. I'll go be a hermit. We'll both go."

"Now would you really call that living?"

"I sure wouldn't. Especially if I had to live only with you."

Moultrie shoved Cicero off balance. Cicero sat hard, rolling in front of the fire. The soup spoon he had been using sailed off into the dirt. Cicero picked it up, turned it slowly, looked at it, blew on it, then handed it to Moultrie, saying, "This one was yours. Too bad it got so dirty."

Chapter 16

The column arrived on the edge of Montgomery late in the afternoon. It was a good deal later when Moultrie finally got away from the prison camp to take a hotel room. The following morning he took a long hot bath and dressed in the fresh clothes he had ordered from Forest Hall. Then he set out to buy a small present to take to Helen. Coming into the hotel lobby, he ran straight into William Hobson and Judge Leander Dupré. Moultrie was dumbfounded.

Hobson looked up, his meaningless smile perfectly in place. "Oh, hello, Ravenel. You staying here, too?" Before Moultrie had time to answer, Hobson gestured to his companion and said, "You know Judge Dupré." Then, catching Moultrie's eye on his bags, he explained, "The judge has been good enough to invite me to stay with him."

The judge colored slightly. He was obviously embarrassed. "Hello, Moultrie. Good to see you. Hobson here and I have some business to attend to. I just thought it would be more convenient if he stayed at the house." The judge coughed. "If I'd known you were going to be here, son, I'd have included you, but as it is, I'm afraid there just isn't room."

How the man was squirming, Moultrie thought. He almost felt sorry for Dupré. "No need to apologize, sir. I understand. You and Hobson want to talk about taking over Indian lands after this war."

Hobson raised his eyebrows in surprise. For a moment, he even forgot to smile. Judge Dupré was white.

Moultrie was pleased with their reactions. Yes, shake the rascals up a little bit. Flog their consciences. Especially the man who is supposed to be my father-in-law.

Outwardly, however, Moultrie's face remained bland.

"Judge, are you all right? It's hot in here. Perhaps if you sit down?"

"No, no, boy. I'll be all right. Just a little shortness of breath. You go on now. Don't let us keep you."

"Sorry, I didn't realize I was interrupting."

Dupré took a deep breath. He was obviously struggling for composure. "Not at all. It's just that you came down those stairs so purposefully."

"That's right, Judge. I was off to find something for Helen."

Hobson raised his eyebrows again. "You know the young lady?"

Someday, Moultrie thought, I'm going to feed him those bloody eyebrows one hair at a time. "We're engaged," he explained.

"How nice." Hobson had recovered his smile.

The judge was looking better, too. "I'm sure," he said, gasping slightly, "that she will be delighted to see you, Moultrie, though I'm sorry to say she is slightly indisposed today. Perhaps you'll call tomorrow. Come for dinner. I look forward to visiting with you." He held out his hand.

Moultrie took it, noticed it was damp with sweat, then shook it lightly. "Thank you, sir. I look forward, as always." Then, as the judge turned to go, Moultrie added, "I hope you're all right. Perhaps you should see a doctor." He was sincere. The man seemed in genuine physical distress.

"I'm all right, Moultrie. Thanks anyway. So long."

"So long."

Hobson nodded and smiled.

Moultrie stood where he was for several moments to give the others time to leave. That Hobson's a disease, a rot, a fungus, he thought. Hell, the man is spreading himself everywhere. Even around Judge Dupré. Too bad. Well, you get the coffin you pay for.

Coming from the hotel onto the street, Moultrie had a strange thought that made him smile bitterly. His sudden suspicion seemed logical. Judging by the way Helen's father had just behaved, Moultrie wondered whether he was hoping to replace him with Hobson, as Helen's future husband. How vigorously might the judge be trying to promote Hobson in Helen's esteem?

And how indisposed was Helen, truly?

Moultrie shook himself. No, stop this line of thinking. Remember what Cicero said—no fretting. No doubting until you have good reason. Doubting is the road to madness. He strode off to buy Helen some flowers, if any were to be had.

He found yellow roses—her favorite.

Coming back to the hotel at noon, he was sur-

prised when the desk clerk handed him a note. It was
from Helen. It read,

> Dear Moultrie,
>   The flowers are lovely. How thoughtful
> of you. You need not have. Papa exaggerated
> my indisposition, I am afraid. If anything, I
> am suffering from an excess of good health.

Well, well, the old man had lied. Why? The letter
continued . . .

>   Of course, I look forward to seeing you
> here at dinner tomorrow. But perhaps if you
> are riding west on the river road this after-
> noon at about four, we shall meet then. I
> hope so.

Moultrie found Helen where she had said she
would be.

He did not dismount from his horse immediately.
He leaned with both hands on the pommel, looking at
her as she smiled at him from her carriage. She wore a
mint-green dress and a straw hat. Green was her color,
Moultrie thought. Sunlight screened by the latticework
of the hat streaked her face. She controlled her horse's
reins easily. Moultrie liked this picture of Helen
Dupré. He realized he should say hello and make
courtly gestures. Instead he simply sat and imagined, as
he so often had, the rise of her breasts beneath the
green silk, the smoothness of them in his hands, the
taste of them on his lips.

He liked that vision. The physical intensity of
desire was marvelous.

Helen's smile faded. She too stared. Moultrie saw

she had quit breathing once more, as she always did when she was overwhelmed. Finally, she said, "You mustn't look at me in that way of yours, Moultrie. I feel like I'm naked with you. I know what you're thinking."

"That means you're thinking the same thing, too."

Her breath came back again and she giggled. "Yes, but I don't like to think it, not if the thought can't become the deed. It's been so long since I've seen you, Moultrie."

He hurdled from his saddle and extended his hand to assist Helen from the carriage. "If I've behaved like a rogue and made you feel like a tart, it's my duty to kiss you like a gentleman and make you feel like a lady again."

He pressed his mouth lightly to hers, then stepped back. She swayed before him. "If you had kissed me longer, I think at this moment I would have fainted," she declared. "Thank you for being so gallant, my Moultrie. But in my own thoughts I still feel like a tart. Does a woman always want a man when he's been gone a while?"

"The man hopes so."

They laughed together, evaporating the tension. They could talk with ease now.

Moultrie tethered their horses to a bush. They walked along the river arm in arm. "Thank you for coming," Helen said.

"How could I not come? You've never invited me to a tryst before."

"You're awful, Moultrie Ravenel," she chortled. "Really, I do thank you for coming, because I think we should talk." Her expression became troubled. "I felt I had to see you before you came tomorrow, and I didn't want to embarrass Papa by asking you to come to the house this afternoon after he'd asked you not to because of my being sick."

"What's the matter, Helen? The judge looks awful."

"I don't know. The doctor says he's too excitable. He says, too, a lot of men like Papa, hale and hearty at fifty, are dead five years later. He's trying to scare me, so I'll keep Papa from getting agitated. I'm frightened all right, but what can I do? Papa's even more stubborn than you."

They had just come to a bluff. Below them the river curved around in an arch of gold and silver. Across the river, forests and farms were bathed in a golden haze.

"Oh, Moultrie, it's lovely. I always feel refreshed coming here."

They sat down on a grassy spot. After watching the river for a while, Moultrie asked, "Why doesn't your father retire? He has enough money."

"That's just it, Moultrie," Helen replied. "He doesn't. I didn't know until recently, but he's made several bad investments, and the cotton market right now is bad. He's frightfully worried. He wants to leave me with what he considers money enough, and he's afraid he doesn't have much time."

"I see." Moultrie pulled at a blade of grass and stuck it in his mouth. "I have money I could lend him."

Helen squeezed his arm. "You're a dear, Moultrie. I said I was sure you'd help as soon as I found out how bad the situation is. Papa was furious, furious that I'd found out his predicament and furious that I'd suggest you as a source of help. You don't know how much you hurt him the last time you were here in Montgomery."

"I did?"

"He thinks you called him a meddling fool. You didn't. But the thought counts. That's part of the reason why he wrote all those silly letters to Madden in Washington." Helen took a deep breath. "I apologize again, Moultrie. I think you're foolish to be doing what you're doing. You know that. But I know you're doing a good job. Papa was wrong, even if he did think he was doing us a favor by trying to have you dismissed."

Moultrie suddenly understood many things. Remembering his reactions over the last months, he felt foolish.

"What are you thinking?"

"I was contemplating some silly things I'd been thinking about that correspondence. But enough of that. That's in the past. Tell me, is your father in debt to Hobson?"

"Yes."

"How badly?"

"Very. Mr. Hobson virtually owns Hope Chest."

"Oh, my God." Moultrie shook his head. "Better to owe the devil."

"Don't say that, Moultrie. Mr. Hobson's been very kind and understanding about the debt."

"I'll bet." Standing up, Moultrie smacked his palm with his fist.

"Yes, he has," Helen hissed.

Moultrie turned and looked at her. When she met his gaze, he cast his eyes down. It was no use. If he told her what kind of person Hobson was, he would just worry her. And for what? "It's time I got you back to your carriage," he said calmly, reaching to help her up off the ground. "We don't want your father out hunting for you. Not in his condition."

They started back in silence, each lost in thought. It

was only when they reached her carriage that Helen spoke. "I love my father, Moultrie," she avowed, "and I'd do anything to keep him alive and happy as long as possible. Anything." Bursting into tears, she buried her face against his chest.

"I know, Helen. I know." Moultrie stroked her hair to comfort her. "Remember. I lost *my* father. Mother meant all the more to me because I no longer had him. And now she's gone, too."

Breaking away, Helen looked up at him through her tears. "I'm sorry, Moultrie. I don't know what came over me. But I'm so worried about him."

He handed her a handkerchief and patted her chin. "Cicero told me the other night that fretting does us no good. It prevents us from doing the things we ought to do. We have to keep a grip on ourselves."

Helen dabbed her eyes. "He's right." She brightened. "Yes, I'll get a grip on myself all right."

"That's my girl."

Moultrie gripped her waist with both hands. As he lifted her to her carriage, she suddenly twisted about, put her arms around his neck and lowered her mouth to his.

The kiss lasted. At first it was gentle. Then it became almost viciously hard. Helen slowly relaxed against him. He felt her thighs, her knees, her breasts melding into him. Their lips crossed back and forth. At last her mouth opened, and her tongue probed for his. He heard her sigh contentedly.

"No matter what ever might happen between us, no matter what," she whispered, "I don't think I'll ever want to feel like a lady when I kiss you."

Moultrie attempted both grin and gallantry. It was difficult, all things considered. But he succeeded. "Maybe I took you back to the carriage too soon."

"Upsy-daisy, Mr. Ravenel," she responded, twisting from his grip and stepping lightly into her carriage.

"Another crisis bravely passed," Moultrie beamed.

"And aren't we both relieved."

She was right. They both were.

Moultrie untethered Helen's horse from the bush and handed her the reins. She nodded in thanks and then frowned suddenly. "Moultrie, I'm unforgivable. I'm terribly sorry. I've been so lost in my own worries and other distractions with you. I didn't tell you how much I grieved for you at the news of your mother's death."

"Don't put yourself down like that." He swung into his saddle. "I suggest that you return to Hope Chest by yourself. We don't want someone telling your father that they saw us together. You *are* supposed to be indisposed."

She waved and wheeled her horse and carriage about.

Moultrie watched her go. When she disappeared around a bend, he shook his head. Holding her, he had known exactly what he wanted to do: marry her. Alone, he no longer was so sure. So much for the temporary power of lust.

His doubts about their relationship returned. He did not want to think of them, for if he did, he would have to deal with them and try to resolve them.

Cicero, he knew, would accuse him of fretting again.

The following morning, Moultrie and Cicero went their separate ways. Cicero wanted to be with Little Hawk. Moultrie was to meet with Major Peter Churchill at the temporary camp where the Creek Indians were held.

They agreed to meet in two hours at Major Churchill's headquarters.

Moultrie and Churchill then set out together on an inspection of the camp. They were about half-finished when William Hobson and Colonel William McElveen came cantering into the perimeter. Moultrie nodded. "Seeing them ride up," Moultrie whispered to Churchill, "I feel as though two good friends just left. What the hell are they doing here?"

Churchill frowned. "I knew they were coming. I just didn't know when."

"But what for?"

"To figure how many of their alleged bad debts we're taking with us. They intend to sue Uncle Sam for the money they claim."

"Lord spare us." Moultrie was astonished. "I thought nothing those two did could surprise me. I was wrong."

Churchill's laugh was bitter. "You have to give them credit. They've got brass."

Hobson's hint of a smile was perfectly in place, as usual. Observing it, Moultrie wondered if the merchant put it on every morning after shaving.

McElveen was his usual self as well: glowering and glum. What a pair, Moultrie thought. Beauty and the beast, Page had once called them.

"Well, gentlemen, shall we proceed?" Hobson put on his smoothest manner. Moultrie gritted his teeth.

"Right." Churchill led the way. As they walked along, Moultrie covertly surveyed the merchant, trying to view him in the same light as Helen Dupré would. Looking at the man from her perspective, he had to admit Hobson was plausible. Good-looking, smiling, soft-spoken, discreet, graceful. Moultrie's anger rose. The snake.

"Is something the matter, Ravenel?" Hobson asked, noticing that Moultrie was staring at him. "Do I have a spot on my coat? Is my cravat loose?" Hobson raised his eyebrows quizzically as he spoke.

"No. Everything's in perfect order." Moultrie smiled. He knew he should be embarrassed for being so blatant in his contempt. But he wasn't.

Coming to the end of one row of Indian dwellings, the group turned up another row. Moultrie saw Crazy Wolf watching them. He went ahead to speak to him.

"Hello, Big Hunting Brother."

"Hello, Little Hunting Brother."

"Your children are well."

"Good. Remember your promise."

Something in Crazy Wolf's way of speaking suddenly jolted Moultrie alert. He did not like the flatness of his tone. Moultrie felt he was looking at a man who was so dissatisfied with life that he no longer cared about anything. Moultrie grabbed his old friend by the shoulder. "Big Hunting Brother, are you all right?"

"Ravenel." Moultrie turned. It was McElveen. As Moultrie turned, Crazy Wolf let out a bloodcurdling war cry and launched himself at the colonel. Somehow, he had gotten his handcuffs off and was free. Not only that, but he had a knife.

McElveen was unprepared for the attack. Startled and disoriented by the cry, he had glanced about to see what was going on. As he did this, Crazy Wolf tackled McElveen. The two men fell with a crash and rolled on the ground. McElveen was a strong man, but he was helpless against the demonic fury of Crazy Wolf. The Indian, one hand around McElveen's throat, raised his knife arm and gave an exultant cry. As he did, a rifle boomed.

Moultrie and the others who had seen what had transpired could not discern what the exact sequence of events had been. Did the guard standing next to Churchill fire first or did the knife plunge first? Was it McElveen's or Crazy Wolf's cry which sounded as the bullet hit and the blade cut?

The questions almost did not matter. McElveen and Crazy Wolf were both dead, their blood mingling as it welled up from their wounds. Their two-man war was over at last.

In death, the red man and the white man had become blood brothers. Moultrie stared down at their bodies and shook his head sadly. He shuddered as he saw the peaceful look on Crazy Wolf's face.

Later, a cloth containing a blacksmith's rusty file was found among Crazy Wolf's possessions. This explained how he cut his chains.

Whoever had given him the file had also given him the knife.

There was an investigation. Nothing ever came of it.

Moultrie stayed at the Indian dwellings all afternoon and mourned the death of Big Hunting Brother.

Chapter 17

Hobson was smiling as he nodded to Moultrie in Judge Dupré's library. The man's control was amazing, considering the killings he had just seen. "Hello, Moultrie," he greeted. He'd never used Moultrie's first name before.

Moultrie did not reply with the same familiarity. "Hello, Hobson."

The judge came up and shook Moultrie's hand, then clapped him on the back. "Bill, here, tells me there was a most unfortunate incident this morning."

"That's right." Moultrie stared at Hobson. "We both lost close friends."

"You call that murdering savage a friend?" Hobson spat out.

"That murdering savage, as you call him, had never killed a man in his life until McElveen's militiamen burned his village and raped and killed his wife."

"He was harboring runaways. Hell, he had one of

205

my slaves." There was hate behind Hobson's smile.
"You might just recall an unpleasantness with Scipio."

"He was on land you wanted." Moultrie shook his
head and passed a hand through his hair. "Sorry,
Judge," he apologized, turning to the older man. "This
isn't any way to share your hospitality."

"We're all overwrought, boy. We'll talk of something else."

Moultrie nodded, observing how much the judge
had aged. His hands were shaking.

When Helen came into the room a few minutes
later, Moultrie and the two other men were chatting
gloomily about the current world recession. "I think,"
she stated after returning everyone's greeting, "that we
can find happier things to talk about." As she spoke,
Moultrie saw her glance anxiously at her father.

They talked about horse racing. Hobson argued
that the best horses were being run by a fellow Vir-
ginian, William Johnson, the man called "the Napolean
of the Turf." Judge Dupré agreed that Johnson had
raced some fine horses, but he maintained that a
Colonel Hampton in South Carolina was doing more
for the sport through his breeding operations. Moultrie
described race day at the Washington course outside of
Charleston for Hobson. Eyes sparkling, Helen told of
going to a South Carolina Jockey Club ball once while
on a trip to Charleston to visit some of her family.

The easy talk continued through the dinner. Afterward, the judge pushed himself back from the table.
"Bill," he addressed Hobson, "why don't we leave
these two young people to themselves for a bit and go
back across to the library?"

Hobson glanced quickly at Moultrie, then at Hel-
en. "Splendid idea, Judge," he beamed. Seeing Hobson's smile, Moultrie glanced up sharply. Whatever he

had thought had been hidden behind it didn't seem to be there any longer.

"Don't go, Papa." Helen had stood up, the men rising as she did. "Moultrie and I will take a turn in the garden and join you two later."

"Fine, daughter, fine," the judge said. "Take your time."

In the garden, Helen took Moultrie's arm. Together they walked to a bench under the jasmine-covered gazebo. "You know, Moultrie," Helen laughed, "when I was a little girl, I didn't know you pronounced the 'e' in gazebo. Gah-zee-bo. I thought it was 'gaze-bo', a place where you came to gaze at your beau."

Moultrie smiled halfheartedly. Why did he suddenly have this arid feeling, as if his heart had shriveled? He shook his head. The small talk now troubled him.

Helen squeezed his arm and briefly rested her head on his shoulder. "You were dear yesterday," she murmured.

Moultrie shifted slightly. Again he felt awkward all of a sudden. "There's no need to thank me, Helen." God, listen to me. I'm being pompous as hell. He kissed her hand. "I love you."

"And I love you." Helen's voice was strained.

"And people in love don't have to thank each other for polite gestures. They can expect them as their due."

His forced smile quickly slipped away as the corners of his mouth drooped in sadness.

"What's wrong?"

"Nothing. I was thinking about love and lovers. I guess it was sort of a sad thought, actually."

"And I suppose you're not going to share it with me."

"Well, all right, I'll tell you. I'm frustrated, because you and I think we're in love and we tell each other we're in love, but we have no way of knowing because we've never been lovers." He took a deep breath, almost afraid to say what he wished to say next, then decided, to hell with it. "So if I leave for long periods to go off and try to unravel this Creek Indian mess, it's partly because there's no compelling reason to stay home." All right, he thought, you've gone this far, now finish it off. "You and I play around with the idea of getting married one day. But sometimes I get the feeling you don't think it would be in your best interest . . . or your father's best interest, to actually marry me. I get the feeling that the man you marry has to be able to give you certain advantages—advantages I don't have to offer, but that someone like Bill Hobson does."

"You really think those things?"

"I wouldn't say them if I didn't. And I'm glad they're finally out in the open."

"I must admit you're right, Moultrie Ravenel, I do often have doubts." She became angry. "But concern for your 'advantages,' as you put it, has nothing to do with my doubts. Your advantages can go to hell." Helen paused, surprised at her own bluntness, then proudly continued. "No, Moultrie Ravenel, my concern is that even if we were married, I wouldn't let marriage, family, or even myself hold you at home. You're a born wanderer, as your Uncle John was before you." She paused. "As long as we're saying things which should have been said long ago, I'll add this. I don't believe you when you say that some greater commitment from me would be inducement enough to make you want to settle down. I don't think you have it in you to ever settle down at all. You're lying to me and you're lying to yourself when you say you do."

And after this, neither of them spoke again for a long time.

They watched a robin flit from branch to branch across the garden. Overhead, a mockingbird warbled its repertoire. Helen coughed gently into her hand. Moultrie cleared his throat and shifted.

When they finally spoke again, both said simultaneously, "This is awful."

"Helen, I. . . ."

"Moultrie I. . . ."

And then they laughed nervously.

"Ladies first," Moultrie allowed.

Helen bit her lip. "It's not going to work, Moultrie, is it? The gulf is too wide."

Moultrie kissed her gently, first her forehead, then one cheek, then the other. "I know."

Throwing her arms around his neck, as she had done the day before, Helen kissed him on the lips. "I do love you, Moultrie. I always shall."

"This is quite a situation, isn't it? Here we are, probably really in love, but never to be lovers because everything we've just said about each other is true. Yes, I think the gulf is too wide."

And, having said this, he knew he had just put an end to things with Helen Dupré. In a way which surprised and even shamed him a little, he was glad it was over. The truth was out. No more fretting. For that, at least, Cicero would be pleased.

Taking her hands from around Moultrie's neck, Helen struggled to get the engagement ring off her finger.

"Here, let me help."

"Ouch."

"Sorry. There it is. That wasn't so bad, was it?"

Helen smiled. "No." Gently stroking Moultrie's cheek, she stood up. "We'd better go and rejoin the others. I'll wait to tell Papa until later."

"He'll be relieved."

"Moultrie! How can you say that?"

"It's true."

They walked back to the house. Helen and Moultrie found the others in the library. Looking up as the two came in, Judge Dupré smiled. "Back, are you? I hope you had a pleasant visit."

"Yes, Papa. It *is* too bad Moultrie will be leaving again in a day or two, isn't it?"

"Humph. Yes, very."

Moultrie almost chuckled. The judge knows already, Moultrie realized. He knows I know he knows. He isn't in the least bit sorry either. In fact, he's finding it damned difficult not to show his glee at the news.

Hobson, as usual, was in perfect control. Rising gracefully as Helen came in the room, he smiled winningly, inclining his head in a token bow. Moultrie was not sure, but he thought Hobson's smile widened slightly when he saw Helen's ringless hand.

Moultrie left a few minutes later. At the door, Helen stopped him. "I know you'll be busy getting ready for this trip, but I hope you'll let me come and say good-bye. I hate the thought of you going without at least seeing you once more."

"Yes, Moultrie, we all look forward to saying good-bye to you." Hobson drawled the words, the corners of his mouth twitching.

"I bet you do," Moultrie said. "Don't trouble yourself, Hobson. I know you're a busy man."

"No trouble. No trouble at all." Hobson continued to smile. "In fact, I shall be delighted if Miss Helen would permit me to drive her to the landing to see you off."

"Splendid idea, Bill," the judge boomed. "I'll join you." Then, turning to Moultrie, he added, "We want to give you a proper sendoff, boy. You're going on quite an expedition."

"That's very nice of you, Judge." He kissed Helen's hand, said good-bye and left, barely suppressing a sigh of relief.

Once the parting had been decided between them, the actual leaving had been easy. It was done. There was no sense looking back. He knew it had been the same for Helen.

Helen Dupré did not come to the landing to say good-bye after all.

But this did not upset Moultrie Ravenel. In fact, he was glad she hadn't come. Now he faced a clear horizon.

The Indian problem remained, however. . . .

The next night from on board the *Meridian,* one of the two small steamboats in the flotilla, Moultrie wrote to Page. "The loading of twenty-five hundred Indians, their pitiful possessions and their guards on two little river steamboats and four barges was a real job." He was understating the case. Even the newspapers had carried editorials on the subject of how appalling the conditions for the Indians were. The editorials had done no good. They had come too late.

Moultrie stopped moving only once. That was while taking women and children down to a barge. Jim Henry was there, talking to his family. As Moultrie came up, Henry's wife threw herself into the chief's arms, tears brimming in her eyes. Henry looked in mute appeal at Moultrie. Turning his back, Moultrie stared off across the river, his eyes unseeing.

Five minutes. Ten minutes. Finally, he felt a light touch on his arm. He looked around and found one of the most beautiful women he had ever seen standing beside him. "My sister and I are ready now," she told him.

"Your sister?" Moultrie was confused.

"I am Jim Henry's sister. I was talking about his wife."

"Ah. You are Moon Shadow," Moultrie said in recognition. He escorted the two women to the landing. Coming back up the slope, he saw Jim Henry still standing in the same spot. Moultrie's heart went out to the man. "Is there anything I can do for you?" he asked.

Jim Henry shook his head. "You can't set me free and give me back my home. Until you can do that, don't ask me if there is anything."

He turned and nodded to the two guards watching him, holding their rifles at their sides. "All right, I'm ready."

The next day, the flotilla arrived in Mobile. At a landing just below the city, the Indians were moved ashore. Disembarking, Moultrie and Cicero looked among them for Little Hawk, his brother Fast Raven and sister Flower Bird. It had been two days since they had seen the children. Together with their aunt, Flying Cloud, they had boarded one of the barges in tow behind the *Meridian*. Cicero had fretted and fussed about the children being too young to go on the barge. Moultrie had said, "There is nothing we can do to stop it. It is unfortunate, but this is the way it has to be."

Cicero had become accusative. "What do you

mean, saying it has to be this way? It is this way because your people lied and cheated and have all the soldiers and guns to back you up. But that does not mean it is right." He spun around, biting his lip. "Your people are very good at pushing other folks around. You've had lots of practice pushing mine for more than two hundred years now. But you, you're supposed to do something to make it easier for them. So do it. Start by watching out for those children the way you promised their daddy you would."

When the children got off the boat, they still looked as if they were in shock. Their eyes were red. The little girl was sniffling. Little Hawk's face was pinched and grey.

"What can a woman do?" Flying Cloud shrugged. "They eat. They sleep. Maybe sometimes they have nightmares, but then who doesn't after these last moons? No, time is the only healer. Eventually they will laugh and talk again. Do not rush them."

"That is stupid talk, woman." Cicero was still upset and inclined to argue, but he remembered he was in public and stopped. When he spoke next, he spoke in the manner expected of a black man. "Sorry for my mouth. But ain't nothing going to happen good if we do nothing, auntie."

Flying Cloud just glared at him.

While the two were arguing, Moultrie squatted in front of the children. "Your father loved you," he told them. Little Flower Bird wailed. Reaching in his pocket, Moultrie pulled out peppermint sticks. One of the last things he had done before leaving Montgomery was to buy a supply of them. He passed one stick to each child, then gave one to their aunt and one to Cicero. Then he started sucking on one himself. To begin with, the children just looked at him. They had never had peppermint candy.

Moultrie could see the chain reactions in the children's faces. First suspicion, then curiosity, then, after they'd taken their first tastes, wonder and delight. Flower Bird's face broke into a smile. She came forward and threw her arms around him, clamping the remaining bit of peppermint stick in her hand against the nape of his neck. First Cicero, then the girl's aunt and brothers, began to laugh. So did a woman passing by.

Moultrie looked up. It was Jim Henry's sister, Moon Shadow. He smiled at her. She returned the smile, then moved on. Little Johnnie had described her well. Brilliant brown eyes, and black hair thick and long enough to wrap twice, perhaps three times, around a man's hand. Sculpturesque features. A woman taller than average, but well-proportioned; Moultrie imagined her bearing and nursing half the children of her tribe.

Moon Shadow was riches enough for any man.

Moultrie patted the little girl on the head and gently pried her from his neck. A fly landed on the handprint of peppermint stickiness she left behind. "I have to go now and write a lot of dull reports which you wouldn't understand," he explained, "but I'll be back this afternoon with some more sweet stick." She nodded her head. Yes, more sweet stick. Moultrie spoke briefly to the two boys and Flying Cloud. Then he turned to Cicero. "Time to go?"

"Let Daca stay?" Little Hawk said softly.

Moultrie nodded. "All right, have your friend Loudmouth for a while. But he'll have to meet me in a few hours. I'll be very angry with both of you if he's late. Cicero and I have things to do before sailing tonight."

Cicero grinned and performed a dancing bow, saying, "Why thank you, Marse Moultrie, thank you sir." But he winked at Moultrie as he did it.

Moultrie strode across the grounds of the make-shift camp of lopsided tents and bent lean-tos. We're doing all of this to them, he thought. Look at this place. Am I the only one who feels remorse?

He scanned the grounds again: the women hunched over small fires, too depressed and weary to brush insects from the food they cooked; men manacled in groups; confused, dirty children; tiny bundles of clothes, pottery and jewelry. These were the only possessions permitted on the migration—one small bundle per person.

But Crazy Wolf's children had something else the others did not have, Moultrie thought. My promise. And they do have Cicero, who is more security for them than an infantry.

The thought of Cicero's enthusiasm for Little Hawk forced Moultrie to grin. Mother Hen Cicero. He blessed Cicero for his big heart, but sometimes he wished Cicero did not have such a big mouth.

Daca was a fine Indian name for Cicero. Loudmouth, indeed.

Chapter 18

Moultrie wrote to his brother, Henry Ravenel:

> I guess that if you're a Creek who has
> never even seen a sailboat, the sight of a
> large schooner with three masts must be
> pretty intimidating. It's as large as some of
> their villages. The thought of actually sailing
> in one must scare the hell out of them.

The Creek Indians were frightened, all right.
Cicero said they had cause to be. "I may not know
boats, but I know neglect and rotten wood when I see
them," he told Moultrie.

Moultrie did not share his gloom. "Suddenly
you're a naval architect. You aren't just afraid of being
seasick, now, are you? It's going to be calm sailing
tonight."

"And suddenly you're an old sea dog who knows

all about weather. Calm tonight does not mean calm tomorrow, Ravenel."

Cicero guessed correctly. The first night out from Mobile to New Orleans was beautiful, clear and warm. Once outside the keys at the mouth of the bay, the ships picked up a following breeze. Even grossly overloaded, the vessels made five knots an hour.

The next day promised to be fair too, but gradually turned greyer and greyer. As the sky darkened, the seas began to pick up. By midafteroon, it was obvious that a storm was coming.

The first rainsqualls hit at about nine o'clock that evening. The seas were already heavy. The high winds and thunder and lightning followed. Wails of terror went up from some of the children. Their parents sat frightened, chanting to their gods. They knew that if the ships floundered, they and their children would drown. Many of them could not swim. The men were manacled, the women had their children to save and the seas were growing rougher by the minute.

Moultrie and the sailors moved forward to transport the Indians into the hold. The soldiers were of no help. Most of them had been green with seasickness even before the storm started. Now they were worse, clinging to the railings and alternately retching and groaning.

Pushing, prying, and prodding, the sailors maneuvered the Indians toward the hatches. Moultrie, while encouraging them forward, looked frantically for Cicero and Little Hawk, the boy's aunt and his brother and sister. Several times he shouted their names, but the wind seemed to tear the words out of his mouth. Even when the lightning flashed, he could hardly make out the faces close to him, much less those across the deck.

"The winds are building to gale force," the mate shouted to the ship's captain. Moultrie believed it. He had barely been able to hear the man's words over the roaring gusts. He saw the deck watchmen fastening safety harnesses to the deck life lines. A rush of water breached the port side and blanketed three sailors. Moultrie himself hugged one of the huge stays supporting the mainmast. His feet were lifted by the water and he imagined his shoes being carried away.

When the water cascaded from the deck back into the sea, the three sailors were thrashing about on the ends of their safety harnesses like hooked fish.

The waves had knocked both the Indians and the crew down like a child sweeps a table clear of toy soldiers. To the sailors' credit, they embraced the Indians in twos and threes and pulled them to the deck as they themselves went down before the onslaught of water. Moultrie realized that the sailors were rolling with the punches, so to speak, and were trying to tell the Indians to do the same. The Indians would try to remain erect against the waves and in so doing would be at greater risk of being swept overboard or slammed against rail and cabin.

A slope of waves lifted the stern and Moultrie was filled with fright. Lord, if a boat this large could be so easily lifted, it could just as easily be broken in two. God did not intend man to go to sea, Moultrie thought.

Then the force seemed to take the bow of the ship. The bow wave grew higher and spread out, lifting the ship, then dropping it like a stone. The entire boat began to hum and vibrate, but Moultrie barely heard it over the roar of the storm.

Moultrie's knuckles whitened as he gripped the stay, praying for salvation. Everyone around him held onto whatever was handy. He wondered whether anyone was steering the ship. It seemed to be steering itself, and not doing too well at it.

Yet, he found it exhilarating as the boat slid over the peak of a wave and began its downward slide bow first into the trough. He knew there would be no stopping until the ship bottomed out.

And when it did, the suddenness of the stop rocked the mast. The force almost broke his grip on the stay. Shouting Indians and deck hands rolled by him like children tumbling down a hill.

Moultrie called out again. "Little Hawk! Cicero! Answer!"

A form lurched against him and other hands gripped the mainmast stay, clamping over his own.

"They're already down below," a voice yelled. A rush of water pressed them together face to face. It was Moon Shadow who had been hurled against him.

"What?" Moultrie yelled.

She placed her mouth close to his ear. "The children and your slave. They're already down below with the others."

Another rush of water broke over the rail, and in trying to support one another, Moultrie and Moon Shadow lost their hold on the mainmast stay. The water rolled them over and over. Moultrie grunted in pain as she accidentally kneed his groin. She cried out when a sailor unwittingly kicked her. He embraced her head to protect her. She wrapped her arms around his waist.

Moultrie yelled out, "Please, Lord, do not wash us overboard."

Then the only thing they could do was hold each

other tight and keep rolling until the deckhouse stopped them.

And there they remained as the storm dumped water on them and tore at them with its winds.

Lightning split the sky. In the brilliance, Moultrie saw Moon Shadow looking straight into his eyes.

Another lightning flash. She was still looking.

And when the rush of water subsided, they still held each other close, even though there was, for the moment, no immediate need.

Then Moon Shadow leaped up and was gone.

The following morning was calm and sunny.

The deck crew cleaned debris, salvaged wreckage and helped pull the Indians from the holds.

The Creeks pulled themselves up weakly. Most were seasick. A repugnant stench was left behind from vomit, sweat and sewage.

Once on deck, many rushed to the rail to be sick again.

Cicero appeared. "Morning." Then, suddenly, he clamped his hand to his mouth and elbowed his way to the rail with the others. All three children followed. So did their aunt, Flying Cloud.

Moultrie was struck by the look on Flying Cloud's face. Crazy Wolf had worn the same expressionless mask during the few days before he attacked McElveen and was killed.

Moultrie reached for her, but he was a second too late.

Flying Cloud suddenly bolted, hoisted herself quickly to the railing, stood teetering for a moment, then let herself fall over the side. She turned head over feet and splashed down into the sea, which was still rolling after the storm. She made no attempt to swim. She looked back at the rail once, then was gone.

Throwing off his poncho and seaboots, Moultrie climbed over the rail. He looked for some trace of Flying Cloud. He was going to jump for her. But as he searched the dark foam, there was no one.

He came down from the rail and ran among those on the deck to the stern. He shielded his eyes and searched the wake. Nothing. No one. And no one seemed to even care that she was gone. He was the only one who had made an effort to stop Flying Cloud.

"Don't any of you give a hoot?" he raged at the crewmen. "Are they really just animals, not to be missed if one goes astray?"

The first mate of the ship stepped forward. "No way to know when they're going to do it," he blared. "They don't tell anybody about it. They just jump."

Moultrie pushed him away, almost knocking the man down.

"You! Creeks!" Moultrie yelled. "Does the loss of one of your own make so little difference? Do something, damn it!"

They too turned from him.

But Moultrie realized with a shudder that they did care. They cared a great deal.

On every Indian face he could see, there was just a little more hatred showing.

The rains came again.

At midday the two schooners limped past Lake Borgne southeast of New Orleans, their rigging torn and still hanging loose after the storm. Standing at the bow of his vessel, Moultrie peered across the water. He could not see the distant shore through the rain. But in his mind's eye, he could visualize British warships anchored there twenty-odd years earlier, during the War of 1812.

Uncle John Ravenel had described the event and the time often. How General Andrew Jackson, alerted to the British advance against New Orleans, had started building a defensive line at Chalmette, south of the city between the Mississippi River and Lake Borgne. How Sir Edward Packenham, British, after waiting two weeks for reinforcements and not receiving them, had attacked the American positions in a frontal assault and had died along with two thousand others out of the nine-thousand-man British force.

"It was simply slaughter," Uncle John had recalled. "Our breastworks were piled high with their dead. In some places, the British had to climb over their wounded and dead to be shot."

Whenever he had told the tale, Uncle John's eyes would light up at the memory, not just the battle but of General Jackson and Jean Laffitte, the pirate, who'd been there with his Cajun buccaneers fighting with the Americans against the British. The excitement, the roar of the guns, the surge of the attack, the desperate hand-to-hand fighting, the rumble of drums and the call of the bugles, and the shrill wail of the bagpipes had all been in Uncle John's voice and face as he had told the story.

So too had been the sadness. He would shake his head and say, "Yet the battle was pointless. The peace treaty between the British and ourselves had been signed in London by the time Packenham attacked. We didn't know. We just didn't know. War is a harder mistress and a better wife than any woman. But a man grows old. Or maybe grows up. He wants peace, a family. He begins to think before he acts. Then he looks back and it all seems such a waste. Such a bloody waste."

Only once in all the times he had heard the story had Moultrie interrupted with a question. "Why haven't you ever married, Uncle John?"

Uncle John had looked as if he had been shot. He had turned white. He poured himself a stiff whiskey, then sat down again. For the longest time, he had just sat there, staring into the fire. He had not even touched his glass. Finally, he had tossed off his drink, shuddering and making a wry face. Then he had started to talk.

He had told his nephew of being in love with a beautiful girl, of losing her to another man, of leaving South Carolina for the West and of joining the army at the outbreak of the War of 1812. Years later his rival had died, and John had gone back to South Carolina for a year, then asked for the widow's hand. She had refused. He left, swearing never to return.

That part in his story had startled Moultrie. He'd suddenly remembered something. "That was just what you told Mother, too, wasn't it?" As he had said it, the realization had hit him. Uncle John had been speaking about Moultrie's mother all along.

Having seen the realization flooding his nephew's eyes, Uncle John had nodded and cleared his throat. "That's right. Your mother is the only woman I've ever wanted as a wife. That's why I have no family of my own and why I treat you as my son."

That was the year Uncle John had given Moultrie the shotgun for his birthday.

*   *   *

Moultrie shook his head. He was soaked by spray and rain. Wiping his face, he turned and looked back along the deck. The Indians were peering through the rain, looking toward their landing.

The prisoners came to shore from the schooners and barges on Lake Pontchartrain by Bayou St. John. From there, they walked up the bayou and along the Carondelet, the Old Basin Canal, dragging a barge filled with the old people, children and baggage to an empty area below the basin at the foot of Julia Street along the bank of the new canal. The Creeks had no tents. Scavenging, they found lumber along the new canal where laborers had been working. With these bits of board, a few branches and some blankets and pieces of canvas, they set up makeshift shelters.

It was hardly worth the effort. The rains cascaded over and through the shelters, turning their floors to mud. Several tents simply collapsed under the weight of the water.

Earlier that day, another cadre of guards had joined the contingent, a platoon of light infantry commanded by Lieutenant Wallace Barry. Barry was a bright, aggressive young man who enjoyed soldiering. Moultrie liked him.

Barry passed his enthusiasm for his work on to his men. They formed a jaunty platoon, marching into the new holding compound to join the twenty-five hundred Creeks and their custodians.

But on this day of constant rain they fared no better with creature comforts than the very Indians they were to escort and supposedly protect.

Their food was soaked and their tents fell, casualties to the rain and wind. They had no fires, only piles of wet wood and grass.

Cicero, in trying to start a blaze for Little Hawk and the other children, finally threw his matches into the mud. "Marse Moultrie, even the devil wouldn't burn on a day like this." Water ran off the rim of his hat, down his face and across his lips.

But for one night, the terrible wet did not affect Moultrie. For one night he did not share the conditions in the camp. He had to be in New Orleans that evening, to be ready to meet John Sanford the following morning. He took full advantage of the opportunity.

He took a room at the Maison Chartres in the Vieux Carre. It was a relatively new hotel with a fine reputation.

He ordered a hot bath and soaked the salt, sweat and mud from his skin. His cold bones warmed.

When the water cooled, he ordered a second bath and soaked some more.

That night, as he lay between linen sheets, he thought of the others out in the rain, but only for a little while. Before long he had collapsed into the deepest sleep he had ever known.

Moultrie's earlier impressions of John Sanford were confirmed when they met in the morning. Sanford had no sensitivity toward Indians and no particular concern for their rights, but he was not a bad man. He was just a Southerner with distaste toward anyone not white.

There were several others at the meeting by the time Moultrie arrived. One was Dr. Eugene Abadie, the physician assigned to travel on the migration and watch over the Indians' health. The others Moultrie did not recognize. They were officers of a private company formed by John Sanford. The entire purpose of this company was to provide food and transportation for the Creeks as the Indians made their way westward.

Sanford was acting in a private capacity as a civilian at this time. He no longer wore his Georgia Militia general's uniform. He insisted on calling Moultrie by his first name. He asked Moultrie to call him John.

When the pleasantries were over, he quickly got down to business. "My company," Sanford began, "was formed to remove these Indians under contract from the government. The government has not been generous. If we are to make even a modest profit, and we will, then we are going to have to husband our supplies in every way possible."

He pulled out cigars and offered them to Moultrie and the others. After everyone had had a chance to light them, he continued. "Unfortunately, we're at the mercy of the people selling supplies and transportation along our route, and they know it. That means we're going to have to pay top dollar most of the time. There's nothing we can do about it."

"Yes, there is." Moultrie stood up and walked around the room to the map on the wall. "Threaten them. Threaten your suppliers with loss of business. Tell them you'll take different routes other times and by-pass them entirely. Tell them that you're going to go up the Arkansas River or the Ouachita, that you'll bring the Indians to Memphis overland instead of up the Mississippi."

As he spoke, Moultrie pointed out the alternate routes on the map with the glowing tip of his cigar.

"Hmmm." Sanford was polite but not agreeable.

"Have you ever sailed on the Arkansas, Moultrie?"

"No, John, can't say I have."

"Well, it's the worst bit of river of its size in the whole United States. Hell, you'll get water depths between twenty-five feet or more at one point and less than five feet at another point, all within twenty or thirty miles. Taking a boat or even a barge up there is asking for trouble."

"I see."

Drawing deeply on his cigar, Sanford let out a stream of smoke. "Let me review for you, gentlemen, the arrangements we've made so far." He stood up and came over to the map. Moultrie stepped back.

"Here at New Orleans," Sanford started, "we'll embark on three side-wheel steamboats we've rented, the *Lamplighter,* the *Majestic,* and the *Revenue.* Lieutenant Barry and his troops will ride in the *Lamplighter,* I in the *Majestic.* Moultrie, you and Dr. Abadie will be in the *Revenue,* towing a barge full of women and children. You'll have the greatest number of Indians. We should make it to Rock Roe at the confluence of the White River and the Mississippi in a week or ten days at the outside." He pointed to the spot on the map, then continued. "From there, as soon as we've gathered enough carts for the supplies, and for the sick and the elderly, we'll go overland past Little Rock along the Arkansas River to Fort Gibson. There our responsibility ends."

With that, the meeting was over. The embarkation date was July 21st, giving Moultrie two days to write letters and reports, eat well, drink well, sleep between linen sheets and buy peppermint sticks for Little Hawk, Fast Raven and Flower Bird.

He also thought of buying a gift for Moon Shadow. He decided not to. Thinking of how her face had appeared, staring at him during the lightning flashes during the storm, he was not certain she would even accept.

Nevertheless, thoughts of her would not leave him.

Chapter 19

The traffic on the Mississippi River was like no other water traffic Moultrie had even seen. He had sailed the Gulf of Mexico, the Atlantic Ocean to and from Europe and the rivers of Alabama and Georgia and the Carolinas. He had seen ships crowding the great ports of two continents.

But never had Moultrie seen so many ships and boats of different kinds as those in New Orleans harbor and upriver on the Mississippi.

For miles and miles to the north, keelboats, barges, clippers, side-wheelers, stern-wheelers, sloops, ketches, even rowboats carrying single bales of hay, brawled for right of way.

Through this patternless traffic, the three scaly paddle-wheelers bearing the Creeks and their escorts bored steadily northward in single file. Their hulls vibrated as engines labored and their fluted stacks threw sparks and smoke into the air.

Uncle John had sailed often on the river, even

back before the United States bought Louisiana from France in 1803. He had told Moultrie and Henry about those trips when visiting in South Carolina.

With Uncle John's stories in their heads, the brothers had spent endless days on the small river which flowed past their father's plantation. There they had looked behind every tree for Indians, Spanish hidalgos in their shining armor and black-robed priests standing in the bows of boats. The swamps had whispered with mystery and adventure.

Smiling at the memory, Moultrie looked up. God, it felt good to be in sunlight again, even if it was hotter than Hades on the riverboats and noisier than Babel with the clanking of the engines and the splashing of the great side wheels.

He turned and looked over the prisoners. They were chatting and even laughing at the rails of the riverboats as if they felt right at home. There was a definite improvement in mood over that of a few days before. But how long would it last? For now, the Indians were passing through country that looked a lot like home. The sun was shining. They were getting enough to eat. The new vistas were exciting, not threatening.

But the Indian Territory where they were going would look very different. Even with fellow tribesmen already there, some of them for fifteen years or more, it was going to seem a forbidding place, with the plains stretching as far as the eye could see, Piutes and Osages and other Plains Indians threatening the settlements and winters colder by far than along the Chattahoochee.

"You goddamned little whore. I said give me a kiss." The words were followed by a slap, then another, then a yelp and a string of curses. They were coming from the stern. Pivoting, Moultrie pushed his way aft. And there he saw Moon Shadow. A deck hand had pushed her against the rail and was trying to pin her arms.

"Sailor!" Moultrie started to run, dodging between piles of possessions and clusters of Indians. As he did, the woman managed to bring up her knee into the deck hand's groin.

"You bitch," the man cried. "I'm going to kill you, you whore. I'm. . . ."

He did not finish the sentence. Moultrie grabbed him, spun him around and hit him hard in the stomach. The man doubled over, gasping. Moultrie threw him on the deck. He landed with a jarring thud. As he did so, the *Revenue*'s captain came running from the pilothouse.

"What's the meaning of this?" Captain Tobias Glenn demanded.

"The man assaulted this Indian woman," Moultrie answered.

The captain bristled. "How the hell do you know?"

"I saw him."

"Why didn't you stop him?"

"I did." Moultrie stooped and picked up his hat.

"And nearly killed the man. I won't stand for it, Ravenel."

Moultrie looked the captain up and down. "You won't have to, Captain, if you do your job and keep your men in line. Now I suggest you get him out of here."

The captain glared, but stooped and pulled the deck hand upright. The man was gasping. Clutching his groin, he looked at the captain, then at Moultrie. "I didn't do nothing, I swear."

Moon Shadow spoke for the first time. "And that is why I have bruises all over me. You are a liar, mister."

Someone in the crowd called out, "Listen to the Indian, will you? Damned if she don't speak English better than me."

The deck hand clutched his groin and tried to stand. "Call me a liar, will you!"

"Calm down, mister. Calm down." The captain pressed down on the deck hand's shoulder.

"Captain Glenn, you going to believe a lying Indian instead of me?" The sailor was incredulous.

"Course not."

"Am I a liar, too, Captain?" Moultrie stepped forward and looked at the sailor.

Glenn ignored Moultrie and turned to his deck hand. "You want to call him a liar."

The deck hand did not answer. The captain told him to get back to his job and shoved him away. "All right, folks, the show is over," he called out. Indians and guards were already turning to look out over the water once more.

"Thank you." The Indian woman had come up beside Moultrie.

Moultrie took a deep breath. "Not at all." He looked at her. "Are you all right, Moon Shadow?"

"I am fine."

"Why did you use an Indian name when your brother chose an English one?"

"I never wanted to be white like my brother." Moon Shadow shook her head. "No, that's wrong. I never hoped to make my way in the white world. Besides, my father didn't care if I carried his name. He just wanted a son."

"I see."

"You try to be a good man, don't you? Like my brother."

"I'm flattered by the comparison," Moultrie responded. Under his breath, he added, "I think." He paused. "I've got a cousin who keeps reminding me that the road to hell is paved with good intentions."

"Your cousin is right," Moon Shadow laughed. Becoming serious once more, she added, "Thank you again."

"Are you all right?"

"Better off than that sailor anyway."

They smiled at each other for a moment. Then Moon Shadow turned and walked away. Watching her, Moultrie muttered to himself, "Remember Uncle John, remember Uncle John."

Riding back from Bear Chief's village seven years before, Uncle John had told Moultrie about his affair with Little Johnnie's mother. "She was beautiful," Uncle John had said. "And full of life. At first I just talked with her casually in her father's lodge. Then we met, quite by accident, a couple of times in the woods. Finally, I asked her to make love with me. She said, 'Yes.'"

"Just like that?"

"Just like that. And just like that, she got pregnant, too."

"But why keep coming back to the woman and her boy? There are lots of children in Indian towns who don't know their fathers. Hell, Uncle John. Indians, the Creeks anyway, belong to their mothers' clans. Being a bastard doesn't carry the same social stigma that it has in our world. Right?"

Uncle John had just shaken his head and ridden on in silence. It was miles down the trail when he had suddenly said, "Making love to Little Johnnie's mother was different. It made all those visits to houses in New Orleans seem cheap. I felt whole then, for the first time in my life since meeting your mother. I didn't just make love to the woman. I took her to live with me for almost a year. I went native."

"But you came back. What happened?"

"I began to miss being a white man."

"Why?"

"Books. I wanted to read. And wine. I wanted to drink a good Madeira again."

"And Forest Hall?"

"Forest Hall was the dream that finally drove me down the mountain."

"But I thought you didn't build until after the Creek War?"

"I didn't. I'd bought the land when I came down from Bear Chief's village to the cotton country. That was just before the War of 1812. I decided to join the army to learn how to be a white man again."

Moultrie could still hear Uncle John's laugh and the bitterness in it. Moultrie turned from where Moon Shadow had just been standing. He made his way toward the ship's mess. He was not really hungry. He just wanted something to do so that he would not think about Moon Shadow.

Yet he still thought of her.

And he wondered what it would be like, living with Moon Shadow as Uncle John had lived with Little Johnnie's mother.

Picturing her extraordinary good looks and fiery ways, Moultrie found himself smiling. Riches enough for any man. And any man would probably stay with Moon Shadow a lot longer than a year.

*   *   *

Later, while he was thinking about living with Indian women, Moultrie asked Cicero about his relationship with Red Wing. "You've no doubt persuaded her to talk to you by now, and probably do other things with you, too," Moultrie ventured. "You could talk the shingles off a house."

Cicero's eyes narrowed. "Well, you're wrong this time, Ravenel, and I don't think I want to talk about her any further."

"Why not? I'm sorry I teased you. I didn't realize it was such a serious thing with you."

"Same old reason," Cicero sighed. "I just can't convince myself there would be any future in it. And even if I did see a future, I'd still have to persuade her. No, Red Wing still doesn't think I'm worth talking to."

Cicero started polishing Moultrie's boots.

"Cicero, you can be aggravating as hell. That kind of talk coming from the man who lectured me about fretting. 'The worst thing in the world you can do is nothing.' Remember?"

Cicero nodded.

Moultrie continued. "And that certainly includes going after the woman you want. Cicero, you've got a great heart and you've been faithful to me as a friend, regardless of the slave status. And I've told you again and again, as a friend in return, your freedom's yours any time you tell me to draw up the papers." Moultrie thought for a moment, then added, "Cicero, let's stop talking about it. Let's set a target date. Take your freedom when we get to the Indian Territory. The things that matter in the South don't matter so much out there. Nobody cares much in the West whether you were a slave or not. Oh yes, some. But not as much. It's what you yourself do that matters most. Take your freedom, Cicero. Then you'll have something to offer

Red Wing. You'll be your own man, to do as you choose, not someone's baggage any longer."

As an afterthought, Moultrie added, "And even if she still turns you down, you've got a whole new life ahead anyway. You have nothing to lose."

Cicero's answer was different than it had been before. "I'll think about it."

Moultrie was so surprised that he sat down, absently took the boot from Cicero and began brushing it himself. "Hey, Cicero, you know, you've never answered me like that before when I've told you to take your freedom."

"I've never had anybody I wanted so much before. I never had any reason to want to be free."

"I repeat, Marse Cicero. Any time you want them, your papers will be drawn. Think about it."

"I *have* been thinking. And *I* repeat, the men in my family have been other men's men for so many years that the thought of being my own man truly scares me to death. What if I don't know how? Slavery is white folks' way of life. And it's black folks' way now, too."

Moultrie felt as though the emotion and tension of their conversation would smother him. It would be good to put some distance between himself and Cicero for a while. He believed Cicero thought the same. Cicero's eyes glistened.

"Well. I'm going out for some air," Moultrie said finally.

Cicero made no effort to follow.

Outside, the air on the river was warm, wet and still. Moultrie took a deep breath. The night was thick with the smells of river mud, pines, the smoke from the stacks of the three riverboats in their convoy and a hint of jasmine. Moultrie turned and strolled past the starboard side wheel, hunching his shoulders and trotting to avoid the spray flung by the orbiting paddles and tines.

He listened for disagreement in the whispers of the Indians on deck. He heard none. He nodded to those he recognized. Whatever hatred they held, they seemed to have at least set it aside for the moment. He did not believe that he should hope for permanent forgiveness from them. But for the moment, even respite was blessing enough.

Moultrie made a full circle of the upper deck. He did not see Moon Shadow. I am not looking for her, he told himself. Liar. You *are* looking for her.

He made his way back to the stern rail and was watching the wake of the boat splitting the moon streak on the water. It occurred to him that he would never have gone looking for Helen Dupré as he had just looked for Moon Shadow.

"Ah, Helen," he whispered. "I hope you and your father have seen through Bill Hobson by now. He has nothing you need. You have everything he needs, beginning with the Dupré name." Moultrie gripped the rail. "That bastard. Well, I've done all I can to warn them." Moultrie suddenly felt bittersweet. Now that he and Helen were no longer engaged, whatever took place between Helen and Hobson was not his affair.

Moultrie peered through the night at the barge in tow behind the steamboat. He could not make out faces, just bodies. Little Hawk and his brother and sister were probably there. Poor children. This has been a difficult journey for them. It will all be over soon.

I hope they're safe back there, he thought. The deck on that barge behind the *Revenue* looked nearly rotted through. Moultrie gripped the aft railing in sudden anger. Damn this whole shoddy enterprise. The feeling welled up in him, setting his pulse racing, turning his knuckles white as he gripped the railing. So help me, he thought to himself, if anything happens to those three children on that barge, I'll hunt down the men who put them there and break their legs, starting with Charles Madden's.

Moultrie made his way aft for the second time the next morning. There was still no sign of Moon Shadow. It was curious, the disappointment he felt. Hell, he thought, I don't even know her. I just know she's beautiful and has character. Jim Henry isn't the only strong person in that family. Moultrie smiled suddenly, remembering Moon Shadow's anger at the sailor who had tried to maul her. She had been spitting fire.

I wouldn't want her mad at me, he decided.

"Little Hunting Brother!" The call came shrilly over the water.

Moultrie looked, then waved. Standing at the bow of the barge, Flower Bird pointed excitedly toward the right bank.

Moultrie turned and looked. In the distance, the busy town of Columbia was visible. The *Revenue* was pulling in to dock.

If he lived to be one hundred, Moultrie would never forget the next moments. Turning back toward Little Hawk's sister, he heard a loud rending noise, then saw the barge's deck collapse. All three children—the girl and her two brothers standing beside her—disappeared into the planks and rubble.

The captain of the side-wheeler had seen the deck collapse and quickly made a sensible maneuver. He purposely overshot the mooring on the town dock and in so doing brought the barge right into dockside with the steamboat at the same time. Otherwise the barge would have needed to be hand-towed in. There was room enough on the dockside for both.

Moultrie did not wait for the *Revenue*'s gangway to be lowered. He hurdled the railing to the dock below, stumbled, picked himself up and ran aft to the barge.

The cries and sobs were terrible. Hundreds of Indians had fallen with the deck. Most were just dazed. They and the others who were on the part of the deck which still held were already lifting people out when Moultrie got there. He shouted back to anyone on the *Revenue* who could hear him, "The doctor! Get Abadie out here!"

Eugene Abadie was already there. Stooping down, he began to examine people as they were brought ashore. Without looking up, he ordered, "Start a fire. Boil some water." Then he went on with his examinations. There were lots of cuts and bruises, and a few broken bones.

And, at first, this was considered a small blessing. There was almost an air of rejoicing as everyone looked about and found everyone else still alive, if battered. Things were not as bad as everyone had feared.

The good spirit was dampened quickly.

While everyone was on deck, Moultrie felt that the worst injuries would have occurred below among those who took the weight of deck beams and planks in the collapse. He was right.

Below, he came upon a group of Indians in the dark who were hurling themselves at a jackstraw pile of wood. Pinned beneath it was Little Hawk's sister, Flower Bird.

Her face looked calm, placid, as though she were merely asleep. But her body was all but flattened by the beams around her.

Moultrie reeled and thought he might become ill. The rage which inflamed him almost sent him out of control. He imagined Charles Madden's face in the sights of a pistol.

Moultrie brought the little girl's body up. Her hands were sticky with blood. Laying her on the ground, he turned to her brothers. There was nothing he could say. He knelt down before them. The little one, his face working, burst into tears and came to Moultrie's arms.

Little Hawk stood with the same stoniness in his face that Crazy Wolf had had that night after his village had been burned down.

It took the rest of the afternoon to repair the barge deck. Sanford, on the *Majestic*, arrived about half an hour after the accident. Like the *Lamplighter*, the *Majestic* had already steamed around a bend in the river ahead of the *Revenue* at the time of the incident. It was not until the signal came from the *Revenue* that the *Majestic*'s captain had realized that something was wrong. Reversing, he had brought his boat back down to Columbia and docked her.

Coming ashore, John Sanford met Moultrie. "What's happened, Moultrie?"

Moultrie gestured toward the wreckage. He told Sanford to count the wounded cluttered about Eugene Abadie.

"Isn't it plain what happened, Sanford?" Moultrie asked. "How can you still ask a question like that after seeing all of this?"

Sanford ignored Moultrie's hostility. "Was anyone critically hurt?"

Moultrie grimaced. "Oh, not really. Just a little girl who was killed when the deck fell in on her."

"Your sarcasm is neither helpful nor welcome at this moment, Ravenel," Sanford returned. "I am concerned, believe me. And I am greatly relieved that things are not too bad after all."

Moultrie grabbed Sanford's shirt. "You swine. You bloody swine." He felt his frustration and anger peak once more. He envisioned Sanford's face in his gun sights, and Madden's face too. "You lease a rotting, unseaworthy scow of a barge unfit to carry even pigs, overload it with human beings, and then you're glad because only one little girl is killed. Only one. That's beautiful. Just beautiful. You son of a bitch, one little girl dies and you're pleased because it's only one!"

Moultrie hurled Sanford away. "The real crime here is that no court or tribunal will ever do anything bad to you for it." He wheeled and strode off, calling over his shoulder, "You'll pay for this, Sanford. You'll pay for this."

The convoy resumed the trip upriver at nightfall.

Moultrie was standing at the aft rail watching the *Revenue*'s wake in the moonlight when Moon Shadow came and stood beside him.

"I am sorry about what happened," she said softly. "This day will never be forgotten. My people will remember."

She stood in silence with him, watching the foamy track of waves the boat and its paddles made. Finally, she turned to go.

"Don't go. Please." As Moultrie spoke, he took her arm for a moment. She pulled away gently once, then relaxed in his grip, as though deciding she was comfortable there.

"Tell me things I don't know about," Moultrie requested. "Make me understand what it is to be an Indian who tries to be white, when white is really no better than Indian."

Moon Shadow stiffened.

"I apologize if I sound rude," Moultrie soothed. "But my uncle fathered a half-breed son and taught him to use the blunt word. Little Johnnie. I don't understand my cousin, though I want to very much."

"You are rude," Moon Shadow said. "But I shall try to explain to you anyway. It's very simple, really. Unless the father goes away or goes native, you end up living in two worlds at once, and those worlds fight inside you all the time."

"And."

"And so you get my brother working as a clerk for Hobson one day and leading the Yuchis' revolt the next."

Moultrie understood. Being half-breed was the worst of both possible worlds. He turned to look at her. "What about you?" he asked.

"My father let me be an Indian. I can't read or write. I've never worn dresses. Except for the fact that my father's a white man and I can speak English, I'm an Indian inside."

"I see."

Moon Shadow smiled and put her arm briefly on Moultrie's. "You are a good man, Indian Agent Moultrie Ravenel. I've even thought of falling in love with you, but that is ridiculous. You will never be an Indian. I shall never be a white woman. We shall always be in separate worlds."

Moultrie arched his eyebrows, then grinned. "I admire your frankness." Suddenly, he confessed, "I suppose I was beginning to wonder if I wasn't attracted to you, too."

Moon Shadow tilted her face toward the moon and gave a throaty laugh. Moultrie grinned.

"I don't wonder," Moon Shadow told him, "that you are attracted to me as I am to you. I am a woman and you are a man. But it is more than that. Man and woman do not look at each other and hold each other as we did during the storm unless they are attracted to each other. My want for you was great then." She ran her hand over his rough cheek. "Have I surprised you?"

"Yes."

"You would have to accept my boldness if we ever became lovers."

"I know."

"And you wanted to make love to me? During the storm?"

"Yes," Moultrie said again.

"I—I must say good night now."

"No," he said firmly. "You must listen to me now. You have told me you wanted to make love with me. You've told me without really saying it that you still want to. And then you say good night, yet you still have your arm hooked around mine. So, no good night. I'm going to kiss you now, the way we both wished I had done the other night."

She did not release his arm. In the moonlight, Moultrie could see the same intense look on her face that he had seen during the storm. She did not have to vocalize an answer. He knew what it was.

He clamped both hands hard on her shoulders and pulled her to him slowly. She resisted. Moultrie knew she was testing his determination. He pulled hard.

"Gently," she scolded. "You do not have to be rough with me if I am willing."

And that was how it all began.

Their lips came together, brushing back and forth gently against each other. Moultrie was quickly aroused. When her lips parted, her tongue searched for his. She hooked one leg behind Moultrie's knees, anchoring her body to his, and began to rub against his thighs.

Moultrie could not help but respond as Moon Shadow gently squeezed the hardness of him between her thighs. He closed his eyes and concentrated on the unfamiliar feelings of pleasure. It was all so easy. Moon Shadow made him feel so good.

"Touch me," she murmured.

Her blouse parted easily. A trickle of sweat fell slowly between her full, rounded globes. Moultrie gently fondled one, then the other. He took one breast in both hands and squeezed gently. The nipple swelled. He bent to meet it. It was hard. He sucked it in deeply, rolling his tongue around and around it.

For a brief moment, he tried to compare Moon Shadow with Helen Dupré. But there was little to compare. What Helen thought about doing but did not, Moon Shadow did without thought.

Now, he looked into Moon Shadow's dark brown eyes—all-knowing eyes—and he felt free. He cocked his head, kissed her lightly and then stared again into her dark pools.

A pellet of water broke on Moultrie's head, seeming to stun him. Then there was another pellet, then another. Drops were exploding on the rail and deck.

One minute the night had been clear. The next minute, Moultrie and Moon Shadow were blinking in a downpour so intense the water stung and robbed them of vision. The rainstorm struck that fast.

Now figures collided with Moultrie and Moon

Shadow, fleeing through the darkness. A man slipped and bounced along the water-slick deck planking, rolled to his feet and ran on. Two other people crashed together, not seeing each other in the gloom, and then staggered around yelling and holding their faces. There seemed to be shapes everywhere in the dark, wet and glistening, fighting for shelter.

When the first lightning turned darkness into daylight, Moultrie had a feeling of déjà vu. Moon Shadow's face was intense before him. Her eyes were wide with terror. Moultrie seized her hand. They ran with the others, crowding, squeezing.

They tumbled down the gangway leading below. At the bottom, Moultrie pulled Moon Shadow from the mainstream. He carried her along a narrow corridor. They kicked up puffs of dust from a neglected and threadbare carpet which had once been elegant. They left behind lines of water drops trailing from their clothing.

Moultrie did not stop running and pulled her along until they were leaning against the door inside his tiny stateroom, both of them heaving. Once there, in the quiet and darkness, it was as though they had never been interrupted by a storm at all.

They collapsed on Moultrie's bed and waited to catch their breaths. After a few minutes, they were once again able to relax. They both looked at one another and began laughing—almost uncontrollably—at their sorry states.

"We'd better get out of these wet things," Moultrie advised.

He started to undress Moon Shadow, kissing her glistening skin as he did so.

When she stood naked before him, he grabbed a

towel and threw it to her. "Here, catch. Dry yourself before you get a chill."

"Why, yes, Mr. Ravenel," Moon Shadow replied in her best imitation of a southern accent.

Moultrie quickly got out of his own wet clothes and dried himself with the same towel Moon Shadow had used. Moon Shadow just stood there looking at him. "You are beautiful, white man," she whispered.

In one motion he swept her up and carried her to the bed.

"Make love to me, Ravenel."

This is it, he thought. At last. . . .

Chapter 20

"The passage of time cures infatuation. War and work are the only two antidotes to love." Uncle John had said that again and again. He had also said that "death is the only cure for lust." Moultrie was not certain which he was coming down with, love or lust. Maybe neither. Just in case, though, he gave himself a stiff dose of work.

He sent letters to John Page, Helen, the judge, Little Johnnie, his brother Henry, and a detailed report to Charles Madden in Washington about the dysentery, cholera infantum, diarrhea and bilious and congestive fevers plaguing the prisoners. "Muddy Mississippi drinking water, green fruit, exposure, cramped quarters, general filth and low spirits together are pretty devastating," he wrote. "The remarkable thing is that so far we have lost less than one in every three hundred. Most of these have been children."

At Jones' Landing, Cicero went ashore first while

Moultrie finished his report so that he could leave it for a steamboat carrying mail downriver. Coming out of his cabin, he saw six flatboats tied up above the three steamboats. Then he heard shouts and laughter.

"Dance, boy. Dance." A shot rang out. Then another and another. Someone was playing a lively tune on a mouth organ.

"What's going on?" Moultrie called to a deck hand up ahead.

"They got your slave," the man answered. Laughing, he added, "They're teaching him how to dance."

Moultrie bounded along the *Revenue*'s deck. On the dock below he saw Cicero circled by flatboat men and steamboat deck hands. He was dancing a jittery series of step-skip-jump movements. Someone was playing a harmonica. Cicero's footwork was in no way synchronized to the music. He stopped, breathless. A man fired a pistol ball into the planks just in front of Cicero's feet, saying, "Hurry up and dance some more or you ain't ever going to dance again."

Several other men were reloading their weapons. They had already served as Cicero's dancing masters.

Moultrie gritted his teeth. Damn them. His first inclination was to leap from the *Revenue* swinging and kicking and bring down as many as he could. No. He turned and strode back to his cabin. From his gun kit he took the double-barreled shotgun he used for duck hunting. He broke the gun open, loaded it with bird shot. Next he took out his brand-new Colt revolving-breech pistol. He could still hear the pistols banging to accompany Cicero's dance. The mouth organ played off key.

Moultrie trotted back along the side-wheeler's deck. He stopped above the men on the dock, steadied the shotgun on the rail, took slow aim, then squeezed off both barrels.

A man with his pistol ready to fire at Cicero's feet took one barrel in the seat of the pants. The harmonica player took the other; his instrument sailed high into the air and fell into the water.

Silence. The men in the circle turned, gazing up at Moultrie. Cicero stopped jumping and breathed heavily in relief.

"The next time, it won't be birdshot. It'll be pistol rounds. Who wants the first one?" Moultrie held his Colt easily on the rail.

No one answered back.

"All right, let the man go. Now!"

"Says who?" The man who asked stepped forward, his hands on his hips, his hat pushed back on his head.

Moultrie walked out into the glare at the railing. "I do."

"And who the hell are you?"

"I'm that man's owner. You've been messing with my property."

The man laughed. Turning, he said, "All right, men, let the boy go. I guess we just paid for our pleasure."

"Like hell, Jack," one of the men protested. "You ain't going to take that kind of guff off any damned aristocrat."

"And why not?" Jack retorted. "A man has a right to defend his own property."

"You didn't get your tail peppered like I did, Jack." Now the harmonica player was yelling.

Jack grinned. "Stop complaining, Joe. You've been bellyaching about your gas problem. Now you have plenty of holes to let it all out."

There were several guffaws. Cicero stood still, his face twitching in anger. "Go on, boy, get out of here." Jack waved him toward the boat. As Cicero made the gangway, Jack turned and shouted up to Moultrie, "You got your boy now. That's fair, seeing as he's yours." He spat, then continued. "But I don't take none too kindly to being shot at by a stranger, particularly when I'm just having fun. I expect you sort of owe me an apology, mister."

Moultrie grinned. "That's debatable."

"Why don't you come down here and debate it with me man to man?"

"When there are twenty or thirty of you?" Moultrie snorted.

"Now that isn't even nice, mister. Accusing me of wanting to get these here fellows to do my debating for me. Jack Slade don't let nobody talk for him."

"Neither do I, Mr. Slade. Neither do I. I'll be right down."

Moultrie handed his shotgun to Cicero. Then, stripping off his jacket, he strolled down the gangway.

Slade was at the bottom to greet him. "Pleased to meet you, mister. The name's Slade. Jack Slade. There isn't a 'gater, wildcat or whore between Cincinnati and Orleans who hasn't heard of me."

Moultrie shook Slade's hand, gripping harder, and harder as Slade did. "Even I've heard of you, Slade," he said. "It was a mosquito who told me you've got a tougher hide than a rhinoceros."

Laughing, Slade clapped Moultrie on the back. "He got it right, I reckon. I'm a wild horse, I sure am. I eat rattlesnakes for breakfast and comb my hair with porcupines. Yes, sir. When I go to hell, they're going to have to make a special fire for me. I don't burn like most folks." He gave his barking laugh again and clapped Moultrie once more on the back. "And who might you be, mister?"

Moultrie recognized Slade's stylized, bloated boasting as part of a traditional, if somewhat juvenile, ritual among men who worked the southern rivers. It was their way of challenging and dueling to demonstrate manhood. Though it sounded crude, Moultrie knew one should not be deceived by it. It was a code, a way of life to these men.

Any man who wanted acceptance on the river had to follow the code when challenged or he would never be taken seriously as a peer by river men. Taking this into consideration, Moultrie decided to play the game. He knew he was going to have to fight Jack Slade sooner or later. Win or lose, he knew he would be treated far better afterward if he fought on river men's terms.

And when he answered Slade, he spoke in river men's language.

"I'm a whirlwind. A rip-roaring, tail-twisting son of a gun. People call me Moultrie Ravenel."

Slade laughed. "I'll say it again, Moultrie Ravenel. Pleased to meet you."

The two were still gripping hands. Giving another squeeze, Slade said, "What say we stop squeezing and start grappling?" Letting go, he backed into the circle of men on the dock. Moultrie followed. Looking at him from across the ring, the flatboat man grinned. He took a deep breath, then suddenly bellowed, "Yahoo," and charged.

Moultrie danced aside. "What's the matter, Slade?" he called. "Your aim getting poor?"

"Stand still, you rabbit." Slade grinned wolfishly. "I'm no fox." With that, he charged again. Springing straight at the man, Moultrie was almost horizontal to the ground when he hit him with his shoulder and back. Grunting, the flatboat man grabbed at him but could not keep his balance. He sat down hard as Moultrie landed and danced out of reach.

"Told you I was a whirlwind. Had enough?"

Slade got up and shook his head, then started to circle. Moultrie feinted once, twice. The third time the flatboat man caught him. The man's strength was incredible. Moultrie felt himself being pressed backward and downward, felt his grip slipping. Behind him the men were cheering wildly.

Letting out a roar, Moultrie pretended to push hard against Slade, then slipped sideways and down on one knee. Braced for the push, the flatboat man was overbalanced. He fell forward hard. He let go of Moultrie with his right hand to break the fall. Catching the man's other arm with all of his weight, Moultrie broke his grip and swung behind him, bending and twisting the arm as he did. Gasping for breath, he called for Slade to give up.

"Never." The man surged to his knees. As he did so, Moultrie thrust upward against his arm and shoulder. Slade yelped in pain and reared backwards. Moultrie let go and danced back and away. As he staggered to his feet, the flatboat man's breath was ragged. His left arm hanging useless at his side, he shook his head to clear the sweat out of his eyes. The men forming the ring were silent. One of their own was being whipped by a stranger.

Slade circled. As he did, Moultrie came in jabbing. The flatboat man swung wide with his right, trying to grapple, and Moultrie stepped inside and drove a left uppercut to the jaw. Slade grunted and stepped back, spitting blood and a broken tooth.

"Hey, Jack," a voice from the circle rang out, "let me take over."

The flatboat man stopped and straightened. "No," he groaned, trying to smile, "Mr. Whirlwind Moultrie Ravenel's just beat me fair and square. I asked for it, and he gave it to me." With that, Slade came forward, his hand out. "Shake," he said, "and no squeezing."

Wiping the sweat from his eyes, Moultrie took his hand. They shook. "You're a bear, all right, Slade. I thought you were going to crush every bone in my body."

"If you'd just sat still long enough, I'd have been glad to oblige you." The flatboat man started to laugh, then stopped, gagging as he spat some more blood. Slade shook his head as he felt the gap in his teeth. "You haven't done much for my looks, I reckon," he drawled.

"The doctor'll fix you up. Come on." The two men, now walking arm in arm, moved slowly through the circle and up the gangway. By this gesture, Moultrie knew he had satisfied the requirements of the code and earned his place among river men.

Moultrie nodded to Captain Tobias Glenn and started to pass.

"Not so fast, Ravenel. You've wasted enough of my time. You can give me a moment now."

"What is it?"

"I just wanted to tell you that the next time you hold us up by fighting with the loaders, or any other way, we'll leave you. I don't care if you're wrestling Jacob. Time's money, and that's what makes this tub go. Understand?"

"Perfectly."

"Good." The captain started to turn away.

"Not so fast. I've listened to you, Glenn, now you listen to me."

"This is my boat, mister. I listen to who I damn well please." The captain turned to go again.

Moultrie blocked his path.

"Get out my way, or I'll have you removed. This is mutiny."

Moultrie grinned. "You want a mutiny? Think of the six hundred Indians you've got on board."

"All right what is it?"

"Just this. If anyone of your crew messes with my slave again, I'll have your head."

"If I don't get yours first. Threatening mutiny with Indians. Wait till Washington hears about this."

Moultrie raised his voice so that everyone within fifty feet could hear. "If you say to anyone that I threatened mutiny with Indians, then you're a liar, Captain Glenn, and I'll have to challenge you. All I said was that when you thought of mutiny, you'd better think about the possibility of the Indians on board mutinying. That's a very different thing."

The captain was suddenly white beneath his mutton chop sideburns. "All right," he returned, his voice low, "maybe I misunderstood you."

"Of course you misunderstood me." Moultrie's voice boomed as the captain winced.

Moultrie waited for Moon Shadow on deck that night after mess. How badly he wanted to hold her close. He was still tense from the fight and the confrontation with Captain Tobias Glenn. He wanted to make love with her and then sleep for a long time gripped tightly in her arms.

At the rail, he lit a long cigar, took comfort in its

strong and bitter smoke and looked out across the Mississippi River to the darkness of the forested shoreline.

Moultrie knew she was coming even before she appeared in the darkness. He heard her voice. There was impatience in it. Moultrie believed he heard her say something like, ". . . for the last time, no! And don't go running off on your own. I'll report you and stop you."

And he thought he heard a man denounce her as a traitorous snake on the bosom of her brother, Jim Henry. He recognized the voice. The man was Deer Warrior.

But Moultrie could not really be certain exactly what they were saying. The thumping of the steam engines and the wash of the side wheels made the actual words unclear. But the tone of their voices was not. In Deer Warrior's voice there had been bitterness.

God, Moultrie thought, once again there is misery aboard this vessel. He walked toward them. Deer Warrior saw Moultrie and suddenly walked off.

Moultrie went to her, pulled her to him, grabbed handfuls of her black hair and kissed her. He marveled at her. Each time was like the first time he had seen her. He was curious, though. Even as she kissed, she seemed distant. Mind and emotion were missing. Clearly, she was disturbed.

"What was the trouble with Deer Warrior?" Moultrie asked.

She held him at arm's length for a moment. Moultrie sensed she was wondering whether she should tell him. "I trust you," she answered finally. "You are not one of those who would punish him merely for his wild talk and anger. He wanted me to bring some of Jim Henry's band together and run with him south to the Texas country."

"Lord. And what did you tell him?"

"I told him, no. And he is angry now."

"All right, but why exactly."

"Because if I do not go, he cannot go, unless he goes alone."

"Why is that?"

"Because Jim Henry's people will not go without me. Or without Jim Henry himself. And Deer Warrior knows this. He has no influence over them. Or respect for them."

"Doesn't he know that he'd only put everyone in the middle of the war going on between the Mexicans, Americans, Comanches and Apaches? Deer Warrior is crazy."

"He is not." Moon Shadow pushed Moultrie gently away. "He is lost. And bitter. Yes, you have taken off his handcuffs and chains, but each time he sees a guard standing near him, he chokes. He is being eaten alive with frustration."

Moon Shadow erupted with anger, and Moultrie realized that there had been more causing her remoteness than one unpleasant scene with Deer Warrior.

"I am sick to death of you men and your petty honor. Fight, fight, fight. Must it always be that way?"

"What do you mean?" The bitterness in Moon Shadow's voice had startled him.

"Deer Warrior and his stupid hatred, my brother and his idiotic revolt, which killed him, you and that silly fight with that flatboat man this afternoon. It is always so unnecessary. You are not bucks in mating season. You are men. You have brains in your heads, not horns on them, although you do not often seem to remember the fact."

Moultrie was stung. "What the hell was I supposed to do this afternoon? Let them dance Cicero to death?"

"Not enjoy the fight. Don't tell me you did not."

"You were watching?"

"Of course I was watching." Biting her lip, Moon Shadow turned away. "Good night," she muttered.

Moultrie stared after her, his blood surging.

He reached for her. She swung around, anger boiling inside her tense body. Coldly, she warned, "Don't ever try to make love with me when I don't want to be touched."

Her sharp tongue sent a chill down his spine. He was at a loss for words.

Realizing the anguish her words had caused him, she soothed, "Please, Moultrie, I want you next to me, too. But right now I am too angry and full of contempt for men. Tomorrow I will probably want to throw myself into the river for having been so stubborn. But for now, I must act as I feel. And I feel too angry with men's foolishness to allow you or any other man to touch me. I hope you understand." And then she was gone.

To his own great surprise, Moultrie found that he did understand.

Chapter 21

Cicero had said, "I'll be glad to sleep on dry land. I sure will."

Hearing him, Moultrie had replied, "Why? So you can feed the chiggers and the ticks and sleep with snakes?" The truth of the matter was, though, he was as happy as anyone to disembark finally at Rock Roe after eight days on the Mississippi and White Rivers. Now he could take a real walk. Better still, he could go to bed without hearing the damned paddles splashing and the engines clanking all the time. Even wolves and coyotes howling would be better than the *Revenue*'s creaking and groaning, clanging and clunking.

Being on land was going to be nice. Getting there was not. Not because there was so much to take off. God knew the Indians had little enough, and there were only about forty barrels of stores. But how did you set up a camp when half the Indians and a fair number of their guards were glistening with fever sweat or shaking from dysentery.

And how did you set up a camp when you were called away from it to a meeting twenty minutes after you had come ashore? Yet that was what Sanford had done to Moultrie, Barry, Abadie, and the members of the removal company. Moultrie cursed. The last person in the world he wanted to see was Sanford. He had been avoiding the man for days. Well, there was nothing to do but go to the meeting. He grimaced at the thought.

Sanford avoided his eyes, even when he offered the ritual cigar. "Gentlemen," he began, looking at Lieutenant Wallace Barry, "the next couple of days are going to be busy. To begin with, we've got to hire carts to take the supplies and the sick in."

Dr. Eugene Abadie snorted. "If you're going to be taking the sick in carts, you'll have a train a mile long. I've got hundreds of cases, bad cases."

Sanford went on as if Abadie hadn't spoken. "Of course, we've only got a limited amount of money to spend on the carts."

"Of course." Moultrie did not even try to disguise his sarcasm. Lieutenant Barry coughed and shifted in his chair uncomfortably.

Ignoring Moultrie's response too, Sanford continued. "We can't stay here too long either. We've only got so many supplies with us and there's just so much we can spend for foodstuffs we buy from settlers along the way."

This time, Moultrie came from his chair to protest short rations. He was interrupted by shouts and cheers, followed by several loud splashes and then more cheering from down by the landing.

"What the devil is that?" Barry was up and on the way down the path. Moultrie and the others followed.

There were about six hundred Indians, mostly

Yuchis, milling around the water's edge. At their center stood Deer Warrior, a triumphant smile on his face.

"What happened?" The question came from Barry.

One of the guards answered. "We were up there at the camp showing these people where to put stuff when we heard this here shouting. I got down just in time to see them rolling a couple of barrels down into the water."

"Those were the barrels with the handcuffs and chains in them?" Moultrie asked, stepping forward from behind Barry.

"Yes," the guard answered, spitting out a stream of tobacco juice. "Can't say as I blame them, neither."

"Neither can I." Moultrie heard Barry mutter the words behind him.

Back in the meeting, Sanford was indignant. "Barry," he admonished, "your men should keep better watch. That should never have happened."

"Mr. Sanford," the lieutenant replied, "if you want us to serve as guards, let us be guards. Don't ask us to be nursemaids and storekeepers, too. I have only a small platoon to watch over twenty-five hundred people, and half of that platoon is coming down with fever. We're spread too thin to guard them and be responsible for their supplies and transport, too."

"If I were in command of your platoon—" Sanford began, only to be interrupted by Barry.

"Well, you're not, sir. I am. Can we get back to the business of the meeting now?"

Sanford did not like the rebuke. But he was wise enough to drop the matter, Moultrie noticed. Slapping one knee, Sanford cleared his throat. "Now," he began again, "we've got to keep the Indians from stealing from settlers on the march or we're going to have big trouble. What do you suggest?"

"There is only one way," Moultrie stated emphatically. The others waited. "Get the chiefs together, explain the problem and let them decide what they want to do." As Moultrie spoke, he looked carefully at Sanford for the first time since coming ashore. He wanted Sanford to believe his suggestion. "I'll speak to them if you want."

Barry leaned forward. "What if they aren't going to be vigilant enough, Moultrie? I don't want settlers telling me how to do my job, too."

Moultrie grinned. "Don't worry," he assured, glancing at Sanford. "For the chance to police themselves instead of being policed, I'll bet they'll do whatever's necessary."

Sanford's voice, when he spoke, was taut with his effort at self-control. "You've every reason to be concerned, Lieutenant Barry," he agreed, "but I have to admit Moultrie is right. If we have trouble, then we'll just have to do something else. I don't think we will, though." He turned toward Moultrie again. "Thanks for your offer to go and talk to the chiefs, Moultrie. It's a good idea. I suspect they'll take more kindly to the notion if it comes from you."

Moultrie stood up. "I'll do it. Is there anything else?"

"Not tonight anyway." Getting to his feet, Sanford nodded to the group. "Thank you, gentlemen."

It seemed only a few minutes later that Cicero was shaking Moultrie awake. Moultrie groaned and sat up. God, but he felt like a pincushion. How many mosquitoes had gotten under the netting with him last night? It must have been hundreds. Moultrie shook his head. Most likely, there had been two or three. However many, the little buggers sure had done a job.

Worse than the mosquito bites was the heat. At six in the morning, when Cicero had waked him, it had already been hot. And it grew hotter. By lunchtime Moultrie felt as though he had been boiled. It did not begin to cool until late in the afternoon. Watching the Indians playing ball then, Moultrie shook his head. You would not catch me out there on a day like today, Moultrie thought.

Cheering along with other spectators, Moultrie did not hear Barry come up. The lieutenant touched his sleeve. "Moultrie, can I see you for a second?"

"What's up?"

"Liquor."

"Christ."

Deer Warrior and a few other Indians were out cold. There were a dozen more sitting on the ground, leaning against trees or weaving back and forth, staring straight ahead with pained looks of concentration on their faces. They were drunk, yes, but trying to keep a grip on control and dignity. Seeing them, Moultrie felt a surge of anger. "How'd it happen?" He asked the question through clenched teeth.

"You were helping us run whiskey sellers out of camp this morning. Well, this afternoon, this fellow comes into camp, says he and a neighbor, knowing what alcohol does to Indians, came to warn us of the demon spirit in the camp."

"Those Indians didn't get drunk by eating words."

"No, they didn't. Let me finish the story. I'm standing there thanking these fellows for their concern when an Indian comes up to me and says these same fellows have a wagon back in the woods where their confederate is selling the stuff."

"You're joking," Moultrie laughed. "Where are these entrepreneurs now?"

"I've got them hard at work. Under the gun. Come see."

There were three men. Each one had an axe and was smashing in the ends of kegs mounted on the wagon. Corn whiskey was dripping between the planks of the wagon to the ground. Another keg burst open. Moultrie danced aside as the liquid cascaded over the tailgate.

"Phew." Moultrie held his nose. "I wouldn't light a match around here."

One of the settlers stopped to wipe his brow. As he did, the guard standing beside him poked him in the thigh with a bayonet. "You don't need no rest now, mister. Keep at it."

The settler looked resentfully at the soldier, but picked up his axe again.

Moultrie walked up to one settler. Barry had told him he was the leader. "Howdy," Moultrie greeted.

The man glared at him.

"Good year for corn?"

The man said nothing.

"How much you make on a keg?"

Still nothing.

Grabbing the man by the lapels, Moultrie threw him back against the side of the wagon. "I'm talking to you, mister."

"Just you wait. The governor's going to hear about this." The man spat out the words.

"Hear what?" Moultrie was shouting in the man's face. "That you're trying to get our Indians drunk, so that they'll mutiny and run over your precious governor's state?"

"If you can't control your savages, that's your

problem." The man grinned. "I'm just a businessman selling something people want."

"You're a swine." Moultrie dropped the man's lapels. "Get out of here. All of you."

The man started.

"First, though, pay back everything the Indians gave you for whiskey."

"That's robbery."

Moultrie grinned. He turned to Lieutenant Barry. "Wally, we've got three choices, it seems to me. We can turn these men over to the Indians for their punishment."

"You wouldn't." There was outrage in the settler's voice.

Moultrie ignored the interruption. "Or," he continued, "we can accept their generous offer of their cart. Or they can pay us back what they made."

"There's a fourth choice," Barry said evenly. "We could arrest them for trespassing, illegal sale of spirits, conspiracy and disobeying military orders on a military post. That's for openers. I can find more charges."

"Hell, Wally, you don't want to do that. They'd be in prison for the rest of their lives."

"That wouldn't be so bad."

"Bad! Have you seen the rats? Me, I'd rather be turned over to the Indians. At least they kill you quick. In about a week or two."

The settlers left Moultrie their wagon.

Moultrie wrote to Captain John Page a few days later.

Even paying what the thieving suppliers ask, getting enough carts has been almost impossible. We have been here a week and have gotten only twenty. That number is not half enough, but we cannot risk staying any longer. Someone is certain to find ways to bring whiskey to the Indians again. There is much profit in whiskey. The Creeks sustained their dignity and basically behaved well during their first binge. But they are ready to explode in their anger and resentment of us. I fear whiskey could release violence, and then there would be bloodshed and more fighting. It seems that the things said about Indians not holding liquor well are true, although I do wonder if the generalization is not merely a self-fulfilling prophecy. Everyone gets out of hand when they drink too much. Anyway, Page, if I have to bust open any more whiskey kegs, I shall be drunk and unruly myself, just breathing the air in this camp.

The column moved out shortly thereafter traveling at night. John Sanford had decided that the days were too hot and exhausting for the journey.

Cicero commented wryly to Moultrie, "If God had wanted men to travel at night he would have given us eyes to see in the dark."

"What does God want men to do at night?" Moultrie asked.

"Bed down with as many women as he can. Me, I'd just like enough time to bed down with just one woman."

Moultrie knew Cicero was speaking of Red Wing. She had finally accepted Cicero and had slept with him on the trail. Cicero had not mentioned the change.

Moultrie understood why. The relationship was new and fragile. Red Wing might change her mind.

"I share the predicament, Cicero," Moultrie confessed. It was true. Moving at night as they were, Moultrie found little time to be with Moon Shadow.

During the days, while others sheltered themselves beneath the wagons from the intense sun, there seemed to be no time either. There were always conflicts to resolve, stores to be tended, sick to be treated. And in addition, Moultrie found he had to police Sanford and his men to keep them honest. He found them short-rationing the Creeks often. He had many face to face confrontations in forcing them to give what they were supposed to give.

Nonetheless, at dawn, between the end of the night march and the beginning of the day's demands, Moultrie and Moon Shadow found time to be together.

One morning, beside a ravine with a stream running along the bottom, Moultrie pressed a finger to her lips and said, "No talk, we do not have time for talk." Moon Shadow grinned. She liked his directness. They dropped their clothing where they stood. Then they embraced and allowed themselves to sink to the grass at the lip of the ravine.

But there had been times at dawn when all they did was talk. . . .

"I know so little of what you have been and what you have done," Moon Shadow said. "A man such as you, who loves women and needs a woman so much. . . . Why are you here instead of being settled down with one woman?"

"I do not have a woman at home," Moultrie answered. "Not any longer." He had never told Moon Shadow about Helen.

Moon Shadow did not believe him. She said that all men had women who were special, somewhere.

Moultrie felt it was time to tell Moon Shadow about his relationship with Helen Dupré. He described Helen's great beauty and how she had stirred him. He told, too, of his inability to settle down, of the months when they had grown apart, and of the awkward ending to their relationship. Then he made a confession that he had not yet made even to himself. "Looking back, I wonder if we really did love each other."

"Why?"

"Because," he said haltingly, "saying good-bye, when it finally came to that, was so easy."

"That's no explanation."

Moultrie grinned. "You're right." He paused to gather his thoughts. "I guess what I mean is that as Helen came to understand me, and I her, we no longer seemed so close. In fact, the deeper our understanding grew, the farther apart we seemed to grow. By the time we said good-by, we each saw a different person than we had seen when we thought we were in love."

"You're a romantic fool," Moon Shadow laughed. She stopped as suddenly as she had begun when Moultrie asked her if she had a man.

At first, she said nothing. Then she stood and turned away from Moultrie. "He's dead." She let out a long sigh. "Killed in that hopeless war."

She looked across the ravine at the horizon, where the sun had started to come up. "I do not understand this Helen you speak of. I do not think I understand you, either. I lost a man before we had time to know each other. You and this Helen had time and lost each other anyway. Such a waste." She shook her head. "Can you explain this to me?"

Moultrie could not. He was sad. For the first time

he felt they were touching upon the basic differences of their separate worlds. He told her this.

"Differences in some things, yes. But is not love the same for both? And knowing love a part of it? What differences could be so great? Tell me."

If you have to ask, he thought, you'll probably never know.

Chapter 22

"The dust and the heat and the mosquitoes are not the worst of things out here," Moultrie wrote to Henry Ravenel.

The damned locals. Out here they are called sandshakers. They are the worst. The whiskey they sell is poison. The carts they lease are deathtraps. Their version of the Ten Commandments is a mockery. Thou shalt love thyself before all others. Thou shalt take from thy mother and thy father whatever thou canst before thy brother does. Thou shalt love thy neighbor's wife, pigs, ducks, cows and everything else he owns that moves. Thou shalt do unto others whatever thou canst get away with. Thou shalt steal. Thou shalt rape. Thou shalt murder. Thou shalt worship no god but the golden eagle.

Sandshakers do have one redeeming

quality. Unlike most we know, these people obey their Ten Commandments to the letter.

In another letter, to Charles Madden at the Bureau of Indian Affairs, Moultrie wrote,

> We have had very little trouble from the Indians, which is an irony, since the Indians were supposed to give us the most trouble. There have been some petty thefts. These were quickly dealt with according to the law as set down by the chiefs.

Moultrie did not explain that he had witnessed one such punishment, the brutality of which had made him ill.

It had been at a stopover not even marked on some of their maps. It was known simply as Mrs. Black's.

For what the place lacked in importance, Mrs. Black herself compensated in size. Moultrie estimated her weight at three hundred pounds plus.

The public house this grossly overweight and unwashed woman kept on the Big Prairie midway between Rock Roe and Little Rock was little more than two pens with a short trot in between for her dogs.

Moultrie remarked to Barry, "The place could do without the trot, too. Don't go near it. More fleas there than anyplace I've seen except maybe for one inn outside Tuscaloosa."

Much later, Moultrie said he couldn't imagine there being anything worth stealing at Mrs. Black's. As it turned out, there was. To one Indian woman, at any rate.

That morning, one of Mrs. Black's daughters

came charging from the smokehouse while the Creek column was camped nearby. Screaming for her mother, she said some thieving savages had made off with their hams.

Mrs. Black was going to send a messenger to the governor, call out the militia and complain to the President of the United States if the thief was not found and flogged, and if someone did not pay for the hams.

As it turned out, the thief was not hard to find. Flower Sun, another sister of the deceased Crazy Wolf, was found before her shelter, openly feeding ham to Little Hawk and his brother Fast Raven as quickly as she could tear meat from bone.

Moultrie was the one who found her. And he knew exactly what he was going to do next.

Take the ham from her. Feed the boys himself. And then, if discovered, say that he had found the ham partly eaten where the thief had probably taken fright and discarded it. Well, he figured he might as well give the rest to the boys and pay Mrs. Black for her ham.

Moultrie felt the lie would be acceptable to everyone. He prayed it would be. He wanted to spare Flower Sun the punishment he knew would come from the Creek chiefs if it was not.

However, Flower Sun misunderstood. She saw Moultrie only as someone trying to take away the meat. She slammed the ham down hard on top of his head and said that no one was going to take this food from her nephews.

The tug of war that ensued was seen by everyone.

Later, the chiefs of the tribunal asked Flower Sun to explain how she came to possess the stolen ham. Proud defiance showing on her face, Flower Sun recalled how she had kicked Mrs. Black's watchdog in the head and deliberately stolen the ham to feed her nephews, as she had promised her brother Crazy Wolf she would feed them

The chiefs said she must accept the penalty for the theft. Moultrie wanted to speak for Flower Sun. He did not, in the end. The chiefs themselves had decreed the punishment in their agreement on the rules of the march. They had promised to police themselves. Honor forbade their breaking the promise. They could have no mercy, even for the sister of one of their greatest chiefs.

And Flower Sun herself said she would have things no other way.

The chiefs summoned all Creeks on the march. They stripped Flower Sun to her waist. They asked whether she wished to be tied to a post for support. She said she would not, that she would stand alone until the punishment was done.

Then one of the chiefs began the twenty lashes. The whip was a leather braid ten feet long. It cracked against her back and came around her torso on each stroke, leaving a red welt each time.

Flower Sun fell only once during the beating. She never cried out at all.

Later, Moultrie paid for the stolen ham and bought two more. He carried one and Cicero the other to Dr. Eugene Abadie's tent. Abadie was dabbing ointment on Flower Sun's red, swollen flesh. Moultrie and Cicero placed the hams beside her.

"To share with all the others," Moultrie told her. "They belong to you. You have earned them."

Flower Sun accepted Moultrie's gift. Moultrie thought he saw her smile, just a little, in triumph.

Little Hawk and Fast Raven were there. Fast Raven was sniffling. Little Hawk simply stared at Moultrie, then turned away. Moultrie put his hand on the boy's shoulder. Little Hawk punched it.

"Now what did you do that for?" Cicero asked softly in the boy's own Creek tongue. "The man brought a gift saying he is sorry for what was done. You don't do that when a man brings a gift from his heart."

In answer, Little Hawk scooped up a handful of dusty dirt, then let it flow between his fingers over the two hams.

"Boy," Cicero said, "you're acting as though Marse Moultrie himself done the whipping. It was your people who did it."

"He is the one who found her." Little Hawk's voice was fierce.

"Yes. And then he tried to take the ham and pretend he had found it, so your aunt, Flower Sun, would not be punished for feeding *you*, boy. You."

"That is true, Little Hawk," Flower Sun told him. "I did not understand. I fought to keep the ham. He is a good man." She suddenly appeared very old and weary to Moultrie. Yet she was probably not older than thirty, he thought.

Little Hawk turned, an expression of hostility still locked on his face. "Is this true?"

Moultrie nodded.

"Then in the name of my father I say that I am sorry for my ingratitude. I shall clean the dirt from the hams."

Forgiving but not forgetting, Moultrie thought.

Moultrie reported to Sanford on the outcome of

the theft, just as the removal agent had instructed him to.

It was hours before Moultrie saw Cicero again. When he did, Cicero was in a volcanic mood.

"All right, what is it?"

"Deer Warrior is as much trouble as ever," Cicero fumed. "He stopped me near the blacksmith's tent and asked in a way he knew would rile me what I thought about Indians getting whipped like slaves. I tried to tell him black people aren't the only ones who get whipped for stealing. Back home, I've seen white men whipped in public for it."

"And?"

Cicero sighed. "It wasn't the woman being whipped for stealing that he was really mad about anyway, it turns out. After I said I'd seen white men get whipped, he came out with it. He said he would whip me the same way Flower Sun was if I didn't stop it with Red Wing."

"Don't turn your back on that rival."

"It's not even that he wants Red Wing for himself, really, you know? He said that slaves are slaves and they aren't supposed to mix with his Creek people, only work for them. Like slaves."

"What did you say then?"

"Then? Nothing. I decided it was best to say nothing." Cicero reflected, then added, "He was looking for a fight. He's going to keep looking. One day I may have to give him one."

"You'll do what you have to do when the time comes," Moultrie counseled. "And when you do, try to make sure it's on your terms, not his. You know that if you don't do it that way, you'll never have any peace."

Cicero nodded. He knew.

*   *   *

Later, Moultrie reassessed his judgment of Deer Warrior. He had once told Lieutenant Wallace Barry he believed Deer Warrior would threaten but would not overtly act. He still respected and feared his Creek chiefs.

The whipping of Flower Sun had demonstrated the intentions of the chiefs to enforce obedience among their own in honoring their agreements with the United States government.

But, considering the incident with Cicero and the fact that Deer Warrior recently had been drinking heavily, Moultrie's uncertainty and concern deepened.

Where was he finding the whiskey? And, Moultrie wondered, where was he getting the money to pay for it?

They moved from Mrs. Black's, past Little Rock, then west along the turgid brown stretches of the Arkansas River, past Cadron and Lewisburg and the old Dwight mission. They passed over Illinois Bayou, rolled beneath the looming mass of Spadra Bluff, then crossed the Illinois River into elm forests of brutal, unending heat.

Night after night they moved. Day after day they sweated, swatted insects and tried to sleep.

Cicero, not given to complaining, decided to start as he and Moultrie bathed in a stagnant pond that left more dirt on their bodies than it washed off. "My feet are hurting bad. Red Wing is too tired for anything but sleep. I shall be happy to see an end to this marching, marching, marching. If we march much longer we are going to be halfway to heaven before we get a chance for joy on this earth."

*   *   *

Chuckling, Moultrie repeated what Cicero had said when he talked to Moon Shadow late that afternoon.

She laughed. "I have been ready to stop walking ever since we started."

"And to think, when I was a boy, I always looked forward to traveling." Moultrie shook his head.

"You did it lots?"

Breaking off a leaf and pitching it into the little creek below, Moultrie watched as it was sucked into an eddy and whirled around before being pulled under. "Every spring and fall." He smiled at the memory.

"Tell me."

"The family used to go in the summer to an island off the coast away from the swamps and fevers. It was wonderful. We'd be packing for weeks. Boxes and boxes. Food, clothes, books, my father's violin. Enough to stay until the first frost. I'd get so excited I could hardly stand it."

"Why?"

Moultrie laughed. "I was a little boy. Going there meant adventure. And the island was a paradise for me. Sand dunes to gallop over. Surf to fish in. Besides, half the summer I was free from schoolwork. My brother and I had all day to explore, hunt, fish, playing at being Indians."

Moon Shadow shook her head. She took her feet out of the water and stretched her legs, then lay back and closed her eyes against the sun. "Your world is so foreign to me," she admitted. "When you talk about it, it sounds unreal, like places storytellers talk about."

She felt Moultrie's eyes gazing at her breasts. Leaning over, he wrapped his arm around her and kissed her softly.

"No." Moon Shadow pushed him back. "Not now. Not here. Later." She smiled and reached up to trace the lines around his mouth. "I want to be with you alone, not where we're going to be stepped on by fifty people. And I want us to have time, not to have to rush because the column is moving out in twenty minutes."

Time. There was precious little of it. Cicero had been right, Moultrie thought. Walking sure got in the way of living.

The marching, night in and night out, made things difficult enough. For a while, politics made things impossible. Not white politics this time, but Indian politics. Word arrived in the form of a letter from General Robert Arbuckle. It was sent from his headquarters at Fort Gibson on the northwestern edge of the Indian Territory. It caught Sanford, Moultrie, Barry and everyone by surprise.

"We have a potential civil war on our hands," Arbuckle wrote.

"What the hell does he mean, civil war?" Lieutenant Wallace Barry looked around the table. Everyone had the same question.

"That's why I called this meeting, to tell you all that I myself know." Sanford looked up from the letter. "The general is very specific."

Moultrie sat up. He clenched his teeth to stifle a yawn. He wished John Sanford had remembered the ritual cigars. Strong smoke would help keep him awake. He needed something to cure his weariness.

Being with Moon Shadow during the day and marching all night is grinding me down, he reflected. He covered another yawn. I must break the pattern

and sleep for a couple of days. My work is suffering.
But Lord, what a way to suffer.

He realized that no one was talking. All were
watching his battle with sleep.

"Sorry to keep you awake, Moultrie." Barry was
teasing him. "We all know you're putting in a lot of
overtime these days. But you don't have to flaunt her
by falling asleep on us."

Moultrie was now serious and wide awake. "And
what the hell do you mean by that, Wallace?"

"Moultrie, Moultrie," Barry soothed. "We're all
envious as hell of your splendid Indian woman. Any
one of us would gladly be so fatigued for so good a
reason."

So they knew. He was surprised. He had hoped
no one would have noticed. He should have known
better.

Everyone at the table laughed. Even Sanford.

"Back to business," the removal agent grumbled,
clearing his throat. "This is the problem, according to
Arbuckle:

> "At a meeting at the Creek agency yes-
> terday, August fourteenth, Chief Roley
> McIntosh and his council decided that they
> would not submit to government by the new
> arrivals."

Sanford looked up. "That's our Indians," he said, then
read aloud again:

> "McIntosh and company have threatened
> resistance. They mean it. To forestall trou-
> ble, I've written to Governor Jones at Little

Rock asking Arkansas for ten companies of
volunteers. I ask you to come and confer
with me at Fort Gibson as fast as you can,
and for God's sake, ahead of the main body
of your removal column. Something has to
be worked out. And by God, something will
be worked out."

Sanford was finished reading. He looked up. "Any
comments, gentlemen?"

Moultrie was suddenly no longer sleepy. The news
of possible renewed conflict had jolted him. "When
does this diplomatic mission leave and who goes on
it?" he asked.

"I had hoped you'd ask," said Sanford. "You and
me, Moultrie. It has to be you and me."

"And that's what I hoped your answer would be,"
Moultrie returned.

"But do you think you can manage to tear yourself away for a few days?"

Moultrie was puzzled by the question. "I don't
have anything going on here that someone else can't
handle for a few days." Then he grinned, realizing Sanford had been teasing him about Moon Shadow as
Barry had done. They were all laughing once more.

Moultrie trotted to Moon Shadow with the news.
He wished it could have been more cheerful.

She was there, waiting, a smile on her face.

Moultrie told her about the letter from Arbuckle.
"I'll be gone a week, at least."

"That's not so bad." She tried to sound positive,
but her smile was gone.

"Yes, it is."

"Just think how good it will be to see each other again after a week."

"Parting is not such sweet sorrow." Moultrie shook his head. "It's rubbish." Then he laughed. "At least I won't have to take Wally's humor for a week." He told her about the lieutenant's teasing at the meeting. Her face lit up in amusement.

Moultrie reached forward, feeling her smooth face with his hands. They kissed lightly and quickly, then slowly and tenderly. Moon Shadow lay back with a sigh, pulling Moultrie down on top of her. He looked down into her eyes, kissed her face, then eased down to caress her breasts.

Moon Shadow ran her fingers through his hair. Suddenly throwing her arms around his neck, she kissed him again, this time fiercely.

She had been right, Moultrie thought. He would have to get used to her boldness.

Later, as they lay side by side, the sun drying their perspiration, Moultrie realized how much he was going to miss her.

"You've become far more than just a physical comfort for me," he told her. "I want you here when I come back, for the comforts and rewards of the spirit you give me as well." He hesitated. "I think you'll miss me that way, too."

She studied the clouds and did not answer.

"It's all right," Moultrie soothed. "You once said it would be hard for you to commit yourself. You don't have to say it now." But her reticence frustrated him.

He had to defuse his depression. Finally, Moultrie

said, "I want us to make love one more time now. I want the memory of you to burn in me."

"Good," Moon Shadow said. She looked straight into his eyes. "I was thinking the same thing. I want very much to make love with you once more."

Chapter 23

"I'm going to be leaving for the Indian Territory tonight," Moultrie told Cicero. "I'll be gone a week. You should stay and watch out for Little Hawk and his brother."

"Did you think I'd do anything else?"

"No. I knew you wouldn't. I'm just saying it, that's all."

Cicero smiled. "We're going fishing tomorrow. They like fishing now."

Moultrie grinned, remembering a different time and two different boys who had learned to like fishing. "Remember, Cicero? On the Cooper River back home? We were on that river, or back in the swamp, all the time."

It had worried his mother a great deal. Moultrie recalled the fight she and his father once had about their adventuring and fishing. It was one of the few bitter arguments he had ever recalled his parents having.

Stephen Ravenel had been on the boys' side. "Let

them grow up, Elizabeth," he had argued. "They'll never be able to look after themselves unless they learn how."

"Are they going to teach themselves?" Elizabeth had been sarcastic. "Are they going to kill themselves in this life, so they'll know what not to do the next time around?"

It had gone back and forth. Finally, Stephen had compromised. "I'll send Bram with them, all right?" Elizabeth had agreed. Bram was Cicero's father. And Bram taught the boys—Moultrie, Henry and Cicero— how to set traps, how to recognize good fishing holes and how to track small game and birds.

"We ever going back there?" Cicero had a distant look in his eyes.

"Someday." Moultrie shook his head. He slapped his leg and stood up. "Now I've got to get on the trail."

There was a squad of soldiers going along with Sanford and Moultrie. Finding mounts for all of them had been hard. The "diplomatic delegation," as Barry was calling it, could not take the cart horses, and the guards that had been left with the main column needed some mounts. That meant renting more horses. The removal agent was in a foul humor about it. "How the hell," Sanford asked as the delegation rode out, "am I going to pay for all of this?"

Moultrie shook his head. "You should have made a higher bid, John."

"And lost the contract." Sanford's tone was savage. "Lost it to a shark who would have made a hell of a lot more per head than me. All at the expense of the Indians."

"Of course, you're doing it purely for humanitarian reasons," Moultrie teased. Yet, despite the cheating, the deck collapsing on the barge and killing

Little Hawk's sister, he had to admit that Sanford was doing a better job as removal agent for the Indians than a lot of others might have done. "Besides, John, you can rent the horses again." Moultrie grinned. "Rent them to another removal company."

Sanford laughed. "I always did think that you were a wise guy, Moultrie."

"Judge Dupré told me I was wasting my talents trying to be Mr. Nice Guy."

"He might have had something there." Sanford fell silent. They rode another five miles before he suddenly asked, "Hobson going to marry the Dupré girl, you think?"

Moultrie clenched his teeth. "I don't know." Inwardly he hoped to hell not.

He remembered Helen's angry defense of the merchant, and also the way she said she would do anything, absolutely anything, to protect her father's health and happiness. Reflecting on this, he despaired. Then he recalled other things: Helen's common sense, her perception, her good judgment. Surely, she would come to see Hobson as he really was. She would not, could not, be fooled by his smoothness. She would see what a snake he was.

Even so, he was left with nagging questions. Would Helen marry Hobson because her father was in debt to the man? Moultrie just did not know. He did not think Helen would sell herself like that, but she might if she thought she was helping her father. Well, she might not realize what kind of man Hobson was until it was too late.

They rode on in silence, making good time. When they got to Fort Gibson, General Robert Arbuckle told them they had arrived within a day of the courier.

The general was relieved to see them. "Roley

McIntosh is too used to being the boss. He's damned if he's going to give it up," Arbuckle told them. "The man really resents the way some of the chiefs in your party, Sanford, treated him and his brother back in Alabama and Georgia."

"What do we do?" Sanford's fatigue could be heard in his gruff voice. Fourteen hours in the saddle every day to get to Fort Gibson had been killing. Sanford turned to Moultrie. "You got any suggestions?"

The Indian agent shook his head. "We could put new arrivals in different parts of the reservation, but frankly, I don't see how long we could keep the groups separate. There'd be quarrels over boundaries and so on, sure as shootin'."

"Hell," grunted Arbuckle, "we've got them already. Under the surface. McIntosh is strong enough to keep the lid on, but he might choose to make trouble, if only to flex his muscles for us."

"So what do we suggest to these chiefs when they meet with McIntosh and his people?" Sanford asked.

"First," Moultrie interjected, "we need to know what McIntosh will accept." As he spoke, he puffed on a cigar. Sanford had remembered them this time, thank God. Moultrie could hardly keep his eyes open.

Arbuckle cleared his throat. "That's the problem. He isn't going to compromise." The general suddenly grinned. "Hell, the man's a McIntosh. Those bleeders don't know how to bend. I ought to know. My great-grandfather was fighting them back during the 1745 uprising in Scotland."

Moultrie shook his head. "If McIntosh isn't going to give, General, it looks as though we're going to have to bludgeon Eneah Mathla, Eneah Micco and the other chiefs in our party into letting McIntosh have his way."

"It does, doesn't it?"

Moultrie rubbed his eyes with the heels of his palms. They itched and burned from saddle fatigue. "You want us to tell the chiefs that they won't get their government allowance unless they cooperate?"

"Do we have any other choice?" Arbuckle looked from Moultrie to Sanford and back again.

"No." Moultrie hated to say so, but Arbuckle was right.

Withholding the allowance would be cruel, but it would work. The Indians would have to swallow it. They could not afford not to. They did not have plows, axes, horses, corn seed. All they had were a few pieces of pottery, jewelry and some clothes. They were totally at the government's mercy.

Sanford and Arbuckle were pleased. Moultrie was in a sour mood. The whole business graveled him. The poor Indians had had to swallow so much already. It did not help to think about it, though. He would think of something else.

Moon Shadow. God, he wanted her. He admitted he wanted to make love to her, but he also wanted to talk to her, be with her. You're beginning to sound like a lovesick boy, he thought.

He and Cicero were both fools. Neither had any business being involved with an Indian woman. Least of all, himself. He couldn't bring her back to Forest Hall. What would Helen and Judge Dupré think? And even if he ignored them and the rest of society, how could Moon Shadow possibly live there? She'd said herself that Moultrie's world was foreign to her. No, it was impossible. Come next summer, he'd be saying good-bye. Moon Shadow would marry Little Johnnie or some other Indian and Moultrie and Cicero would go back to Alabama.

Helen was not the only eligible woman in the

state. Moultrie would find one to marry someday, a woman to be a lover and a friend like Moon Shadow, but also the mother of his children, the mistress of his plantation, and a hostess at dinners and balls. Yes, and with her to enrich his life at Forest Hall he would go back to planting, maybe run for the district legislature and raise a few horses. Wasn't that the life he had always imagined for himself? It was a good life, a solid life and a comfortable life. But there was one more thing about it. He would die of boredom from it.

When Moultrie rode into the Indian camp, a smile played across his lips. He spoke to Cicero and Little Hawk. They had had no luck fishing, but had enjoyed themselves.

He spoke to Barry, too. Barry's first question was, "Get much rest while you were gone, Moultrie?"

But where was Moon Shadow? No one could, or would, tell him. He looked for her everywhere. She couldn't have just disappeared, he thought. This camp isn't that big. She's avoiding me. Maybe she's hurt, has fallen out of the column. No, someone would have said something. She must be hiding.

He looked from group to group scattered around him. There, on the right, was one woman with her back to him, huddled in a shawl despite the heat. It was Moon Shadow. Moultrie called to her. At first she looked as if she was going to try and flee, but then she shrugged, stood up and turned around.

"My God." Moultrie was horrified at the bruises and scrapes on her face. "What happened to you?"

"I fell."

"The hell you did." Moultrie looked more closely. "You've been beaten. Badly."

"No, I. . . ."

"Who did it?"

"I am not going to say." Moon Shadow looked Moultrie in the eye for the first time. Taking a deep breath, she said, "It does not concern you."

"Is this why you've been avoiding me?"

"Yes. I knew you were going to ask questions."

Moultrie tried to keep calm. He could not. "Damn it, Moon Shadow," he exploded, "you couldn't hide forever."

"Long enough for this to get better." She touched the bruise at her temple and winced. "I thought."

"Have you seen Dr. Abadie?"

"Of course not."

"Do I take you to him, or bring him to you?"

"Neither," Moon Shadow insisted. "There is nothing he can do for bruises."

"Are you hurt elsewhere?"

She shook her head. "No, just where everyone can see."

"I've got to admit that you're noticeable," he said sternly. He wanted to know what had happened that had caused her to be beaten so badly.

"So now I disgust you," she said. She covered her face with her hands so he could not see. "But that was his intent, I suppose. To disgust you."

The revelation was painful. He had prayed that the truth would be that she had fallen off a horse. But somehow he had known that someone had beaten her.

"Whose intent?" he asked, measuring the words and controlling his temper. "Who did it to you?"

Moon Shadow shook her head. The motion hurt and she winced. "I won't tell you. It was a mistake to even hint there was someone. I was off guard." She covered her face. "I am so happy you have returned, Moultrie."

"Why won't you tell me?"

"What would you do?"

"Talk to him calmly. Ask him for an explanation. And unless he had one that would satisfy God Himself, I'd open up his face."

"And cause great trouble and maybe killing. All because you want revenge. Just who do you think you are, Moultrie? I am the one that is hurt. What right have you to revenge? If anyone has right, it is me. And I choose not to seek it. My bruises will heal easily. The trouble would not."

Moultrie ground one toe into the gravel. He could not look at her. He could not even speak further to her for fear he would lose control and shout at her, his rage was so intense.

He wanted to know who had beaten her. He wanted to know the reasons. He knew she would not tell him. "All right," he said, feeling awful. "Have things your way. You won't tell me, so there's nothing I can do. I have no choice. But one day I'll find out."

"By then you will not be so angry, and it may not matter."

"I'll always be angry. It will always matter."

"Then I hope you never learn." She touched his cheek gently. "If you hurt one person because of this, you would involve many and cause even more hurt. Moultrie, I need to be alone with you. Please, make me forget this ever happened. Hold me."

Moultrie held her tightly in his arms as she wept.

Chapter 24

The huge column of Indians was on the move once more. It alternately bunched up in sections and then thinned out with no observable pattern, resembling a caterpillar inching along.

Moultrie was still greatly disturbed by the beating of Moon Shadow. He was frustrated by her refusal to name the one who had brutalized her. There seemed to be no end to the problems surrounding the Creek Indian removal.

He decided to put some distance between himself and everyone else. He wanted solitude. He had had none for many weeks.

He told Lieutenant Wallace Barry he was going to ride ahead for about ten miles to reconnoiter the route of march, and that he would report back if he saw anything which would pose a problem. Otherwise he would simply stop and wait for the column someplace down the road.

Barry observed that they had never sent scouts

out so far ahead before on the march. "What's the need now?" he asked.

"Don't question it," Moultrie told him. "Just be a friend and accept what I want to do."

Barry swatted Moultrie on the shoulder good-naturedly. "No problem. Go ahead."

Moultrie spurred his horse and cantered off into the darkness. He did not drive the animal, letting it find its own pace. He did not want his horse to tire. He wanted it to carry him many miles away from everyone.

It was well after midnight when the line of march overtook Moultrie. He was sitting on a pyramid of rock about ten feet above the road. He was listening to crickets and tree frogs, tracing constellations and feeling much better.

His horse sensed the approach of people and wagons before Moultrie did. The horse pawed the ground and dropped its ears back.

The column was several hundred yards off. Moultrie came off the rock, stretched, then tightened the saddle girth. He swung onto the horse and rode out to meet the group.

Barry was at the head of the column. Their horses faced each other in the moonlight. The lieutenant looked unhappy. He did not observe the customary formalities of greeting. "You picked one hell of a time to go off by yourself and sulk."

"What do you mean?"

"Hell, your black man suddenly turned tiger and nearly killed Deer Warrior."

"What for? What happened?"

"Damned if I know." Shrugging, the lieutenant

added, "Neither of them will talk to me. I've got them both in cuffs and under guard."

"Where are they?"

"Not close together, you can bet. Never seen a fight like it in all my life. Eugene Abadie says those two make you and Slade look like pikers. Those boys meant it."

Moultrie grimaced. "If they were fighting harder than Slade and me, Lord, it must have been awful."

"You said it. Which one do you want to see first?"

"Cicero."

"He's your slave. Let's go."

Cicero was pacing back and forth in the darkness, his eyes unseeing. His hands were manacled together and a guard was riding along the column beside him. Blood was seeping through a bandage around his head. Moultrie looked at it and concluded that the old wound, the one Peters had given him, had reopened. The swelling around the eye and the split lip were new. So was the limp.

Moultrie and Barry were almost beside Cicero before he saw them. He looked around when Moultrie called his name, then quickly turned his head away.

"Cicero, you all right?" Moultrie spoke softly.

Cicero did not answer.

"What happened?"

Cicero still said nothing and kept staring away into the night.

"Was it Red Wing?"

He nodded.

"Did he beat her badly?"

Cicero grinned. "No. I get there first!"

"You hurt him?"

Still grinning, Cicero replied, "Anyway, he ain't

ever going to look the same again. That's the Gawd's truth."

"I'll vouch for that, Moultrie," Barry agreed. "The man's a mite rearranged, I guess you could say."

"I'm sorry I wasn't here," Moultrie said viciously.

"So am I." The lieutenant shook his head.

"Not me," Cicero said, trying not to grin or grimace, for facial movement was painful. "You'd have tried to stop me, Marse Moultrie. . . . And it was time for Deer Warrior and I to go at each other, yes sir. It had been coming a long time. It's good we got it over, Marse Moultrie, Lieutenant Barry." Cicero paused. "I don't think he'll want to do it again soon."

Moultrie marveled once again at Cicero's ability to play the darky when on public display, while still retaining his dignity.

"Barry, undo the man's chains," Moultrie requested.

"Will he go after Deer Warrior?"

"I'll vouch that he won't start anything." He looked to Cicero.

Cicero nodded.

"But if Deer Warrior starts it," Moultrie added, "I'll not stand in Cicero's way. He'll do what he must do."

"Fair enough," Barry conceded. He dismounted and unlocked Cicero's chains. He tossed them to the guard on horseback. "Come on, Moultrie, and we'll go see if the other half of this latest battle in the Creek Wars is willing to make truce."

Moultrie did not follow immediately. He whispered to Cicero, "It was Deer Warrior who did it to Moon Shadow, wasn't it?

"So Red Wing tells me, Ravenel," Cicero said softly. "Don't you do anything stupid."

As they rode up to Deer Warrior a few minutes later, Moultrie knew Cicero had not exaggerated the damage he had done. Deer Warrior's face had an off-center tilt. Moultrie guessed the tilt would probably be permanent. Deer Warrior's nose was broken. One ear was partly split from his head and needed bandaging. Several teeth were gone.

Moultrie felt no sympathy for him.

In spite of his condition, the Indian's spirit had not changed. He glowered past his guard at Lieutenant Barry and Moultrie through his swollen eyelids the way a cat, with its back up, does at a dog.

"Handsome devil, ain't he," the guard chuckled. "He's a real talker, too."

Barry laughed. "If eyes could talk, and talk could kill."

"We'd be playing poker in hell with old Beelzebub," the guard said.

Moultrie did not pay any attention to the guard. He just sat on his horse and looked at the Indian. Deer Warrior returned the gaze for a moment, then spat and looked away.

"What's so fascinating, Moultrie?" the lieutenant asked.

Shaking his head, Moultrie glanced at Barry, then back at Deer Warrior. "I'm just asking myself," he said, "why I shouldn't kill him." He envisioned the damage to Moon Shadow's face.

"Whoa." Barry put his arm on Moultrie's. "Did I hear you correctly?"

Moultrie didn't say anything.

"Kill the Indian because he and your slave got into a fight? Man, talk sense."

Without shifting his gaze, Moultrie said, "Deer Warrior's also the one who beat up Moon Shadow."

He swung his left leg over the pommel of the saddle and dismounted on the off side, away from Barry.

"Moultrie. . . ."

Moultrie waved him off and started toward Deer Warrior.

Barry unholstered his pistol. "Moultrie," he cautioned once more. Then he fired into the air.

Horses reared and men and women yelled in protest.

Deer Warrior blinked at the shot, but he did not move. He stood bearing his chains as if they were victory garlands.

Moultrie stopped and called back over one shoulder, "Don't worry about me, Barry. I just want a look at this splendid hero up close."

Moultrie realized what he was doing, yet he could not stop himself. He imagined himself doing something bad to Deer Warrior. He wanted to. He could almost taste the bittersweet revenge. But he knew he could never go through with it. Violence done in immediate response he could condone. Premeditated violence he could not.

Deer Warrior suddenly grinned. He seemed to sense Moultrie's change of mind. "So," he said, "this is the lying white coward who sends slaves to fight for him."

Moultrie gave a short, barking laugh. "A man who makes war on women," he returned, his voice low, "must know a lot about being a coward." Turning, he looked up at Barry. Still speaking in Muskogean, so that the Indian would understand, he said, "Let your guard set this woman-fighter free." Then he mounted. He looked down at the Indian and grinned. "I'm going now, to tell all the column that they need to protect their women from the brave and mighty fighter of women, Deer Warrior of the village of Bear Chief." He kicked his horse and started to ride away.

"Eeeeahha!" Deer Warrior's cry echoed as loud as Barry's pistol shot had. "I will kill you, Ravenel, or die trying!"

Reining up, Moultrie looked back at him. "No, you won't, Deer Warrior. Not unless you shoot me in the back."

"You're afraid?" The Indian's voice was taunting.

"I don't fight cowards."

"Come on, white man," he called, "defend the honor of a whore."

Moultrie's face reddened with anger. He kicked his horse forward, and without turning around, said, "Tomorrow morning, Deer Warrior. Tomorrow morning."

The chiefs arranged a large circle. Almost the entire camp was there. Looking around, Moultrie did not see Moon Shadow. He felt a sudden pang.

Eneah Micco came into the center of the circle and explained the circumstances surrounding the fight. Striding to the center behind the chief, Deer Warrior looked around him with a grin.

Cicero whispered in Moultrie's ear, "I don't like that 'gator mouth. I sure don't trust him."

"You and me both, Cicero."

Turning to Moultrie and giving a mock bow, Deer Warrior started speaking. "The white man, Ravenel," he bellowed, "wants to fight me for punishing two women. He shall get his fight—gladly. But first I must tell the reasons for what I did.

"I should not have been angered that the sister of Jim Henry sleeps with a white man like a common whore or that Red Wing sleeps with black slaves. I should not have felt shame for them, but I did. So I hit them and hit them. My anger was at the dirt our people have been made to swallow by these same white men and their slaves. It is an anger I shall always have."

A murmur went up from the crowd and there was scattered applause. Moultrie felt his blood surge. He turned to Deer Warrior and said, "A man who beats on women and children is a coward and a brute. If you were a man, you would have attacked me or my slave, not Moon Shadow or Red Wing. But you are not a man."

With a yell, Deer Warrior lunged at Moultrie. Moultrie leaped to meet him. They grappled in the middle of the circle, swaying back and forth, panting, kicking up clouds of dust as they dug into the ground with heels and toes, trying to get better footing. Suddenly shifting his weight to his back leg and pulling Moultrie across his other leg, the Indian flung Moultrie to the ground.

"Eeeahhh!" The cry was triumphant. Deer Warrior threw himself at the fallen Moultrie. Moultrie rolled to one side and kicked at the same time, catching Deer Warrior's chin. Springing up, he danced back, waiting for Deer Warrior to get to his feet again.

The Indian stumbled as he got up. He shook his head and spat out blood and another fragment of tooth. "What's the matter, coward?" Moultrie called to him.

Roaring, Deer Warrior charged. Moultrie came forward and then swerved. At the same time he kicked out and up, catching Deer Warrior in the stomach. The Indian fell to his knees, gasping for breath. This time, as the Creek brave staggered to his feet, Moultrie attacked. He came in low and fast, tackling the brave.

Deer Warrior grabbed for him but couldn't keep his balance. Instead, he fell back with a thud.

Bounding back up, Moultrie stood waiting for Deer Warrior. The Indian started to raise himself, then fell back. "Come on, white man," he breathed. "What's wrong? Are you afraid to kill me?"

Moultrie started to walk away. At the edge of the circle, he turned and looked at the Indian still on his knees. He caught his breath, and with his voice ringing, he called, "Deer Warrior is a brave fighter. He fought a fair and brave fight. I take back my insults to his courage."

The Indians murmured their approval, the soldiers their surprise. As the crowd disintegrated, Cicero grunted his disapproval. He slapped his forehead. "Sometimes I just do not understand you, Marse Moultrie. Why did you say a thing like that? About a pig like him?"

"Because I think it might be true," he replied. "You beat the hell out of the man once only a few hours ago. And still it took everything I had to do it a second time." Moultrie's head hurt. "He almost had me, Cicero. Fair and square he almost beat me. Deer Warrior may be a son of a bitch, but he's not a yellow one."

"So you say."

"Besides," he said, "it made lots of friends among the chiefs." He put his hand on Cicero for support.

Deer Warrior, still rocking on his knees, watched the pair go from him.

After a moment, he smiled bitterly and nodded at Moultrie in grudging respect.

Moon Shadow was waiting for Moultrie. Exhausted, he all but fell into his tent and found her there.

"I saw it," she told him. "I hated it. Men acting like boys pretending to be men. I could not bear to be close. I was standing far away. I wish you had not done it." Her eyes welled with tears. "I am honored that you did."

"Whether you feel honored or not, it had to be."

"I now feel truly valued by you. Even when you leave me and return to your home, as I believe you will one day, I shall remember that you made me feel honored and valued."

She touched his battered face with her fingertips, barely brushing the skin. He pulled her to him and hugged her tightly, as tightly as his sore body would allow.

"The way in which you showed respect for Deer Warrior," she remarked, "makes me proud. You could not have done a better thing. It brings honor to you, too. My people respect your gesture. I do not believe they will cause trouble over this fight now, after all."

"I might not have fought him if he had not called you a prostitute before the entire camp," Moultrie sighed. "After he had beaten you, calling you a prostitute was too much for me. You do not deserve that."

"I know." Moon Shadow's smile hinted at resignation. "But it doesn't matter. The whole camp knew about us anyway."

"But that is my point," Moultrie continued. "If he had not said it about you and me, everyone could pretend it was not happening. You would still be sought after by others as a wife. But now that he has announced it for everyone to know, no one can ignore it. Few Indian men will want to marry you after this. And if I took you back to Alabama with me, you would not be accepted by my kind, even though I would take you as my wife."

"I am prepared to see you go away alone. I am even prepared to be left behind with your child in me. Nothing lasts forever. The spirits promise no one a life without trouble."

She took his head gently and began brushing her lips across his bruises. "But why do we talk about something sad that has not yet occurred, and that no one can foretell for certain. We have each other for now, do we not?"

"We do," Moultrie said. "You know it."

Two days later, in the evening, there was a great disturbance at the point of the column. The night had been so bright and clear that one could read maps without candles or lanterns.

"There it is! There it is!" someone shouted.

Indians and soldiers in the vanguard began to run. Someone on a horse broke from the ranks and galloped ahead, shouting and scribing circles of fiery light above his head with a torch.

Others followed, trotting and stumbling at first, then running too, dropping their bundles as they did.

And soon the entire column of Indians and soldiers alike was running. There were no guards, there were no captives, only a wild mob with a common purpose, running to the fulfillment they had sought for so long at such great cost.

Ahead was a rise in the land. Beyond that the flatlands of the Creek Agency seemed to spread to infinity in the moonlight. No one had to tell them this was the place.

They just knew it.

The trip was over.

They were there. For better or worse, they were there.

Chapter 25

"What are you doing?"

Looking up from the letter he was writing, Moultrie smiled. "Telling John Page how magnificent the new mansion we're building is going to be."

"All two rooms of it," Moon Shadow laughed. "I am sure Captain Page has better sense than to believe you. Mansion indeed."

"Me? Exaggerate?" Moultrie grinned. He closed the lap desk. "Come here, my beautiful." Reaching up, he pulled Moon Shadow into his lap. They kissed.

"My Moultrie," Moon Shadow sighed, "will we never have enough of this?"

"I want you so much, so often, that sometimes I almost feel greedy." He kissed her again, then said, "We can't keep this up. There's work to do."

The cabin construction was new. They still had not laid floorboards or even a bed. They only had a blanket on the ground. But it did not matter to them; they had each other.

Turning his face toward the sun in the doorway, he asked, "Where are Cicero and the boys?"

Moon Shadow shrugged. "What does it matter?"

He patted her head and pushed her out of his lap. As he stood, he said, "That Cicero is never here when he can help with the heavy work. He and Little Hawk and Fast Raven are stretching out the nut and berry picking as long as they can to avoid helping here." He wagered that they already had enough to last two winters.

"Does not your Bible say that even your God rested after seven days?"

Moultrie fell into fits of laughter. Cicero deserved a day off, of course. He deserved weeks off. The cabin, though, would not have a roof until he returned.

Moultrie had been raised a gentleman. He was not a builder. Cicero had been raised a slave. He knew everything about building. He had drafted the plans, cut the logs, shaped the lumber and even framed the cabin and gotten the roof ready. Moultrie himself had watched and listened and learned.

That Cicero sure is a hard worker, he thought. A smile played across his lips.

"Why are you laughing?" Moon Shadow asked suddenly.

Moultrie looked up at her. He had been thinking so deeply that he did not realize he had started to laugh. "It's nothing," he shrugged.

"Only crazy men laugh at nothing."

"Well," he began, "I was just thinking about what Page would say if he saw this place. I told him before this whole thing started that I'm like a bull in a china shop when it comes to working with my hands."

She giggled. "And you would not tell him Cicero built it, would you?"

Moultrie grinned. "Not straight off. He wouldn't know what to think."

"But you should not be thinking of Page right now," she told him. "You should take this time to relax."

"Well, the mission is technically over. I can go home any time I want to. I've decided. I'm not going, maybe not for a long time. Maybe not ever. I want you to see this house as a sign that I mean that."

She thought for a long time before speaking again. "It is too soon to make such promises, to me and to yourself. Let time pass. Think more. And when you really make up your mind to stay, you will probably not have to promise at all. You will simply stay." She paused again. "I sound ungrateful. Forgive me."

Moultrie waved his hand to protest. "No," she continued. "Listen to me. Even if you do go, I am glad for this place. Again I feel honored and valued. It is a great thing for a man to build a house for a woman. And I am glad you did not stay at the fort. I was afraid you were going to."

"Right now, all I want is you."

They held each other. Moon Shadow's voice was muffled against his chest. "What we do together here will cause you no trouble at the Bureau of Indian Affairs?"

"No." Moultrie hugged her again. Stroking her hair, he added, "In the first place, why should they object? Lord. There are at least thirty white men living with Indian women here in the agency. There are even a couple of white women living with Indians."

"And in the second place?"

He grinned. "Who's going to tell Washington?" Certainly not Moultrie. He had written a report for Charles Madden just yesterday. He had told the clerk that he was building a cabin, but he had not mentioned a word about Moon Shadow. It was none of the man's business. What *was* Madden's business was what was being done for the Indians. Moultrie had told him about that. He reminded him of the issuing of the blankets the government had agreed to provide, and of the additional provisioning of about fifty felling axes, froes to rive boards, and iron wedges, so the new arrivals could scatter and start building before winter. They had been overwhelmed by the extent and beauty of the forest along the rivers and the quantity of nuts and fruits. Moultrie had been pleasantly surprised, even though John Page had already described the country to him.

There had been only two other things to call to Madden's attention: the ongoing trouble between the McIntosh Creeks and the new arrivals, and the trouble with the Osages. There had been several incidents, all of them minor, but the trouble was under control. There had not been any bloodshed, but the situation was explosive. There had been another meeting of the chiefs last week when only angry words had been exchanged. Eneah Micco had stood up and called Roley McIntosh a money-gouging cheat for claiming so much of the best land for the old settlers. McIntosh had replied that it was up to the new settlers to make their own way. He said they were not going to do it by staying drunk all the time or by robbing the settlers who had come ahead of them.

There was only one thing besides their mistrust of each other that the two groups agreed on as far as Moultrie could tell. It was fear of the Osages and Delawares and other tribes raiding them.

Moultrie was glad when the meeting was finally over.

Chapter 26

Fort Gibson.

Moultrie had once written about the fort to his brother Henry.

> One sees in the foreground a two-story building. Behind that, on the left, there is a series of lower buildings obscured partly by foliage ranging along the top of a slope. Fort Gibson itself is to the right. In my view it is a sorry place. To some it is the capital of the world.

Since he had written to Henry Ravenel, Moultrie had been there how many times? Twenty? Thirty? He had lost count.

He knew he had come to the place again and again to help newcomer Indians draw their first rations of corn or flour and cattle or pork on the hoof. These were the things the government had agreed to provide the immigrants over the first year, until their crops ripened. He had come over, too, to mail his letters and reports, to meet new arrivals, to confer with officers and to pick up things he needed: bullets, axes and cloth to make clothing for himself, Moon Shadow, Cicero and the boys.

He knew the twenty-five miles from his cabin on the south bank of the Verdigris River to the juncture where the Verdigris met the Arkansas and the Grand in front of the fort as well as he had known the federal road back in Alabama. He smiled at the memory. He patted his mare. They had covered a lot of ground together since he bought her from a Captain William Armstrong back in September, just after the column had arrived. The captain had been right. He had said she was a good horse. "Has bottom," he had said. She did have wind and endurance. More important, she had heart and courage. He had charged her at a group of Osage raiders while firing both his horse pistols at once, and she had not flinched. He had hunted buffalo on her too, down on the plains between the Arkansas River and the Canadian. She had carried him for hours without faltering. He still remembered Little Hawk's glee as the buffalo had thundered past. He would also never forget one bull buffalo swerving and charging straight at the boy sitting there on the pony Moultrie had given him. That had been one time he had thanked God for Deer Warrior. He might be a sodden drunk, Moultrie thought, but he had ridden and shot like a warrior of legend that day. Seeing the buffalo's charge, Deer Warrior had swerved and ridden straight at the bull, shooting first one arrow, then a second and then a third. The buffalo had fallen finally not twenty-five yards from the frightened boy, an arrow sticking straight out of its eye and two others lodged in its massive chest and shoulder.

Moultrie had tried to thank the brave, but Deer Warrior had laughed in response. The laugh had been bitter.

Moultrie shook his head at the memory. Where was Roley McIntosh? Pulling the watch out of his fob, he opened it. Eleven o'clock. Damn. He wished the chief would come soon. He was freezing. He hugged himself, then slapped his arms, his breath white in the air before him.

It was a miserable day, and it was close to Christmas. Back home, the slaves would be coming up to the big house in a couple of weeks to get their presents before going back to the feast in the quarters. He had always loved the time. Now, here, it seemed different. Though he and Cicero had started to decorate the cabin, it was difficult for Moultrie to embrace the holiday spirit. Cicero was having trouble, too.

Little Hawk and Fast Raven were puzzled and amused by the preparations. Cicero had tried to explain the meaning of Christmas to them one day.

"Well, the Creek people have celebrations. Christmas is one of the most important celebrations of the Christian people. It celebrates the birth of the man we believe is the Son of our God. God is like the Great Spirit of the Indians. Christmas is a very religious time, but it is fun, too. There is much food and singing and dancing."

"Do you bring a sacred fire? We do at our feasts."

"No," Cicero replied.

"And do you drink a black drink for the spirits?"

Again Cicero replied, "No."

"Then how can your Christmas be religious when

you do not have sacred fires or black drinks?" Fast Raven asked.

"All religions are different. We celebrate Christmas like a birthday feast. We exchange gifts."

The boys looked at each other, excitement dancing in their dark eyes.

Cicero nodded. "I think they understand what Christmas is now, Ravenel. Uh huh, yes sir, they do."

Moultrie chuckled now in recollection. He hugged and slapped himself again, his breath as white as ever in the cold. Damn, but he wished Chief McIntosh would hurry up.

The mare's ears cocked to the right. Moultrie turned. McIntosh and his train of chiefs were now coming up the road. "Well, girl," Moultrie said, patting the mare again, "let's hope this goes all right." He wasn't really sure *how* it would go. There was no love lost between Roley McIntosh and the new Creek arrivals he was coming to officially greet. The feud went back for years, back to the time Roley McIntosh's brother William had been executed for illegally signing a treaty relinquishing tribal lands to the State of Georgia.

"Hello, Ravenel."

"McIntosh."

"It's plenty cold."

"You don't say?" Moultrie grinned. "I'm beginning to understand why a man wants two wives. Just to keep warm."

The chief chuckled. "That's a fine woman you've got in your cabin, Ravenel."

"And better than six wives."

McIntosh rubbed his hands together and blew on

them. "So we go to greet Opthleyaholo, officially, at last?"

"That's what Armstrong's note said." Moultrie looked across the river at the immense Indian encampment just to the south of the fort. "How many are in the camp now, do you know?"

McIntosh squinted against the sun. Putting his hand over his eyes, he stared. "I don't know. There must be ten thousand of them." He shook his head. "They've been coming in steadily. Two weeks ago there were only half as many." He coughed and cleared his throat. "How are they going to house that many new arrivals in the middle of winter? They haven't even managed to house all the ones who've trickled in since your group arrived at the beginning of September." McIntosh kicked his horse and started forward. "Well, we might as well get this over with." Mumbling to himself, so that Moultrie could hardly hear him, he added, "Poor people. A man wouldn't wish this on his worst enemy."

McIntosh and Moultrie rode along in silence for a minute. Coming to the ford across the Grand River, Moultrie said, "You sent word that you wanted to see me, McIntosh, before you met with Opthleyaholo."

"That's right. I want your advice."

"All right." Moultrie looked at the old chief. He was not particularly impressive in appearance. Wearing store-bought trousers, he looked as if he might be a small merchant. But sometimes his gaze bored straight through you when he spoke, and you felt the enormous force and vitality of the man. Moultrie had not seen him since that first meeting back in August, but he had long ago lost his arrogant, short-sighted assumptions about Roley McIntosh. Only a fool would think the chief was a fool.

McIntosh ignored Moultrie's scrutiny. He cleared his throat. "How, Moultrie, do I make Opthleyaholo feel welcome and still make my position clear?"

"I thought that might be what you wanted to discuss."

"Did you?" McIntosh smiled.

Moultrie pursed his lips. He had thought about this a good deal over the last weeks. He knew of the intense hatred, rivalry and distrust between these two men. Still, Moultrie thought he had come up with a possible solution. "Tell Opthleyaholo," he said, "that you are glad to be able to offer your brothers help in this season of cold."

"And?"

"And that in the spring, after the thaws, you will be glad to help him and his people move."

The chief started to chuckle. "I think I'm going to like this. Go on."

"Say that there are rich, empty lands down on the Canadian River where he and his people can spread out and build villages for themselves, while here on the Verdigris and Arkansas they would be joining already existing villages and getting the second best lands because most of the best have already been taken."

"True, true." McIntosh reached over and clapped Moultrie on the back. "Wise thinking," he commended. "I'll do it."

The meeting between the chiefs went well. General Robert Arbuckle was relieved. So, for that matter, was Moultrie.

Afterward, Moultrie went to speak to Bear Chief again, as he had the week before.

The old man smiled. "It is always good to see a friend of my people," he greeted. Then he shook his head and added, "One who is not a false friend."

Moultrie's heart ached for the man. Only six months earlier he had stood tall and proud in old age. Now he was bent and withered. He had lost too much weight and looked as though he would blow away in a good sneeze. Just like a withered leaf, Moultrie thought.

"You know how I regret all that you and your people have suffered in being forced to come here," Moultrie told him.

"It was hard." The chief looked off across the Grand River. "But we are here now. We can learn to live again." He shook his head and sighed. "I only wish we had our young men with us."

Moultrie nodded. He knew why they were not there. Little Johnnie had written to him that he was leading Bear Chief's warriors to Florida to fight for the United States against the Seminoles. Moultrie had received the letter in September. . . .

. . . And this is how the U.S. shows its gratitude. We cannot do otherwise. Merchants are pressing fabricated claims against the tribe. We, the younger men, cannot leave to join our families where you are until we pay the claims. At the same time, we are being driven from our lands here so that we cannot pay. So this dilemma is what enables your General Jesup to convince Jim Boy and myself and several hundred others to go fight our own brothers, the Seminoles. For money. The U.S. says they will pay us to fight. Then we can pay our debts to the merchants. And in its magnificence, the U.S. grandly tells us that our families may stay in our homes until we return from the war against the Seminoles. In short, the U.S. government will not completely rob us until it has finished using us. This is all your William Hobson's arrangement. One day I may shoot him through the eye to show my gratitude.

"Little Johnnie is a very bitter man," Moultrie told Bear Chief. "And he has a right to be bitter."

"I know." Bear Chief's voice was weary. "He told me he is sometimes sorry now he did not fight with Deer Warrior and Jim Henry and the others, instead of against them. I told him he was a fool." As he spoke, the chief's eyes began to flash and his voice regained some of the richness Moultrie remembered. "All this war did was let the whites proceed more ruthlessly than they otherwise could have done." Looking at Moultrie, the old man smiled, suddenly tired again. "You were wise in your advice, nephew of my dead friend. I am not sorry."

"Has Deer Warrior been to see you yet?"

"Three days ago. He told me of your fight."

"Did he tell you how he saved Little Hawk, the boy I have living with me?"

"No." Bear Chief shook his head morosely. "Deer Warrior can have life in this new country. He won't know what to do with it."

"But you can live here, Bear Chief."

"No." The old man put his arm on Moultrie's. "I am too old." Then he looked back toward the camp. Suddenly the fire was in his voice again. "But I have pride. I will not drink myself to death." He was about to speak again when an officer came striding toward them.

It was Captain William Armstrong. He nodded to the chief, then turned to Moultrie. "There are a couple of letters for you, Moultrie. Up at the Fort. Came in by steamboat only a few hours after you left last. Four or five days ago."

"Thanks, Bill, I'll walk up with you in a minute." Moultrie turned back to Bear Chief. "Maybe Deer Warrior will catch life again from that woman he used to court."

The old warrior shook his head. "She is in love with your cousin. And since his fight with you, Deer Warrior doesn't even allow himself to lash out in anger. He just eats at himself." Taking a deep breath, he smiled wanly. "Thank you for coming to see me. Next time we meet, it should be across the river."

"I know. I'll be coming to help in the move. Good-bye, Bear Chief."

"Good-bye." As Moultrie turned to go, the old warrior squeeezd his hand.

"Ready, Bill?"

"Right."

The two men strode off.

Moultrie waited to speak again until they were out of Bear Chief's hearing. "Bill, any word yet on when the Indian baggage arrives?" he asked.

"Nope." As he spoke, the captain clapped his gloved hands together.

"What's the delay?"

"Ask Felix G. Gibson and Charles Abercrombie of the Alabama Emigrating Company." The captain's tone was savage.

"But, damn it, the Indians have no winter clothes!"

"Do you think those gentlemen care?" Armstrong

kicked at a pinecone on the edge of the path. "Hell, no."

There was nothing else to say. The soldier and the Indian agent walked on to the fort in silence.

Chapter 27

"You can read the letters in my quarters, Moultrie. I've got to go check on the stores. Jamie Stephensen is giving out ten thousand rations a day now just for the camp. That doesn't count your Indians."

"I know. Thanks, Bill." Walking over toward the barracks where Armstrong's room was, Moultrie smiled to himself. He wondered what Henry had to say. And Helen. This was the second letter from her within a month. He hoped Judge Dupré was doing better. Helen had sounded worried about him in her last letter.

Inside the captain's room, Moultrie took off his coat and laid it on the bed. Blowing on his hands, he went to the fireplace. The ashes were still warm, thank God, but he was going to have to build a new fire. It would not take long.

Which letter should he read first? Henry's? The sod hadn't written in ages. What was happening on the upper reaches of the Cooper River back in South Car-

olina? If Henry was telling the tale, probably nothing.
Moultrie grinned. His younger brother had no sense of
drama.

The letter, dated November 6th, was short.

> In the wake of Mother's death, I have
> decided to leave the church. My faith has not
> been the bulwark I have preached in my ser-
> mons. Rather, it has become an intolerable
> burden. I wake up every day dreading the
> barrenness of my prayers.

Moultrie looked up from the letter. This was unbelievable. Henry leaving the ministry? All he had ever
wanted to do since he had been twelve years old was
serve the church. He'd always said the Lord was his
keeper. Henry, solid as a rock. Moultrie shook his
head. What was the poor man going to do?

> Having renounced orders, I cannot stay
> here. The pitying looks and reproachful
> stares are enough to choke a man. I have de-
> cided, therefore, to sell my share of the plan-
> tation. You are welcome to buy it, if you
> like, though I do not suppose you will want
> it. Write Cousin Arthur in Charleston of
> your decision. He is handling the matter for
> me and has advanced me the value of my
> half so I can come west. I intend to look for
> land in Alabama or Mississippi. Any recom-
> mendations? If so, write care of my godfa-
> ther, Jim Thorn. I shall be spending
> Christmas and the New Year with him and
> his wife, Sebrina.

That was all, except for best wishes to Moultrie from various family members, greetings to "that lovely Helen Dupré" and a wish that Moultrie and Helen would be happy together.

Putting the letter down, Moultrie stared ahead. The fire sputtered. He added a log and poked up the flame, then sat back down.

He ran his fingers through his hair, then picked up Helen's letter. He opened the envelope.

This was too much. Not only were Helen and Hobson engaged, but they had announced their wedding plans. They would be married on January 23rd.

> I know this seems sudden, but I think it
> is for the best. Papa is so happy, and Bill has
> been such a dear. I am sure we shall learn
> how to be very content together.

Moultrie smiled to himself ruefully. Helen marrying Hobson after all Moultrie's efforts to stop her. The poor girl. Well, it none of his affair. Not now.

But damn it, the woman could not be that blind. She must be selling herself so that her father will have a few feeble years of peace. Her father should not stand for it.

The judge, to be fair to him, had probably believed Helen when she told him how happy she was. Poor man, he was desperate for security—not for himself, but for Helen.

Angel-haired Helen. She would have made a splendid wife for Moultrie. Now she would make a splendid one for Hobson.

Crumpling the letter, he threw it into the fire and watched as the flames licked it around the edges and shot up through the center, turning it into a crumbling ball of black ash.

He went to the bed, picked up his coat and shrugged it on. A drink. That's what he wanted. And more than one. Henry Ravenel's choice to quit the church depressed him. Helen Dupré's decision to marry William Hobson enraged him. The abuses heaped upon the Creeks, despite his own efforts to prevent them, frustrated him.

He wanted to be freed from his cell for a while. Some strong raw whiskey would give him the key.

He left Armstrong's quarters and went to the saloon where the soldiers of Fort Gibson did their drinking.

He told the man tending the board-and-barrel bar that he wanted a glass and a bottle. The men there understood Moultrie's unspoken message. A man asking for a glass and a bottle also wanted to be left alone. They respected this.

Moultrie poured some whiskey and gulped it down. It tasted hot and burned his throat. He drank a second glass a few minutes later. The third glass did not taste bad at all.

Around midnight, two sergeants nearly as drunk as Moultrie lifted his arms over their shoulders and carried him home through the darkness to his cabin. They sat him on the doorstep, wrapped his coat snugly around him and left him sleeping there.

And that was where Cicero found him in the morning.

Moon Shadow was not pleased.

She brought him no breakfast when he awoke at midday. She did bring him water. "Here. My father knew much about drinking. He always said, if you want to feed a thirst, drink liquor. If you want to cure a thirst, drink water."

Moultrie smiled. "I'm grateful. And I don't blame you for being angry. Getting as drunk as that is stupid. I was feeling sorry for myself, and I feel less of a man for it. But I've fed the thirst, all right." He gulped the water. "Where's the man who found me?"

"Cicero is next door with the boys. We've been taking turns staying with them." Her tone became angry. "I wanted you home here with me very much last night."

He imagined a ball of pain growing inside his head. When the ball shrank to bearable size, he answered, "Was there something special about last night?"

"You see me every day. And yet you cannot guess."

"No. And stop posing silly riddles like that to a man who feels like he's about to die. Just tell me."

"If you cannot see for yourself, I'll not tell you. Ask someone else for the answer."

Moon Shadow wheeled and rushed from the cabin just as Cicero came in. And it was Cicero who gave Moultrie the answer.

"What's wrong with her, you ask? Why, nothing, Ravenel," he chided. "She's just pregnant, that's all. No reason why you should have been home last night, just to hear that news."

"Cicero," Moultrie growled, "do not scold me for something I knew nothing about. Of course I would have stayed home. Pregnant? My God. Me? A father?"

"You're right. Sorry, Ravenel. I guess I've got a lot on my mind, too."

"All right," Moultrie grumbled. "Now you're talking riddles. Everyone's talking in riddles. What's yours?"

"I just received the same news from Red Wing. Red Wing is going to have a baby, too."

Moultrie was unable to respond. He and his childhood slave-friend had grown up, had become men together. And now they were both to become fathers.

Moultrie laughed. He was elated. "Congratulations, Mr. Cicero!" he shouted.

"Congratulations, Mr. Ravenel!"

"Really. I mean it."

"I do, too."

They embraced.

It was the first time they had done so since they had grown to manhood.

Moultrie pulled on his coat and trotted out into the bitter cold to find Moon Shadow.

There were few people about on this bitter, bright winter day. A cavalry trooper sat wrapped in a blanket on horseback in the distance. A group of Indian men walked backwards into the wind. A wagon carrying bales of hay creaked past. He saw her walking by the river, her hair flying behind her like a wind-blown cape. Moultrie ran hard to catch her. Each step made his head pound. Pain or no pain, he ran on.

"Hello, little mother," he said, wheezing for breath.

"You know."

Moultrie could see she was relieved that he knew.

"I was going to tell you last evening," she exclaimed. "I had gotten up the courage. And then you were not there. All that courage gone to waste. And this morning I was a coward again. That is why I was harsh with you. There is nothing really so terrible about a man drinking too much once in a while."

"How long have you known?"

"For certain, two weeks."

"Lord. Why were you afraid to tell me?"

"Because." She bit hard on her lip and seemed to be seeking the answer from the sky. "Because I am afraid of what a child will do to us."

He coiled his arms around her. She tried desperately to pull away, but toppled backward against him.

"Please, Moon Shadow." He turned her around to face him. "Don't try to run away from me. I want to tell you that the child will do nothing but make us happy."

Moon Shadow's face lit up. She nuzzled against his navy wool coat.

"And I am happy, too," he told her, caressing her cheek. "Know that I am happy."

Moultrie also knew that now he was not going home, not for a long, long time. With Henry Ravenel's news, there was no need to. With Moon Shadow's news, he did not want to.

He did not tell her he was not going. He remembered something she had once said. When the time came that he decided he was going to stay, he would not have to say anything.

Chapter 28

"What the hell is this, Cicero? It looks like it weighs a ton."

"I think I know what it is," Cicero replied. "But I think you'd best just open the box up and see. Maybe I'm wrong. I hope I'm wrong."

"What are you talking about, Cicero?" Moultrie asked as he took out his knife and cut the rope binding the box. He opened the lid, then quickly slammed it down again.

"Lord," he exclaimed, "it cannot be. What is this thing doing here?"

Moultrie opened it once more, slowly. He lifted out the shotgun he himself had given to Little Johnnie back in Tuskegee.

Moon Shadow was puzzled. "I do not understand. You and Cicero seem so upset. This is a very handsome weapon. Is it a present? Did you buy it? What is bothering you?"

"The letter will tell you, Ravenel," Cicero sulked.

When he was with Moon Shadow, Cicero dropped the public slave manner and addressed Moultrie as Ravenel. He had never even thought of behaving any other way before her.

The letter was from Captain John Page. Moultrie broke the seal with the knife. He read the first sentence, then put the letter down and almost began to weep. "I knew it as soon as I saw the gun," Moultrie sighed. "Little Johnnie is dead."

Page had managed to compile a fairly detailed account from an officer whose squad Little Johnnie had saved. The half-breed, according to the letter, had been on a scouting mission with a troop of his warriors when he had heard guns firing in the distance. Working their way as quickly as they dared toward the sound of the firing, the Indians had come up on the rear and right flank of a party of Seminoles. The Indians had an infantry company pinned down under murderous fire. Giving a yell, Little Johnnie had charged with his warriors. The surprised Seminoles had scattered. The army troops, seeing their enemy pulling back, had moved forward, shooting.

One of the soldier's bullets had caught Little Johnnie in the throat. He had died almost instantly. That was all there was to tell. Page was sorry. He had liked and, in a way, admired the half-breed. Moultrie had the captain's sympathy.

And the gun? Moon Shadow still did not understand the connection with Little Johnnie. Moultrie explained, then read to her from Page's letter, "The shotgun was left in my care by Little Johnnie before he went to Florida. He made me promise two things: not to tell you I had it and to send it to you in the event he was killed. He did not want to lose it in combat."

Moultrie looked up, his eyes watering. "Crazy,

crazy Johnnie," he said, his voice thick with emotion. "He told Page to say that having owned the gun—even for a little while—had meant more to him than anything."

Moon Shadow stood carefully. Moultrie noted how slowly she had gotten up. She had started to swell with their child inside her. She touched his arm gently. "I did not know Little Johnnie meant so much to you."

"Neither did I, until just now. I feel as bad as I did when each of my parents died. And beyond them, I never believed any other loss could be as great. That is how bad I feel. It hurts so much. I didn't realize how much Little Johnnie meant to me."

He did not verbalize his other thoughts; they were about Moon Shadow. Do not let me lose her in any way, dear God, not in any way.

"Ravenel," Cicero whispered softly. "Ravenel. What do you want me to do with this shotgun?"

Moultrie ran his hand along it. He shook his head. He knew that he would never use it again. Never. "Clean it up and put it away. I'll think about it later."

Cicero stood at the kitchen door. He looked across the land. Winter was over. He imagined a warm spring and a hot summer for good crops ahead, if he and Ravenel stayed. He still wondered if Moultrie and Moon Shadow would stay, despite their constant reassurances. He prayed they would.

Behind him, Little Hawk and his brother scuffled on the big bed Cicero had made for himself and Red Wing. They were two reasons why he did not wish to leave. And Red Wing was the other. True, he could always stay if Moultrie left. But to suddenly be separated

from Moultrie would be like losing a piece of his soul.
Cicero sighed. No fretting, he reminded himself.

In the distance Cicero heard someone grunt. The
sound came from the cabin next door, where Moultrie
and Moon Shadow lived. Cicero had said nothing to
Moultrie, but it was his impression that Moon Shadow
often had discomforts in her pregnancy and was keeping the fact to herself.

He was grateful that Red Wing had no discomfort. She was having what appeared to be an easy pregnancy. He felt a pang of guilt for allowing himself
relief at the expense of Moon Shadow.

He hefted the shoulder yoke and buckets and set
out for water at the spring. He looked toward the river.
A fish jumped, shining like a bright silver coin flipping
in the sunlight. "That's lunch," he proclaimed. He
turned back to the two cabins. He wanted his fishing
pole. Water could wait. "If I don't fish now, we don't
eat."

Just as he reached the breezeway between the two
cabins, his own and Moultrie's, he stopped in sudden
fright. An Indian on horseback sat there quietly, not
moving.

A man on a horse had moved up on him and he
had not even sensed his arrival. An unpleasant chill
ran up Cicero's back. Men who move so silently can
kill you before you know it, he thought.

It was Bear Chief.

"Welcome," Cicero said, then waited. When Bear
Chief was ready he would state his business.

"Moultrie Ravenel," Bear Chief stated with final-
ity.

Cicero sensed an overwhelming urgency. Any
other time, had Bear Chief wished to see Moultrie, he
would have summoned him. His age and position

among the chiefs would have merited his doing so. Protocol would have required it. The fact that Bear Chief had come himself to Moultrie meant he had something important on his mind.

Cicero called out, telling Moultrie to come quickly.

"I wish to prevent an uprising and the slaughter of my people," he told Moultrie. "This can be done simply, and you are the only one who can put an end to the white man's robbery. Please. I am shamed to have to beg for your assistance, but we need you."

Bear Chief went on to explain that the white men with whom the Bureau of Indian Affairs had contracted to distribute goods and services on the western Creek Agency reservation had been cheating them, short-weighting them and stealing from them all winter long. Blankets were an example. The Indian Affairs contractors had not even distributed them. As a result, children were ill with diseases associated with winter cold. Some had died.

The Creeks were not going to put up with these abuses any longer. The chiefs had considered the matter and agreed in council that if something was not done to give them what was theirs now and in the future, they were going to attack and take it. And if that meant renewal of war with the United States, so be it.

Bear Chief had suggested to the chiefs that they enlist Moultrie to win redress for them, as he had in the past. They wanted results within the week.

Moultrie promised he would do everything he could so Bear Chief could bring that promise back to his chiefs.

"I told them you would do what you could," the old chief said. "They trust you. They will wait one week. You will come with me to speak to these men of Indian Affairs now?"

"Now," Moultrie nodded. "But I cannot promise anything more, Bear Chief, than that I will try."

The old man stood, ready to mount his horse. "That is all I can ask."

Turning, Moultrie went back inside. Moon Shadow smiled up at him from the bed.

"Are you comfortable?" he asked. "Can I get you something?"

"How long will you be gone?" Her voice was weak.

Moultrie looked down at her worriedly. "I should be back by tomorrow evening," he answered. "Cicero will be here. And the boys. You'll have plenty of company. And help."

Moon Shadow managed a laugh. Tracing his lips with her finger, she snickered, "Maybe I'll have produced some new company by the time you get back."

Moultrie looked down at her swollen belly. "Don't rush." He leaned over, smiling, and kissed her. "I want to be here myself when our child arrives." He stood up. "I'll tell Cicero I'm going." He turned and strode through the open door, stopping only to blow a kiss back over his shoulder.

Moon Shadow sustained her smile, refusing to show the pain burning up her insides, until Moultrie was out the door. Only then did she allow herself to gasp. Now it sometimes hurt so much that she was afraid.

She knew Cicero was aware that she might be having problems, and was thankful that he had not become alarmed enough to tell Moultrie.

In the end, everything will be all right. They will have a fine baby. She swore they would. Then there will be no need to mention the fact that she had ever had pain at all.

Arriving at the Creek settlement, Moultrie rode directly to the weathered wooden buildings which served as the offices, lodgings and supply depot for the contractors. He was anxious to have the showdown with the chief contractor, a man named Kirk.

Jumping down from his mare, Moultrie yelled to a man at a hitching rail, "Where's Kirk?"

"Up there." The man shifted a quid of tobacco in his mouth. "But it ain't going to do you no good to go up there. He's playing cards with some of the boys."

"That so?" Moultrie grinned. "In that case, maybe he'll deal me in for a hand or two."

"Could be." The man spat, then shifted the quid again. "Well, I got work to do. Can't stand around. Picking up a bullwhip from the tie rail in front of the storage shed, the man trudged down toward the cattle pen. At least fifty Indians were waiting there in the choking dust for their cattle to be cut out for them according to their government requisition slips.

Watching them, Moultrie felt his anger grow. Bear Chief had been right. If this was a typical transaction, they were being cheated. The cattle were too few, too scrawny and too old. It is going to stop, Moultrie told himself. I'm going to stop it.

Moultrie hammered on the cedar-planked door, then entered.

A group of men sat around a card table. "You looking for someone?" one of them asked.

"You Kirk?"

"Yup." The man tossed two cards on the table, picked up the two the dealer passed him and arranged them in his hand. "Five dollars," he said, pushing coins from the pile in front of him out into the middle of the table.

"I'm Moultrie Ravenel."

"So?" Kirk flipped another gold piece out. "Call you," he said.

"I'd like to speak to you." Moultrie's voice was tight.

"Go right ahead. I ain't playing with my ears." Slamming the cards down faceup, he chuckled, "Thank you, boys," then raked in the pile from the middle of the table.

Moultrie took a deep breath. He had promised himself he was going to remain calm dealing with Kirk. It was not going to be easy. "I'd like to speak to you in private."

Kirk turned to look at him. "Nothing's stopping you. Talk."

"It's about the false weights and measures you're using. Your company is cheating the hell out of the Indians."

"Yup. I'm listening. . . . Give me three of them cards this time, Willie. . . . What's the problem?"

"I'm reporting you to Washington."

Kirk just continued playing, unconcerned with what Moultrie had said.

Moultrie stepped forward quickly, grabbed Kirk's collar and jerked it, toppling him backward hard onto the floor. As Kirk kicked and flailed, striving for balance, Moultrie seized the barrel of the pepperbox pistol Kirk had produced and twisted it from his hand.

Kirk sat spread-eagled on the planked floor, looking perplexedly at his empty hand.

He started to get up.

Moultrie put his boot against Kirk's forehead and

shoved him back to the floor. Then he pressed it to Kirk's throat. Kirk sucked in wind in distress.

Moultrie eased off of Kirk's throat and put the pistol muzzle to his head.

"Quit jiggling around or I'll push this lead right through you," Moultrie warned. "Now you listen, and listen good."

He looked up quickly. Bear Chief had brought several of his chieftains to the door. They were watching the confrontation with Kirk. Moultrie was pleased. He wanted them to see it.

"I said, listen, man," he repeated. "I was going to give you the benefit of the doubt, kinda reason with you, on the unlikely possibility that there might really be a misunderstanding here and that you were not purposely cheating the Creeks at all."

Moultrie saw the card dealer's hands moving slowly toward the table's edge. "You reach for anything and I'll put the first bullet between Kirk's eyes here. The next one will go right through your heart." He tapped the fat barrel of the pistol. "This pepperbox holds six, so I'll have four left for anyone else who wants to quarrel."

The others stayed still. He couldn't believe it. They were actually scared of him. He was bluffing five men. If only two of them had the sense to come at him from opposite directions, it would be all over for him. He could only shoot one of the men before another shot or stabbed him. He was in complete control.

"Getting back to business, Kirk," he said, stepping hard on the man's windpipe again, "I'm not going to reason with you at all. You are cheating. And you have threatened to kill me, a government agent, if I tell. There is no point in trying to reason any longer." He paused and applied more weight to Kirk's neck.

"So I tell you this. I am writing to Washington, with documentation of your thefts and corruption, and by God, I am going to have you fired. In the meantime. . . ." He paused again. "I deputize Bear Chief and his people standing there in the doorway to punish you in any way they see fit, according to their own tribal codes for thieves, if you steal from them or cheat them again."

He called to the Indians in the doorway, "Do you hear me, Bear Chief? That includes doing what you have to with Kirk here and breaking into his warehouses and taking what is yours, if you must."

Bear Chief heard him.

"You can't do this, Mr. Ravenel," one of the cardplayers said.

"I just did."

Moultrie took his foot away. He seized Kirk's coat and lifted him. Kirk was gasping and coughing. Moultrie pushed him into one of the chairs.

"You understand me, Kirk? Oh, never mind answering. I know you do." He backed away from Kirk and the others, the pepperbox dangling easily at his side. Moultrie prayed they believed him to be as calm as he was trying to appear. He was not going to turn his back to them.

The last thing he said was, "I'll leave your weapon down at the cattle pen, Kirk. With the man who minds the pigs."

Moultrie passed by Bear Chief, nodded and went out the door. He knew he could not actually deputize the Indians, and they knew it too, but he had given them status as peers. And he had made it known to the Indians and the white contractors that the official Indian Affairs position was that Indians were not to be cheated. And hearing a federal agent tell the Indians they had the right to fight for what was theirs would make the contractors careful.

Whether he had done any long-range good, Moultrie did not know. But he was certain that for a while at least, the Indians would receive fair measure. He was certain, too, that the contractor, Kirk, would not wait for official inquiry from Washington to resign. Moultrie had humiliated him before both his colleagues and his victims.

That had been Moultrie Ravenel's final act as a federal agent representing the United States Bureau of Indian Affairs. Shortly thereafter, his life among the Creek Indians ended. It had not ended in a way that anyone could have ever feared or imagined. How ironic, as Moultrie described things later, that this should have been the happiest of times for himself and Moon Shadow. No. The horror of it never lessened in Moultrie's memory.

When he returned from the trip to Bear Chief's settlements, he found that Moon Shadow had begun labor. She was doing badly. She was running a high fever and was soaked with sweat. At times she convulsed. When not shaking with fever, the labor contractions shook her body into spasms.

The labor itself had gone on for several hours. Considering her condition, Moultrie knew that was far too long. Two neighboring women and a third who claimed to know something of midwifery were with Moon Shadow.

The midwife had hung a chicken foot and other things on a string from the ceiling above Moon Shadow's swollen belly to drive off the evil spirits causing the pain.

Cicero was cursing himself for not being more

aware of Moon Shadow's condition and anticipating
the crisis. He had already sent Little Hawk galloping to
Fort Gibson to fetch the army surgeon, Dr. Benjamin
Farquhar. He told Moultrie that Little Hawk was on
the fastest horse they owned—the one Moultrie had
given him—Uncle—so named by Little Hawk, after
Cicero. The boy often addressed Cicero as "Uncle."
Cicero said Little Hawk was shouting to his spirits as
he rode off, "Oh, don't let another of my mothers die."

Moon Shadow yelped in pain when Moultrie came
to her. "I cannot hide it from you any longer," she
panted.

"Why did you hide it at all?"

Moon Shadow gripped his arm so hard that she
hurt him as another spasm stiffened her body. Moultrie
held her head. She was burning with fever. The Indian
women washed her with a wet towel to cool the fever.
The chicken foot above her belly swayed in a breeze
coming through the window.

Her breaths now came in quick little puffs. Labor
had gone on for thirteen hours. The fever had not yet
broken.

"Isn't there something someone can do for her?
You," he grabbed a tearful woman by her shoulders,
"please. Help her. Help me." She stared back at him,
afraid. He ran out to Cicero. "Doc Farquhar might not
even shake his stumps for an Indian boy, and Little
Hawk doesn't really know what's wrong. He doesn't
know what to say, how to persuade him to come." He
pleaded with Cicero. "You must go. Just in case Farquhar doesn't take the boy seriously. Please, Cicero.
She's my life."

Cicero did not even pause to answer him. Moultrie watched him go. He took Moultrie's horse, still

saddled at the rail outside the cabin. He slapped the horse's flanks hard even before he mounted. And as the horse started off in fright, Cicero held on from the saddle as the Indians did, swung like a pendulum, then dug his heels into the earth. He was catapulted into the saddle by the forward motion.

Moon Shadow no longer camouflaged pain or muffled her screams. She loosed another cry and clawed at her belly as if trying to tear the source of the pain from herself. Moultrie clenched his fists tensely whenever she yelled. He felt so helpless, so damned helpless. At one point he tore down the chicken foot and the other charms in anger. He allowed the disapproving midwife to tie them back into place. Moon Shadow seemed to derive some comfort from them.

"Don't be angry. Please don't." Moon Shadow held his left hand, the one closest to her. "We have so little time."

Moultrie took her hands in his. She stiffened and gasped, cold sweat breaking out on her forehead again. "I told you we would live in different worlds." Moon Shadow smiled.

"Shhh. Don't talk like that. The doctor will be here soon." Leaning forward, Moultrie brushed her lips with his.

"I love you, Moultrie."

"And I love you." He swallowed hard. He could not break down in front of her. He must not. He took a deep breath and said, "You taught me to love." His sob racked his whole body.

Moon Shadow reached up and stroked his hair. When she finally spoke, it was with a faraway voice. "You'll learn new love," she murmured.

"No. You are my love." Moultrie's voice was fierce, but his eyes glistened with tears. "You."

Moon Shadow had not heard. She fell into a deep sleep.

Dr. Benjamin Farquhar and Cicero arrived three hours after dawn.

"This must be serious, Moultrie, for you to drag me up here like this."

Moultrie nodded. "Thanks for coming, Ben." Turning on his heel, he started back into the cabin. Cicero followed them.

The doctor cursed as he hit the top of the door frame with his head. Inside, he squinted in the darkness. Moon Shadow was moaning softly and tossing back and forth, her hands clenched beside her. The Doctor started his preliminary examination. When he looked up, his face was grave. "Get out," he muttered. "Both of you. Only the midwife stays."

"No, Ben, I'm staying."

The doctor shook his head impatiently. "You go, or I go. I will not treat her with anyone but the midwife in here." He turned back to the woman. "It's going to be five kinds of hell in here."

Five minutes later, he called for more hot water and towels. He shut the door again.

The two men outside could still hear Moon Shadow's screams, though. Each time they heard her, both Moultrie and Cicero jumped.

They did not talk. Cicero prayed. Once Moultrie looked up suddenly and asked where Little Hawk and his brother were. He lapsed back into silence when Cicero said he had sent them to inspect the fishnets upriver.

The doctor came out just before noon.

Moultrie jumped to his feet. "Well, Ben?"

The doctor shook his head. "I couldn't save either of them, the woman or the child. I'm sorry."

Moultrie's face turned stonelike. At that moment, he imagined he would know for the rest of his life that there could be no greater despair.

A large part of him had just died in that now silent room. And with that knowledge came the realization that nothing in the world would matter to him for a long, long time.

Chapter 29

"Opportunity to resign accepted with pleasure. Thank you for past kindness. Moultrie Ravenel."

The note had not taken long to write. But then neither, he supposed, had Charles Madden's note to him.

> So sorry, but pressure to get rid of you now more than I care to withstand. In case you are interested, the latest push is coming from Governor Conway of Arkansas, an influential man. He says you have slandered the reputation of the firm of Kirk that is supplying rations to the Indians. The governor is a partner in the firm and is dangerously upset that a government servant would make such scurrilous and unfound attacks as those launched by you on a group of businessmen and community leaders who are carrying out

this patriotic task of feeding the Indians with small hope of any substantial remuneration.

The Indian agent—former Indian Agent Moultrie Ravenel—stood up. Walking over to the cabinet, he reached in and took out the shotgun, hefted it and broke it open. Cicero kept it in good shape. Moultrie would now show Little Hawk how to use it.

Little Hawk was chopping wood. Watching him, Moultrie smiled. The axe is almost as big as the boy, he observed.

"Dedzu, can I talk to you?"

The boy looked around, put down the axe and started over. "What is it, Uncle?"

"Have you shot this gun before?"

Little Hawk shook his head. "Cicero won't let me touch it."

"Well it's yours now." He handed it to the boy.

"Mine?" The boy's eyes glistened as he looked up. "You are going?"

"That's right."

"But why? Aren't we a good family to you?" Little Hawk bit his lip, but he couldn't hold back the tears. "Why do we have to lose you, too?" The words were tinged with anger. "Why?"

"You have Cicero, your brother, your aunt, many people."

"But you are deserting us. Despite your promise to our father." The boy looked down at the gun in his hands. Suddenly raising it over his head, he dashed it on the ground. Dust swirled up at the impact and then settled. "I don't want to be reminded of you," he grumbled. Turning, he walked away, only stopping once to say, "I shall tell my brother you said goodbye."

Moultrie bent down and picked up the gun. Pulling out his handkerchief, he wiped off the dust.

Moultrie shook his head. Little Hawk was ten or thereabouts. How sad that one so young should have so much anger and hatred inside him. Perhaps Cicero could make him trust again. . . .

Cicero demanded that Moultrie stay in the settlement long enough to be with him for the birth of his first child. He said he would break Moultrie's legs if he refused. Moultrie told him he intended to stay.

It was a girl. Cicero was delighted.

Moultrie ached during the celebration. The beautiful little girl made him realize what he had almost had, and he ached. For Cicero, however, he smiled the whole day through.

On the day Moultrie finally left, the good-bye was almost wordless. There was no need for lengthy talk. The two lifelong friends agreed that life without each other was going to be strange for a while. Like losing a piece of your soul, Cicero had said. They had been each other's comfort and mainstay for twenty years.

Moultrie speculated that Cicero would probably manage better than he would. Cicero had Little Hawk, Fast Raven, Red Wing and the new little one. And Moultrie? Well, he had an urge he could neither control nor explain, to break clean with everything and go somewhere else. And this time he was doing it alone.

As Moultrie mounted up that last morning, Cicero said, "This is all going to turn out to be a joke. You are going to climb down from that horse now and say you are really staying. It is all a joke."

Moultrie shook his head. "No, Cicero. This is no joke. Here." Moultrie took from inside his shirt a leather wallet. "This ought to prove this isn't a joke.

Take them, Cicero. Your freedom papers. I can't wait any longer for you to decide. If something happened to me, you'd never get them."

Cicero hefted the wallet.

"Well, whether you like it or not, you are now a free man. I've had it noted officially in county and state house records back home and I've put paid announcements in the newspapers out here. In case anybody ever questions you, the receipts showing the dates the notices ran are here." The papers signing over his sharehold and cabin in the settlement were also there.

Cicero helfted the wallet again, then smiled bitterly. "Funny," he remarked.

"What?"

"Now that I'm free, I don't feel any different. In twenty years with you, Ravenel, I've been about as free as a black man will ever be, all along, anyway."

Only once did Moultrie surrender to the lies of sentimentality to make departure easy.

"What the hell, it's not the end," he grinned. "I'll probably be back again this way someday."

"Don't say it if you don't mean it," Cicero sighed. "Just go."

Cicero's bluntness startled Moultrie, and he found he could not respond.

He turned and went.

He did not look back.

The trail led down a long, gentle slope toward some fields. Moultrie reined up, then leaned forward and patted his mare. "The crop's going to be a good one, girl," he said. The mare's ears flicked.

Moultrie took off his hat. He wiped his forehead with his sleeve. "Maybe, just maybe," he murmured, "the Creeks will survive here." He hoped so. They were a proud people. And brave. It had taken great courage to trek west and build anew as they had just done.

He put on his hat, squinting against the glare of the afternoon sun burning high on the horizon ahead of him. He could not be sure, but the man working in the third field down below looked like Deer Warrior.

Moultrie had one more good-bye. He kicked up his mare.

It was indeed Deer Warrior. "I wanted to see you before I left," Moultrie told him.

The Indian nodded. "Going back to Alabama?" There was nostalgia, even envy, in his voice.

"No. No I'm not. I'm going West."

Deer Warrior's eyes showed surprise. "Why? Why go toward nothing?" Wiping the sweat out of his face with his sleeve, he squinted up at Moultrie.

Moultrie shrugged. He held out the shotgun. "Take this," he requested. "Please."

The Indian reached up and, taking the gun, cradled it in his arm. "Good-bye, Indian Agent Moultrie Ravenel."

Moultrie nodded. Spurring his horse, he started westward.

He did not know how long his journey would take. Nor did he know what he might find there. He didn't care.

He had decided to go anyway. And having decided, there was nothing more to think about or discuss with anyone.

There was Forest Hall, one last responsibility to be dealt with. But that could be sold or held in trust by managers. He would think about that tomorrow.

Moultrie had heard it often, from many, that if a man went as far west as the Oregon Territory, he would find it mattered not what he had done, or what he had been, or what his color might be. What he could do was the important thing.

A man could make a fresh start.

And without Moon Shadow, a fresh start was all that mattered.

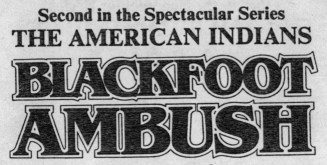

Third in the Spectacular Series
THE AMERICAN INDIANS

by Bill Hotchkiss

A woman pursues her own destiny and learns the lessons that only the mountains can teach her...

The third volume of the AMERICAN INDIANS series — the unforgettable story of Chastity, a beautiful, free-spirited woman who refuses to conform to the Mormon way of life. Betrothed to a man she does not love, she is saved from a life she hates by the scout Aloysius Benton and the gallant Crow warrior, Big Dog, when Indians raid her wagon. Though realizing she will be banished from her own people, Chastity cannot resist the awesome power of the warrior. Yet her love for him will force her to accept a new way of life ... among CROW WARRIORS.

Fourth in the AMERICAN INDIANS Series

CHIPPEWA DAUGHTER

by Jane Toombs

An extraordinary tale of an Indian woman with an unusual past and a passionate young man with an uncertain future.

Young, still inexperienced in the ways of the wilderness, Flann O'Phelan is on a secret government mission: to determine who is supplying guns to the Chippewa. On this assignment, Flann meets the mysterious Birch Leaf, whose powers fascinate him . . . He is drawn to her sensuous grace and beauty . . . unaware that the fierce warrior Black Rock waits to take her into his arms.

Birch Leaf, a woman who knows the ways of the forest and the customs of an ancient people, captures the love of the young adventurer and teaches him the meaning of trust and survival in a harsh, unfamiliar land.